Lingua Timore

Lingua Timore

13 Terrifying Tales

SUSAN H. RODDEY

Shenanigator Books
Chester, South Carolina

Haunted - previously published by Mocha Memoirs Press
Wolfy - previously published in *The Big Bad Anthology of Evil* by Dark Oak Press
Skippin' Stones - previously published in *The Big Bad 2* by Dark Oak Press
Downing Street, Rock 'N' Roll Angel, Easy As Pie, Angel with the Scabbed Wings - previously published in *Lost in the Shadows* by Phoenix & Fae Publications
Worlds Collide - previously published in *An Improbable Truth* by Mocha Memoirs Press
Crippled Playthings - previously published in *Curious Incidents* by Mocha Memoirs Press
The Memory Remains - previously published in *Paying the Ferryman* by Charon Coin Press

Name: Roddey, Susan H., author
Title: Linqua Timore
Identifiers: ISBN: 979-8-9892292-3-9

Published by Shenanigator Books

Printed in the United States of America

In loving memory of Angie P. Small

*Who never once flinched at my imagination,
and whose unfair and untimely death inspired
the final tale in this collection.*

TABLE OF CONTENTS

INTRODUCTION

I LOVE HORROR SO VERY MUCH.

First off: let's address the elephant in the room. Yep, that title is weird. It's Latin, after all. "The Language of Fear." It seemed the most appropriate title, yet was already taken by rather famous (or, thanks to Guns N' Roses, infamous) collection of stories. These... are certainly not those stories.

You see, as a kid, I was terrified of everything. The first horror movie I consciously remember watching was Poltergeist 3, and to this day, the image of Kane in the doorway looking down the hallway still haunts my nightmares. I still shy away from mirrors, and I still have a pathological fear of clowns. But I love the thrill that comes with the fear.

I'm drawn to horror, I think, because of the psychology. I've always wanted to know how things work, why people do what they do. I'm fascinated by the why. I'm that person who, after having just had a baby, watched nothing but true crime shows for weeks on end. My friends and family thought I was cracking up, that I was going to become one of those people in the shows. But it had nothing to do with the crimes themselves. I wanted to know what made these people tick.

Just the other day my husband and I were in a waiting room for one of his endless doctor's appointments. Two Corrections Officers came in with an inmate handcuffed to a wheelchair. I immediately wanted to know everything about this man—who was he, where did he come from, why was he in custody, how long would he be in prison, what's wrong with him?

What's wrong with me?

I know it's not normal to be that curious about people society considers "bad", but I can't help it. I want to know.

Which is where this collection comes in. The stories in this book are... different. Some of the characters are terrible people—I mean *awful.* No redeeming qualities at all. Some of them even get what they deserve. Others are victims of circumstance, driven mad by the things they can't control. But the one thing each of these stories has in common is that they contain the element of fear. In some small way, each of the ideas exhibited here scares me.

I've exorcised many demons through my writing, and many of them are immortalized on the pages within. These aren't happy stories. Some of them are humorous, some will jump up the squick-factor very fast, and others will break your heart.

I slept with the lights on for weeks after writing *Haunted.* To be so broken inside becuase of another person that I'd resort to murder...that idea created *Rock N' Roll Angel.* And *Frozen Ground* was my way of processing the murder of a very close friend. This particular story took three years to write, and it helped me come to terms with what happened to Angie. I'll never get over it and I'll probably be angry for the rest of my life, but now that I've had my revenge, I can at least move on.

Though, the fact that I can now say I know what it feels like to be so angry that you want to kill someone (and I mean that in the very literal sense) still scares the Hell out of me. Like what human death and decomposition smell like, it's not something I ever expected to know. Yet... here we are.

All of that having been said: Prepare yourself, dear reader, for a case study in fear. There are nightmares in this book, and you may not like what you find.

But don't say I didn't warn you.

—SHR
April 2025

Haunted

ONE

"I'LL HAVE AN EGG-WHITE SANDWICH WITH A SIDE of sausage. And a beer, if you've got one."

The waitress couldn't have been more than sixteen. She looked at me strangely for a moment with her faded blue eyes, shot a sideways glance at the clock, then shrugged and turned to call in my order. It was a greasy spoon, and it was deserted, save my ragged presence. From the girl's reaction, nobody had come in here asking for a beer in nearly two years.

"Hey Rick!" she called to the guy on the other side of the pass-through. "Do we have any beer?" Either I was sitting too low, or the guy was really short, because all I could see was the tip of a greasy, white paper hat.

"You know you're too young to drink, Sheila!" he called back. "But for a fee I'll see what I can do for you, hon." I could hear the sarcasm and sleaze dripping from his voice. He had been trying to get into this girl's pants for a while now.

"Not for me, jackass!" she snapped and punched her hands against her hips impatiently. "You know I can buy it any time I want! This guy wants a beer."

"At six in the morning?" he asked, sounding more than a little dumbfounded. I suspected confusion was a typical state of mind for him. "Check the blue box in the closet," he replied, his voice much flatter than before.

The girl, Sheila, smiled weakly over her shoulder at me and disappeared behind a grimy, unplugged jukebox. While she was gone, the heavenly scent of frying sausage filled the dusty air of the little diner, and though I wasn't particularly hungry, my stomach started doing backflips. After what I'd been through, what I could remember of it, I doubted I'd ever be able to eat again.

Sheila reappeared a moment later, her oily pigtails bouncing alongside her ears as she skipped back toward the counter. She blew a thick layer of dust from around the bottle cap, and the telltale blue ring of PBR caught my attention.

"Sorry if it's a little old," she said, nodding her head slightly as she popped the top, "but we don't get much demand for beer around here." She handed the bottle to me, and from the moment my fingers touched it, I knew it was not only flat, but skunked. It didn't matter; I needed the fortification.

I held my breath and took a long draught from the bottle. It was every bit as disgusting as PBR should be, and then some. But it was beer, and it wasn't overly hot. Despite the bile creeping back up my throat to dispel the ghastly taste, the alcohol grounded me slightly. My fingers ceased their shaking a little, and my vision didn't seem like it was confined by quite so long a tunnel.

"What's got you drinking beer at six in the morning, sugar?" Sheila asked me, though she couldn't have sounded tmore disinterested. "You act like you seen a ghost or something." I cringed at her horrible grammar, but kept the comments to myself. Suppose I did tell her I'd seen a ghost; would she believe me? Not likely.

"Just a kick start," I lied, and fought to swallow the beer that was steadily rising in my gullet. I washed it down with another long swig. "Long night."

"So, who's the lucky lady?" she asked, turning those pretty blue eyes back to me. Now she was interested, which was strange. Nobody ever paid attention to me unless I'd done something wrong.

"No lady tonight, hon," I replied and tried to smile. It must have worked, because she smiled just before her lip turned downward into an apologetic pout.

"That's too bad," she said with returning disinterest. *Not really*, I thought. "What's your name, darlin'?"

"Bobby," I said.

She nodded, and I could see the gears in her brain turning to process the new information.

She looked me in the eyes again, this time with building curiosity.

"Well, Bobby," she started, but Rick quickly cut in with a smack to the bell in the window and a loud shout.

"Order up!" he called a little too loudly into the emptiness of the restaurant.

"Jeez Louise, Rick!" Sheila snapped, turning her attention to him. "I'm standin' right here!"

"Just wanted to make sure ya heard me, doll."

"Can it, dickweed!" she snarled, her pretty little pink mouth curling downward into a sneer that could have stopped a truck. Something about the shape of her lips as the word fell from them was disturbingly erotic.

She lifted one perfectly-manicured hand to pick up the plate and turned back to me with another of those flashy smiles. She was definitely too young; her teeth were still too white and too many to belong to an early-morning waitress. She was as dingy-looking as the establishment around her, but that radiant grin could cut through any layer of grime.

"So, Bobby," she repeated and set the plate in front of me, shooting a dirty look over her shoulder I was certain Rick wouldn't be tall enough to see, "what brings you into *The Breakfast Bowl* so early?" As she said it, she motioned to the empty building. "We usually don't see customers until after the sun comes up."

Normally I wouldn't have had a problem answering that question. This morning, though, was a different story. I picked up my fork and toyed with a sliver of egg hanging off the toast. The night had been one for the books, no doubt. I couldn't really remember much of it, but I knew there had been blood. Lots of blood. The memory of it nearly brought back the stale beer.

"Just headed home," I said over the rampage of my own memories, and the sudden eruption of gastric juices settled.

"Where ya from?"

"Wellington, just on the other side of Wichita."

"Well, what're you doing in Newton at this hour if you're from Wellington, Bobby?"

I discovered I couldn't answer her. The events of the night – the clear parts – were still too surreal for me, though when the sun came up and the house was discovered in its current state, it would be all too real. I knew the police would come for me, even though it wasn't my fault.

"Waiting for my friends to wake up," I heard myself say, though the sound of my own voice was distant and alien, "so I can catch a ride home."

"Where are your friends?" she asked.

"Normandy Road."

"Well, what are they doing over there?" she asked, wide-eyed and innocent. In the kitchen, I could hear Rick grumbling about something and slamming dishes. All I could gather was he was angry over my presence interrupting his attempt to woo her.

I hesitated in answering her again. I couldn't just announce what they were doing on Normandy Road was lying dead in someone else's home. That would scare her for sure. No, I definitely couldn't tell her that.

"Investigating," I said, removing as much emotion from my voice as possible. "They've probably been done awhile now." To keep from looking at her, I started sawing at the overcooked sausage with the edge of my fork.

"How'd you get all the way over to Pine Street from Roanoke?"

"Walked," I said, and forced a lump of the sausage-scented charcoal into my mouth. For a moment I was certain it was going to abandon ship, along with the beer and the remains of last night's dinner, but I managed to swallow it without too much trouble.

"Tell you what," she said, her demeanor growing more cheery as the early-morning sunrise filtered in through the dirty windows. She glanced at the clock and leaned across the counter, close enough that Rick was sure to miss what she said. "I get off in fifteen minutes. I can either take you back to your friends, or take you home. The choice is yours."

"I can't do that," I said. "That would put you out."

"I don't mind," she replied, flashing me another of those soul-stealing smiles. I found myself smiling back.

"So, where's home for you?" I asked, and shoved a sliver of egg between my teeth.

"Junction City," she said simply, and I nearly choked. That was sixty miles away.

"I definitely can't accept a ride now… that's too far for you to have to backtrack."

"I really don't mind," she repeated, and something in her eyes appeared to beg me to accept. She seemed a little nervous about getting off work, and I suspected it had something to do with the sleazeball in the short order cook's uniform behind the grubby kitchen wall.

"All right… I suppose you can take me back to Normandy Road, just so I don't have to add too much to your trip." As soon as the words were out of my mouth, I regretted it. I could feel my face pale, but Sheila pretended she didn't notice. When I left that house, I swore I wouldn't go back. For some reason though, something was drawing me back to that street; to that house. Something dark and familiar.

Sheila bopped happily across the room to the other end of the counter, her long, thin fingers quickly turning and rearranging the pies in the old chrome-lined dessert case. She quickly mopped a wet rag across the counter tops, working her way back to me and skipping over my plate of barely-eaten food. She busied herself with menial tasks, all the while glancing at the slowly-ticking clock face.

"Are you gonna finish that, sugar?" she asked after finishing with her salts, peppers, and sugars. I looked down and realized I'd barely touched my food at all. I was right – I wasn't hungry.

"I don't think so," I replied as kindly as possible. "It was good… I just wasn't as hungry as I thought."

"Want me to box it up for you?"

"Sure… why not? Maybe I'll be hungry later."

"Or one of your friends can eat it," she replied. Something about the way she looked at me gave me the feeling she was slightly suspicious of my story. It could have been my lack of appetite, or some of my strange actions, but I was pretty sure it had a lot to do with my hesitation when she questioned me.

Instead of answering her, I nodded and spun around on the stool to survey the restaurant. It was old, with fifties-style black and white flooring and red-glitter vinyl booths. Everything was traced in chrome. The view beyond the lettered windows was of Washington Park—trees and grass and a beautifully landscaped baseball diamond. If someone had taken the time to clean the place up and wash the windows, it could have made a fantastic retro burger joint.

As I stared off into space, an older woman whose red-and-white skirted uniform matched Sheila's ambled up the sidewalk, paused long enough to cough loudly as she checked the too-thick lipstick of her reflection in the glass, and shouldered open the door. From the shape of her mouth, she was missing a few teeth, and her skin had the sickly yellow pallor of a chain-smoker. I was also certain her voice would remind me of Janis Joplin's bluesy growl.

Without looking at me, she rounded the counter, tossed her bag to the side, and kicked open the door to the kitchen. I noticed Sheila had disappeared from sight, and just when I was sure she had ducked out the back to avoid me, she came bounding out of the kitchen. Her uniform had been replaced by a pair of tight, faded jeans and a too-tight David Bowie t-shirt. She really was a pretty girl when she wasn't working.

"Ready, honey?" she crooned and smiled at me again. I found my balance and stood up on shaky feet. Before I could take a step, she skipped over to me and hooked her arm through mine. She led me out the door and turned right. "My car's just behind the building."

"Are you sure you don't mind?" I asked, still uncertain.

"Of course not! But there is one condition," she said, her voice quickly turning serious.

"And that is?" I prodded when she didn't continue.

"If I give you a ride, you have to tell me what's really going on. I don't believe your friends are just sleeping over on Normandy Road."

"Why not?" I asked, trying not to sound guilty.

"Because the only thing on Normandy Road is an old mansion everyone says is haunted." I blanched, and I knew it. She was looking straight at me, so I knew she saw it this time. "Your friends aren't alive." Not a question.

"No," I said quietly. My tongue suddenly felt as if it had swelled to three times its normal size. I swallowed around it as she led me through the alley that led to the diner's parking lot. "I don't know what happened, to be honest."

"How did you get there in the first place?" she questioned, dropping my arm to snatch her keys from her pocket. "I thought the driveway was blocked off."

"I have keys," I heard myself say, my voice thick.

"How the hell did you get keys?" she asked, sounding all too eager. "Did you steal them?"

"No," I said.

"Well? How'd you get 'em?"

"They belonged to my grandfather."

"You?" she asked, puzzled. "You're Elias Gaston's grandson? You are *the* Bobby Gaston?"

"How do you know me?" I asked. "Wait, how do you know my grandfather?" It was my turn to be shocked and questioning. I was pretty sure my grandfather passed away before she was out of middle school.

"We met a few times before… you wouldn't remember me though because we were so young." She glanced back at me to gauge my reaction. "He was my trainer." I stumbled and nearly fell to my face on the pavement. This girl had to be older than I thought. Gramps had been gone almost ten years now—I was sixteen when he died. He hadn't given riding lessons since his stroke, three years before. I didn't remember her specifically, but I did remember being introduced to several of his students on random occasions… though very few of them were young girls.

"How old are you?" I asked. I knew it was rude, but I couldn't help it.

"Twenty-three. Why?"

"No reason. I just thought you were younger."

"Yeah," she replied with a heavy sigh, "I get that a lot." She didn't look at me as she unlocked the doors of a fire-orange Camaro and climbed in. I hadn't known this girl but an hour, and she already knew more about me than most of the people I had come back to Newton with.

Plus, she knew something was amiss.

"So, why were you up at the mansion anyway?" she continued, jerking me back to the present.

"Two of my friends are… were… well, *are* ghost hunters. They own all of their own equipment. Ever hear of *Shadow Nine*?"

She squeaked in surprise.

"Yeah!" Wow, she was enthusiastic. "I used to watch their TV show… all three episodes of it!" I had to laugh.

Had Chad and Tim been there to witness the rush of fan girlishness, they'd have loved her for it. Three episodes, we found out after it started airing, was generous, considering the TV families said it was the lowest rated show in the history of the Public Broadcast System. "So…" she continued, her tone muted, "they're dead?"

"Yeah, I'm pretty sure."

She swallowed audibly. "What were they looking for?"

I sighed. "Grampa used to tell us stories about a woman on the stairs and an imp in the basement."

"An imp?" she asked, her voice thick with disbelief. "You mean like one of those pointy-tailed deals you see in renaissance paintings?"

"Not exactly," I said and slammed the car door just in time to keep her from tearing it off on the side of the building. "The imp in the basement was supposed to look like a man—only short."

"So, a midget?"

"Something like that." She didn't respond; only made a low musing sound as she whipped out onto the highway and into morning traffic.

Sheila was thinking hard about something, and I was pretty sure I didn't want to know what it was. I could feel the unasked questions buzzing around her. She wanted to know how they died; what happened and why I was still alive. To be honest, I wasn't entirely sure why, but I did intend to find out.

"I didn't kill them if that's what you're thinking," I blurted, before I realized I had even spoken. Her eyes left the road for a moment, fixing on my face with deep scrutiny before she slammed on the brakes at a changing traffic light.

"I wasn't thinking that," she said. She was a horrible liar.

"Chad and Tim wanted to go out there for a while, but I wouldn't let them. I kept trying to tell them it was stupid. Ghosts don't exist."

"They don't?" she asked, again with that same hint of sarcasm and disbelief. "Then what happened to them?"

"I don't know. They kept saying they could feel something moving around in the house, but I never saw a thing. The place has been empty for so long, there's no telling who or what might be living in it. And no, I don't know how they died. Truthfully, I'm not even sure they are dead."

"Then why did you leave?"

"Because I didn't want to be there anymore," I said. She glanced at me as she turned a corner a little too fast, nearly taking out a mailbox as her right front tire hopped the sidewalk. "I couldn't find them."

"So maybe they're just hiding from you… trying to play a prank on the skeptic."

"I don't know," I replied and sighed. The whole situation was a little too strange for me. It was possible they would go to such lengths…

But surely they would have come to find me by now. *Right?*

I hadn't been in the house since Grampa died, but I had the keys because it was my inheritance. Reluctant as it was. The house held too many memories for me, both good and bad. My mother didn't want the house, and nobody trusted my sister to have it. Everyone had told me to get out of my apartment and move to Newton, but I didn't want to. I didn't want to be the crazy guy who rattled around alone in the big house at the end of the street. I could have gotten a bunch of cats to keep me company, or maybe found some bimbo to marry and occasionally fuck in between trips up and down the moldering, old staircase, but that wasn't what I wanted.

I didn't want something that was going to be a constant reminder of how horrible a grandson I was – how even when he was dying, I was too busy being a kid and having my own life to bother stopping by and saying hi once in a while. I didn't want to have to face the fact I was a substandard family member and an even less-deserving heir than I had convinced myself I was.

Besides, if something really was in the house, the guilt-riddled grandson knocking around in there would surely be enough to stir up some crap. After all, wasn't that how it happened in the movies? Wasn't the emotional discord what really brought all the trouble on? Maybe, I realized, it actually was my brief trip inside to set up the cameras that caused this whole mess to begin with.

"Bobby!" Sheila called, and snapped her fingers in front of my face. "There you are!" she said when I looked at her. She was glancing at me sideways and smiling. "Don't wander off like that again."

"Sorry," was all I could muster. I was too busy drowning in self-pity to have paid attention to anything she said at all.

"I know you missed what I said, so I'll say it again. Are you going back in the house?" She looked expectantly at me out of the corner of her eyes.

"I guess so… I mean, I need to find the guys and get them out."

"How many people are we looking for?"

"Five. Wait... *we*?"

"Yes, WE. You didn't think I was going to miss out on this, did you?"

"But... what if there is something inside?"

She shrugged, attempting nonchalance even though I could see the fear trickling across her face. "If there is, you don't need to be facing it alone."

I didn't respond, and she didn't offer any further conversation until we pulled up in the driveway. Tim's van and Chad's truck were still sitting there. The back doors of the van were still open, and I could see the monitors from the seat of her car. One was still nothing but static and snow, but the others looked like they had clear pictures.

"Wow... professionals," she muttered. "I never knew..."

She killed the engine, but left the keys in the ignition. "Just in case," she said, her voice barely above a whisper. She had been pretty gung-ho when we left the diner, but now that we were outside the looming, old mansion with its dirty windows, peeling paint, and crooked shutters, she'd begun to turn a sickly green color. She was as afraid as I was. I still refused to let my brain tell me there were ghosts in the house, but something was definitely wrong.

I'd gone with the boys on their little hunting trips before and had always turned up nothing. They accused me of being a psychic rock, but they also said having a skeptic kept the rowdier spirits in check. The running belief was, if I didn't believe, things couldn't eat me. And you know what? I was perfectly fine with that sentiment. I wasn't a big fan of being eaten.

But this time around, everything was different. From the moment we passed through the gates, I was spooked. Those nasty chills of the unknown crawled up my spine and seated themselves at the base of my skull. My arms and legs felt unusually heavy before I even got out of the van.

The boys claimed weird shit started happening as soon as I walked through the door and put out the first of the sensors. Tim said it was almost like something was following me. I called his bluff on it. He'd said that more than once in the past to try to scare me. And before this trip, he had always admitted he was joking.

This time he kept it going, and even after I was outside again, he tried to convince me I'd drawn something out.

"Your grandfather loved you," Sheila said for no reason, snatching me out of my eerie reminiscence. "He always talked about you after lessons."

"Hmm," I grunted.

"He was never upset with you for not coming around more," she said. It was like she was reading my mind and that uneasy feeling of *creep* came back in full force. "He wanted you to live your own life and be your own man."

"That was before the stroke," I reminded her.

"Even after," she corrected. "I used to come by and visit him, you know." Great, she was a better grandchild than me, and she wasn't even blood. "He still talked about you all the time…" She paused to chew on her next statement. Looking over at her, I noticed she'd caught her bottom lip between her teeth and was worrying it in a way that made me shiver. Whatever she was going to ask wasn't going to be good. "Are… are you sure he really had a stroke?"

"That's what the doctors said."

"It's just…"

"What?"

"He wasn't like any stroke victim I've ever seen. The only side effect was a complete change in his personality."

She had a point. The few times I saw him in those last few years, he wasn't the Grampa I knew and loved. Something about him had definitely changed, and it wasn't that he was an invalid of any sort. He just wasn't my grandfather anymore. When he looked in my direction, there was a distance to his eyes, and hollowness to his voice when he spoke. He didn't say my name until I said it first, like he had a hard time remembering who I was. When he walked, he didn't limp or drag. He wasn't a stroke victim, but he wasn't…

He wasn't *right*.

Maybe that was part of the reason I stayed away. Maybe as a child, I could sense the inherent wrongness of his situation. But then again, maybe it was just my own cracked psyche working against me, just like it was doing now.

Guilt overwhelmed me as I climbed into the back of the van to survey the equipment. I'd failed him, whether anyone else believed it or not. I didn't hold up my end of the bargain — at the first sign of trouble, I ran and hid and waited until it was over. Whatever was going on was my fault.

Sheila hopped up behind me, using my knee for leverage to crawl up. Her legs were almost too short to take that step, and her touch was enough to clear my head of the pity party. It put bad things in the pity's place.

"So, what happened out here last night?" she asked, pulling a box over to sit down and see what I was looking at. I started to tell her about Tim's insistence something was following me and how Chad had taken the other four into the house with the radio equipment, when the master bedroom camera started flickering, stopping me cold.

"I think it knows you're back," she said, her voice warbling a little. I had the grim suspicion she was right.

I checked the drives, and everything was still recording. The ten one-terabyte hard drives Chad bought were still buzzing along, quietly recording everything. The mics were still on, but they were silent. There was no chatter from any of the guys, even with the warbling lines of camera one. Camera five was still dead, but it had been since we set it up. It wouldn't even come on with a new battery. Because of it, we never did get a clear shot of the kitchen.

I had read Grampa's journal more than once, and so had Chad. He studied it and made notes on all the rooms where things were supposed to happen. Even after his stroke, Grampa continued to make notes… but the timbre of those entries was different… as if he weren't even the same person. The writing followed the same pattern as his personality – he became someone else. And according to his writings, he was spending more and more time in the basement – a room he'd previously wished to forget. He claimed to find comfort in the dark solitude.

Years ago, he talked about the history of the house, how his grandfather had bought the land from a ranch foreclosure and spent ten years of his life building the house. The old man was obsessed with the house – it was his passion. He'd bought unique accessories from all over the country to build and furnish the place, and over the years, it had become a sort of museum.

It reminded me of that Stephen King miniseries, *Rose Red*, and how the woman believed the day she stopped construction on the house would be the day she died. Granted, my great, great grandfather wasn't that kind of crackpot, but he did love his house more than any man should.

After my great grandfather's death, Grampa started writing about strange noises – starting with footsteps on the stairs. Followed by doors opening and closing on their own, disembodied voices, thumps and creaks and groans... all typical haunted-house sounds that could easily be attributed to the age of the house. Well, except for the voices.

Those noises drove him to research the land before the house was built, and what he found was unbelievable. Picking up one of the older journals, I flipped to one of the entries that always seemed to stick with me and handed the book over to Sheila.

"See if this answers some of your questions," I said. She held the book reverently, as if it were the Holy Grail itself. Her eyes misted, likely with nostalgia for my grandfather. I wished I could have felt some of her bittersweet reminiscence. Instead, I felt only dread.

February 21, 1963

Just returned from the courthouse with some interesting information about the house. Tax records, such as they are, list two previous owners of the land. The owner immediately prior to Pop was a widower named Nate Duncan. The property was only owned by Duncan ten years. Prior owner Sally Ford, daughter of Winston and Juliet Ford, sold it to him for less than one-quarter fair market value.

Winston and Juliet… those names rang a bell, so I went to the vital records office. No birth records or other information, save two death certificates. Both died the same day. That has definitely piqued my interest. Will try the newspaper office, church archives, and funeral home after lunch.

Later.

According to the records of the mortician, Winston and Juliet Ford died mysteriously in the home with no evidence of foul play. Both appeared to have suffocated, though police found no murder weapon and no marks to suggest strangulation.

Coroner's report on the microfiche said their hearts simply stopped. The daughter, Sally, was committed shortly thereafter, reports stating she suffered a massive brain hemorrhage which caused lunatic ravings about an evil man in the basement that killed her parents. Sale of the property was fast and quiet, to Nate Duncan two weeks later.

Strange story, no doubt. While out, I decided to check out Nate Duncan as well, and found the most astounding thing. Nate Duncan married Rebecca Morse, niece of Juliet Ford. That explains the strange connection between families.

The coroner's report states Rebecca died of a stroke eight years after purchase. Nate Duncan, I also found, was Pop's half-brother. My great-grandmother, Edena Duncan-Gaston, was married once before, and bore her first husband a son (Nate) shortly before his tragic death in a train derailment.

According to the tax assessor's records, Nate grew despondent after Rebecca's death, quitting his job and forgetting to pay his bills. The house was foreclosed upon, and in an effort to keep it in the family, Pop purchased the land with money from his farm, sold the cattle, and moved the operation to this house.

It appears, from this new revelation, that our family has quite the history in this house. As far as town records go, only one lineage has owned the property.

Side note – perhaps there is more to Sally's claims of a man in the basement. This needs investigation.

Sheila looked up at me, her jaw slack with either surprise or confusion, I couldn't tell which. A tear escaped her right eye and trailed down her cheek.

"Nate Duncan was my great-great grandfather," she said. "I had no idea…"

This news hit me like a blow to the stomach. The air seemed to have been sucked from the interior of the van, and the rest of the world, for that matter, since the doors were still open. Those words echoed again and again in my head… Never in a million years would I have thought this hot young thing and I were related. At least, I thought wildly, I hadn't acted on the impulse to tell her to pull over so I could fuck her brains out before wandering back into this death trap. Hell, when she touched my leg to get into the van, I briefly considered throwing her to the floor and having my way with her.

But despite her tight clothes barely covering a very tasty-looking body, I'd refrained.

But even now, looking at her curvy, little figure made me want to throw her down and fuck the hell out of her.

"What?" she asked. I looked up.

Oh, hell…

"What's wrong?" The look on her face was one that spoke of both fear and disgust.

"Did you just say what I think you said?"

Oh, shit… "What did I say?"

"You said 'fuck the hell out of her.' I hope you weren't talking about me."

"No," I lied. Damn it, I had said that out loud… I was fairly certain if I looked in the mirror over my head, my face would be the color of a pickled beet. Even so, the shame of voicing inappropriate thoughts refused to dull the longing ache I felt.

We sat in awkward silence for a bit. From the troubled look on her face, I feared she'd had the same thoughts I did, and was now trying to find a way to rationalize it. Great-great grandfathers that were half-brothers – only half of each man's bloodline counted. Grandfathers that would have been half-first cousins with only one-eighth of their chromosomes in sync… fathers that would have been somewhere along the lines of one thirty-second… which put us so bloody distant it really wouldn't matter if I did fuck her and she managed to get knocked up. I could easily tell her the blood tie was so thin we couldn't really be called family, but I thought better of it. Sex should be the last thing on my mind at this point, and to my great surprise, it was the only thing, even if it was irrelevant.

"Well," she said finally, and permanently derailed that train of thought, "I *have* to go now… it's my family too." She had guts… I had to give her that. I shrugged — what else could I do? — and turned back to the panel of monitors.

The basement camera was dark. There weren't any windows that deep beneath the house's foundation, but the thing was running on night vision. It glowed eerily, like the sight from a mutant, green eye. The whole frame was a myriad of shadows and highlights that never seemed to quite line up the right way. But there was nothing moving.

The library camera was a little fuzzy, but otherwise ticking along fine. Light filtered through the grimy windows and thin curtains well enough to show the room in perfect color.

We could see ourselves on a grainy monitor set off to the side. Trying to break the stuffiness the new discovery had caused, I waved at the camera, but received little more than a sick smirk from Sheila.

The other five cameras were still as well. The final drive wasn't hooked up to a video monitor, but to the sound system. According to the laptop, it had recorded for thirteen straight hours, and still had several hundred gigabytes of space to fill.

There were still eight rooms in the house without cameras, and multiple hallways, closets, and other creepy little crawlspaces. Most of those empty rooms were bedrooms and bathrooms, but there were still unattended rooms, and they could have easily been hiding from me, ready to spring out and "get me," so to speak.

"Do you really think they're hiding?" Sheila asked in a thin, reedy tone when I voiced this opinion. I wanted to say yes, but I knew better. They weren't just hiding… couldn't be, without having left at least some sign they were fooling me. Everyone was mic'd, so I'd certainly hear their conspiratorial giggles.

"I'd like to think so," I said instead. I stared at the cameras, hoping I would see one of them shift to shake out a cramp, or show up in the corner of a frame and spoil the surprise. She watched the cameras over my shoulder, and I could feel the anxiety rolling off her in palpable waves.

"Tell me exactly what happened last night, up until you walked into the diner and ordered a beer with your sandwich," she said finally, and turned to face me. My stomach lurched, and I thought about the food lying abandoned on the back seat of her little orange sports car. I didn't even want to think about what happened, much less talk about it.

"We set up at seven. They gave me the cameras since I knew the house the best. All of them worked fine when I walked into the house. Tim kept telling me he could hear voices around me, but the rest of the guys were outside the van laughing. I told him it was probably feedback from them on his monitor." I wiped my hand across my face, trying to hide the nausea rising in my throat. My hand came away damp—I'd begun to sweat. "He said the voices got louder as I got closer to the back of the house."

"So you think he was messing with you?"

"I hope he was. I've never seen anything in the house, and I didn't want to let my mind play tricks on me."

Her skin was just a little bit paler, her eyes a little wilder when she asked the next question.

"What happened next?"

"I set up the cameras. The last one was the one in Grampa's bedroom, and no matter how hard I tried, I couldn't get it to come on. Tim told me to leave it, so I did. He said as soon as I left the room, it powered up by itself. It had lots of squiggly lines running through it." I pointed to the camera one monitor. It was mostly static and snow, but in between, I could see glimpses of my Grandma's antique four-poster bed. It had been part of her dowry… in a time when those were still fashionable.

"So then what?" she asked. Sheila was also getting impatient with me, but my mind wasn't moving as quickly as it should. I kept finding myself hung up on the little details that had nothing to do with the investigation.

"Then," I sighed, "then I went back toward the front door. At one point I thought I heard someone walking down the hall behind me, but nothing was there. I thought it had been one of the guys, but they were all still outside when I opened the door." I spun around and switched the audio controls to playback. Maybe something there would tell me what was going on. "Tim said he could still hear the voices coming through my mic."

"That's a little weird. They followed you out?"

"Apparently," I said with a shrug. "That was the last time I went in…" I paused, shaking off the sudden memory of waking up in my grandfather's bed as a delusion. It seemed like a relevant piece of information, but I couldn't bring myself to tell her.

"Bobby? What is it?" she asked.

I shook my head. "Nothing," I lied. "Chad took the others inside while Tim and I monitored. They were full of piss and vinegar, which was nothing new. We laughed at them as they romped through the house, determined to find something I was certain wasn't there."

"So where are they now?" Her impatience was giving way to fear again. I handed her one of the two pairs of headphones hanging from the nail in the side of the van. Her fingers were shaking as she put the headphones over her ears, and the look in her wide eyes was what could only be considered abject terror. This little game had gotten real way too fast.

"Beats me." I hit the playback button and slipped the other pair of headphones on. As usual, all I could hear at first was the laughter in the background behind the initial system test. Then Tim came on and labeled the excursion.

This is Timothy Conrad, here with Bobby Gaston. Say hi, Bobby. Waiting outside is Chad Wilton, Aaron Saxon, Buddy Kremlin and Martin Pickett. The time is 7:18 PM. Tonight's investigation will take place in the Gaston Mansion on Normandy Road, Newton, Kansas. Local law enforcement has been notified.

The investigation of the Gaston Mansion is based on the journals of the late Elias Gaston, grandson of Tobias Gaston, original owner and builder of the mansion. Journals have been provided by Bobby Gaston, grandson of Elias Gaston and current owner of the property.

This investigation will feature ten digital video cameras, sound system, still photography, EMP reader, and digital temperature recorder. All items belong to Chad Wilton, owner of Shadow Nine Paranormal, LLC. Cameras will be placed by Bobby Gaston.

I paused the playback and looked at Sheila. She attempted to smile, but it was laced with an edge of pure unreasonableness. The need to leave the scene was evident by the thin, hard set of her lips and the tremor of muscle in her left cheek. She would have stopped listening if I had turned the machine off. Even through her terror, though, she was determined to hang on. After all, it was her family now, too.

"You okay?" I asked, and she nodded. The fleeting thought passed through my mind that we should get out of here as quickly as possible, but I smacked it away and hit the button again. As I turned to reach for the house keys, I saw her wipe her eyes.

I restarted playback and let it run through the rest of Tim's introductory speech, scrambling it through until it came to the point where he first started telling me he was hearing voices. Sheila tensed next to me, and I ran the dials around until I could hear the background noise.

At first, there was nothing, and then… then there was a low hum. A cough. And finally, the sound of someone screaming. It was distant and quiet—as if the person were screaming into a pillow or maybe from the bottom of a well. I couldn't tell whether it was male or female.

Then, it happened again, closer to the microphone this time.

I stopped the tape with shaking fingers. Tim was right—there *had* been something there. The voice was familiar and very distinctly female, and there had been no women on-site when we began. Sheila was beyond trying to hide the terror. She was as scared as me, and she clearly showed it, from her shaking fingers to her trembling lower lip.

"Did your grandmother die of natural causes?" she asked. Her question startled me.

"The doctors said her heart just stopped," I told her. My throat was dry and my voice cracked. I didn't like where this was going… the conversation was already too familiar. "But it didn't seem right. She was so healthy, and she wasn't very old."

"What do you think it was?"

"I don't know." But I sure as hell didn't think it was simple heart failure anymore.

We sat in silence for a long time, watching the monitors' blank pictures of the inside of my grandfather's… no, my house. It was time to admit it… this was my house now.

My problem.

"We need to leave," she said quietly, and laid the headphones on the steel desk in front of her. The fun and joking nature was gone from her voice and from her eyes. "We need to get out of here, Bobby… something bad is going on."

"I know," I said, "but I have to find out what it is. Don't you see? I own this house, and if something has happened in there, I'm going to be held responsible… especially since I was here when it happened."

"But you said nothing did happen!" she shrieked.

I never said that.

I only said I *hoped* nothing had happened. I had no idea what really had gone on—I couldn't remember most of the night beyond the first few minutes of the investigation.

While I tried to calm her, movement on camera four caught my attention. The basement camera was still set on night vision. I spun around, clicked the audio over to that camera, and listened as I watched two bodies come into view.

Two police officers were in the house, wandering through the basement with flashlights and weapons drawn. From what I could gather from their stilted and unnerving conversation, they decided to come and check on us when we didn't call in this morning, because Shadow Nine *always* called in. In hindsight, I realized I probably should have called… if for no other reason than to cover myself until I could figure this out.

If I could figure it out, that was. If the boys really were gone, I could have been implicated as the murderer just from that call. Damn it, I was stuck. From the sound of the voices coming through the camera's mic, they hadn't found anything suspicious yet, but they were just as scared.

"I have to go get them," I told her, and started out of the van. She caught my arm and pulled me back.

"Don't leave me!" she whimpered, her eyes pleading.

"I'm going in," I repeated. "I have to get those two men out. I have to find my friends, even if there isn't much left of them." It was my turn to get impatient. I suddenly wanted to be angry with her – my fucked-up psyche demanded the fury, as if it would help sort out the rest of this mess. "If you don't want to be left, come with me," I snapped, and she recoiled. I couldn't really blame the poor girl. I mean, I'd only known her a few hours, and she'd allowed me to somehow drag her into this clusterfuck. She was just being nice and offering me a ride home, probably a free piece of ass for the tip, and a few hours' amusement – not that I could think in those terms anymore. I had to go and ruin it by having a real-life crisis on my hands that in a stupidly roundabout way involved her. I patted her thigh reassuringly as I crawled past her and out the back of the van.

She hopped out and followed closely behind me, her fingers just barely clutching the hem of my shirt. She was shaking from head to toe, and I could feel that tremor along the connection between her hand and my clothing. We were both strung tighter than piano wire, and we knew it wouldn't take much for either of us to snap.

The house loomed in front of us, its peeling, shuttered windows glaring down at me like accusing eyes. This large, dead thing stood before us as a testament to my winsome youth and lack of concern for those long gone. The house seemed to regard me with disgust and disdain as I walked up to the front door.

"I… I think I'm going to stay here," she said, backing down the porch and away.

"Suit yourself," I said with a shrug and shouldered my way through the door. Logically, I knew I had no right to be angry with her, but I was, all the same. She was backing out; abandoning me at the moment when I needed her support the most.

Bitch.

The heavy door opened with a sick creak, alerting anyone inside to my presence. Beyond the threshold, the floor settled in a series of unhealthy crackles and pops, and somewhere deep in its bowels, the house groaned. Inside the foyer, it smelled of stale cigars and old paper. High ceilings arched overhead, giving all of the first-floor rooms an empty, cavernous feel. Sheets covered most of the furniture, but hadn't stopped the accumulation of dust. The great room to my left had several sets of footprints tracked through the layer of grime on the hardwood floors. Two other sets of footprints moved away from where I stood, one going into the dining room on my right, the other passing down the hall. Those tracks seemed almost otherworldly; they were so out of place in the still, stuffy silence of this old sarcophagus. The paint on the walls was faded, and in places, peeling back to show chipped, yellowed plaster. I hadn't so much as set foot in the place since it passed to me, and it really showed.

A hard shiver rattled its way up my spine. This was not a joke. This was not a game. This was real, it was a matter of life or death, and I knew it with absolute certainty. My friends were still in the house, but as I breathed in the moldering air of my dead childhood, I was positive they weren't alive.

I was barely inside the foyer when I heard the roar of an engine and the crunch of tires on gravel. Sheila was gone; having had enough fun she took off while she could still get away. Part of me knew she was doing the smart thing. The right thing. Part of me also had the feeling I should have gone with her like she asked. But this was my problem, and I had to find out exactly what was going on, to warn the officers inside that something strange was happening. Yet another part of me was convinced whatever had my friends was only out to get me, and all the rest of this was just the net to catch me. That sick feeling of inevitability settled around me, roiling in my gut, churning those few bits of breakfast I'd eaten and threatening to bring them all back up.

This house wanted to make me pay for the things I had done. Or rather, the things I hadn't done.

Taking a deep breath, I turned to face the long, dark hallway. It gaped before me like a blackened throat, its jaws agape in preparation. The sickening, paisley wallpaper stretched forward, reaching for me like the ripples in an esophagus. With shaking fingers, I reached to flip the light switch to my right.

Nothing happened.

I toggled the switch a few times just to make sure.

Still nothing.

My sigh echoed down the hallway, chanting back to me in perfect chorus my own shrill terror.

I couldn't help the tremble in my hands as I clicked on the flashlight. The sun was up, but the heavy drapes hanging along the old windows kept the inner sections of the house abnormally dark. Even when this house had been full of love and laughter, the artificial light overhead could never truly keep the darkness at bay.

Grampa spent most of his time with the curtains closed – to save on the heating bill, he said – but the lamps, sconces, and chandeliers scattered through the rooms always sparkled, no matter the time of day or night. When I looked up, I noticed the chandelier in the great room was covered in a layer of grime, many of the crystal strands hanging loosely from rusted chains.

The love was gone from this building. It had been sucked away by years of avoidance and neglect. The jewel of my grandfather's collection, his home, was little more than a rundown shell that housed the souls of things insane.

The rooms I'd spent so much time in as a child were completely unfamiliar now; not at all what I remembered. The darkness permeated the house and its contents, warping my memories and twisting them into nightmarish caricatures of the place I once loved. The walls seemed to lean a bit to the left, the dusty, faded paintings adorning them leaning every other way. The rugs bunched over the old, cedar floorboards like tense muscles, ready to reach up and trip me as I passed. Even those boards appeared to jut from their places like crooked teeth in an old man's maw. It looked hungry, and the more I stared at the shell around me, the more I felt like I was looking at bits of my life from a cell at the end of a long and badly-lit hallway.

I shook my head to clear away the fog settling in around me, but that weird sense of vertigo wouldn't let go. It almost felt like there was another person inside my head, trying to take control of my body. Scrubbing my hand over my face — the scruff on my chin was getting out of control, I realized with a high, maniacal giggle — I told myself to banish those thoughts. Easier said than done, even though they would get me nowhere, and would only serve to allow what was stalking me to win.

I urged myself forward another step. My legs felt heavy and my heart hammered against my ribcage. My footsteps creaked, resounding off the faded and dusty walls. Each groan of the floorboards sounded like a pained exhalation to my stricken ears. Unseen eyes slithered over my skin, reminding me, even though I was by myself, I was not alone. The house itself was watching my every move, and I felt violated.

The front door slammed behind me, hard enough to rattle the glass in the windows of the great room. It wasn't a draft — hurricane-force winds weren't strong enough to blow the beast closed. That caved-in feeling of being hunted fell heavy on my shoulders, as if the unseen sentience was treading silently along behind me, its spindly, death-fingers poised just over my arms, waiting to spring and draw me into oblivion. Above me, the ceiling began to creak and whine, and somewhere, a door opened.

The sound of that door opening upstairs spurred me into motion. I flew down the hall in three long strides, my feet moving of their own volition, taking me to the base of the stairs. I looked up the darkened well, noting each one of the footprints on the dusty running boards. I could count four distinct tread patterns in the layers of grime, but only one of those patterns went up *and* came back down again. If I lifted my foot and looked at the underside of my shoe, it would be pretty easy to see the double set was mine. But the rest of them...

Shuddering, I reached out and gripped the banister. So many times when I was a child, I'd nearly broken my neck sliding down its glossy surface, the feeling of unbridled glee coursing through my veins as I came as close as any human being could to flying without a machine. But what lay under my hand now, cold and knotted from years of neglect, felt foreign and cruel. Like a fist around an artery, the warped wood seemed to pulse under my fingers. Maybe it was my own heartbeat in my fingertips, but as that chalky feeling returned to my throat and my vision started to blur with frightful tears, I sensed something else beneath my own heartache. Something dark. Evil.

Wrong.

Above me, I thought I heard footsteps, but I couldn't be sure. The sound was old and distant, almost like an echo. *Maybe,* I told myself, *maybe they're all upstairs and fucking with me.* If the little bastards were up there, I'd be sure to punch the shit out of each of them at least once for this.

But that little, niggling voice at the base of my skull chuckled as I took that first step up and whispered its sad story to me again. *They're all dead, and it's all your fault, Bobby.* That sickly, inhuman sound made me want to retch, to collapse to my knees with my hands over my ears and scream like a little girl.

I took another step. The image of a familiar-yet-not, middle-aged, white-haired woman flashed before my eyes, her face frozen in an expression of frightful agony as she tumbled down the stairs. I blinked and looked back, but there was nothing in front of me. The image was gone, but the memory was there, ingrained in my memory forever.

I took another step, wincing in anticipation of what vision might assail me next. My shoulders tightened; my spine tingled. Nothing happened. Another step. Still nothing. Another.

A shrill, ear-piercing shriek echoed through the upstairs hall, winged its way down the stairwell, and surrounded me in a wave of nauseous energy. I flew up the remaining steps, clutching at my chest as I slumped against the wall, my heart nearly beating through my ribs. The sound, much like the vision, was gone; replaced by another memory that would never wane.

From this new vantage point, I could see both hallways. The banister near the top of the stairs was missing several spindles, and the handrail at the landing leaned away from the steps, as if straining to come loose and run away. Heaven knew I wanted to run, to make a hasty exit and never return.

When I was finally able to stand without the worry of falling over, I started toward the lower floor, but my feet took me in a different direction. Like I was standing outside of myself, I watched my hands swing back and forth, watched my feet take step after step over the dull, squeaky floorboards until I was standing at the door of my grandfather's bedroom. The paintings on either side of the door—juvenile drawings I'd done for him as presents when I was a child, sat askew, the centers of the pictures seeming to come together like a pair of angry, accusing eyes.

A shrill tendril of fear snaked its way into my belly and coiled around my guts, squeezing me tight and refusing to let go. My hand extended, hovering over the antique latch. I didn't want to know what was behind that door. I had a pretty good idea of what I would find – absolutely nothing – but part of me didn't want that. Part of me wanted to open that door and see all of my friends laughing and giggling, sitting around the rumpled bed with a camera, waiting for me to open the door so they could get that candid *fuck you, Bobby* shot and spend the next six weeks trying to humiliate me for my own fear.

With the last of my own strength, I pulled my hand away and started to turn. My feet seemed glued to the floor, which laid down another layer of panic. Somewhere in the house, a radio began to play.

The smoky, soulful voice of Sam Cooke filled the air, warbling about a party. The happy, carefree clap-beat tapped on every single nerve in my body, already raw with unresolved anticipation, and when I finally unglued my left foot from the floor and took a step, two hands landed on my shoulders.

I know I screamed. I heard the sound bounce back and forth off the walls and resound back to me. Spectral fingers clutched at my biceps, traced down my arms, then caressed — because a caress is truly what it was – my throat.

My feet came unglued, along with whatever shred of reason I'd managed to hold onto until that point. I ran, probably flailing my arms as I did so, down the hallway, which seemed to stretch before me with each step I took, and upon making it to the stairs I think I might have jumped from top to bottom. I don't remember the descent; I just remember doubling over and gasping for breath, holding my sides as I shivered and shook, trying to work the feel of those invisible hands off my body.

When I righted myself, I realized I'd come to stand directly in front of the basement door. The music still played. James Brown sang about a *Man's Man's Man's World*, and I noticed that it was louder down here. The sound wasn't coming from a radio in the bedroom, or even the old Victrola in the great room… it was coming from behind the door in front of which I stood, shaking in my boots. Dust had settled on the hand-carved scrollwork, turning the intricately-etched door into a solid, gray panel. A large handprint rested in the middle of the dirty veneer, and I could count the individual grooves of the fingerprints on the handle.

Something deep inside me — my waning sense of self-preservation, I suppose — screamed at me, begged me not to open that door, but I was helpless to stop my own trembling hand as it turned the corroded lever. My throat was bone-dry and thick, and when I tried to swallow, my tongue stuck to my teeth.

The unused hinges squeaked loudly, and I expected to be told to freeze; not to move or blink or I'd face getting shot. I closed my eyes and gritted my teeth and waited, cringing, but the orders never came. If those officers weren't dead by now, they would be very soon. My friends were dead, of that I was absolutely certain. Even with all the creaks and groans of this old tomb, there were none that could be misconstrued as a sign of life. The air in the house was too still, the rooms too quiet.

As I looked down that black staircase, that other presence in the back of my mind took hold, and the immediate and unwavering knowledge that I was responsible washed over me. Like the voice of a long-buried conscience, I heard the words.

It's all your fault, Bobby.

The acrid taste of panic once again rose with the bile in my throat, and my body went completely numb to my control, even as my brain screamed at my feet to run away. They were dead because of me, and if I didn't get the fuck out, I was going to join them. With that little voice in my ear, cursing me and blaming me, I knew my fate just as surely as I knew my own name. The revelation brought the morning's queasiness back, which threatened once again to bring up the bits of breakfast I had eaten.

When I'd had someone with me, I was able to feel better about the situation, able to blame myself less for being a shitty grandson and even shittier heir. Now that I was alone again, I was as sick as I had been when I ran out into the street at 3:30 this morning. I was filled with fear, anger, hatred, and the heavy nausea of inevitability. Behind me, and above my head, several sets of footsteps moved through the upstairs hall, coming to stop at the head of the steps. If I'd been able to turn my head to the right, I am certain I could have seen the owners of those feet watching me, staring back through spectral and accusing eyes, waiting for me to become one of them.

That, I demanded of myself, was real. Those hands had touched me. Those eyes were the same ones that had woken me from a dead sleep. Those were the things that had put me where I was, scared the bejeezus out of me when I'd woken up in my grandfather's bed, and run me out of the house into the street like a frightened child. Those were the things that were at one time human. The thing in my head, playing on my fears, was not. Those things, all members of my family I realized, as I began to hear their pitying and frightened voices screaming at the thing that had control of me, had been trying to protect me in their own way. That anxiety I'd felt about coming back had been my last, valiant – though sadly ignored – defense mechanism.

When the last voice joined the chorus, his deep, paternal voice so achingly familiar that tears sprang from my eyes and poured down my cheeks as hysterical sobs broke out of my throat, I was afraid then that I knew just why I was here.

As the last male in the family, it was my inheritance. My turn.

As I pried my fingers off the cold door handle, and for the last time told my stupid feet to *start running, goddamn it!*, laughter filled my head and the air around me, drowning out the most loving voice of my childhood. This fucking *thing*; it had gotten all of my friends, and now it was coming for me. My feet came loose from the floor, I turned, and then I stupidly dared one last glance down the dark portal. I realized as that all-consuming darkness crawled toward me, it was too late. That voice in my head confirmed it, its hollow, unholy echo carried on the gust of wind rushing up the stairs.

TWO

"**WHAT THE FUCK AM I DOING?**"

Sheila wasn't far from the turn-off to Junction City when pangs of guilt flooded her. She'd asked—no, insisted—she be part of it. For years she'd nursed the desire to get back into that house and find out for herself if all the rumors were true. But there was more to it now… this was not just Bobby's family. This was her family. Her history. Her heritage.

"Bad idea, Sheila," she said out loud, her own voice a little too loud in the confines of the little sports car. "Not your problem."

But in a roundabout way, it was. It was her ancestors who owned the land and built the house. Her family had suffered at the hands of whatever nasty thing existed there for decades. Bobby, poor, tormented Bobby… the thing had him in its clutches…

"Damn it…" she sighed and hung an illegal U-turn. Stomping the gas, she sped back toward Normandy Road, a sick feeling building in the pit of her stomach. She shouldn't have left Bobby there, and if anything had happened to him, she would never forgive herself.

The grounds were even more deserted than she remembered. The truck and van still sat in the yard. Monitors still clicked along, the quiet hum of the van's generator only amplifying the silence. From the back of the house, she heard the echoing squelch of the police cruiser's radio, unattended and still unanswered. She noticed then, the complete lack of city roar. A tiny, familiar voice came from over her left shoulder. It told her to run—it was too late. There was nothing living on those grounds.

But still, she'd left one time before. And she'd come back.

She had to know.

Sucking in a deep breath, Sheila climbed into the back of the van and looked at the discarded instrumentation. There was no movement on any of the cameras. They were all blank, and the ones that had previously been unreadable had clear, full-color pictures just like the ones she'd watched with Bobby.

That unholy sight alone made her want to scream, to cry and to run away from it all. That one sight would stick with her for the rest of her life, no matter how badly she wished she could unsee the clear, neatly-folded coverlet on the old four-poster bed.

The old journals lay across the table; she noticed them when she pulled her eyes from the monitor. Numbly, she picked up the most recent one and began to read.

August 4, 1994

The noises are growing louder. The sound of Juliet walking on the stairs has grown more frequent since the séance – I wonder, is she telling me something? Perhaps it has to do with the basement. It is a frightening place to be. The imp, as the medium called it, is more insistent that I deal with him. At times it feels as if he is pulling on my very consciousness, trying to get inside. He wails at all hours of the day and night.

And finally, I have contacted a demonologist at the medium's insistence to deal with the repeated happenings in the kitchen and dining room. She swears the thing that taunts me is from the bowels of Hell itself. I have always considered myself to be a pragmatic person, but the sensations have ripped that part of me away. I now fear for my life when I am downstairs. I should probably bar the door somehow.

Sheila dropped the book back to the table. Her breath came in short, ragged gasps. The fear Elias Gaston felt slithered down her spine and seated itself deep in her belly. There was more going on here than even he was able to comprehend, and she feared then that perhaps Bobby's lack of memory was more than just psychological.

She swallowed and stared down at the panel of buttons. She was only a waitress… not technical at all… but she could read, and she was fairly certain the switch that read "master" would control all cameras and sound. When she flipped it, each of the ten cameras skipped backwards several frames and went black. Red lights flashed brightly, then the headsets crackled to life.

Sheila slipped one set over her ears, shuddering at the sound of the woman screaming. Biting down on the terror, she lifted her eyes to the monitors, and learned the identities of each of the missing men. She remembered their faces from the television, and had this been any other situation, she'd have found herself giddy and a bit star-struck by the candid footage.

She noticed as the tapes rolled, grim lines split Bobby's face even then, but he kept a strong façade for his friends.

She skimmed the preliminaries with the master skip button, but a sudden movement in between the static-lines of the master bedroom camera had her slamming all the feeds to a stop. She backed up and watched it again, despite the flood of panic in her stomach. A hand flew to her mouth to stifle a scream as she watched Elias Gaston, ten years dead, walk around the bed as if he were still alive and well. He pulled back the covers, lay down in the bed, and vanished from sight in a settling flutter of sheets.

Sheila bit her knuckles, but the scream still squeaked free.

Camera two showed the foyer and formal living room, and the first shadows of flashlight trails as the hunters entered the house. She pressed the forward button again, watching in double-time as the first group investigated, then the second went in and upstairs. The second pair, obviously called in by the unsure looks from the faces of the first two, made their way up to the master bedroom too. Movement on the tenth camera caught her attention then.

Bobby was out of the van, standing between the open doors, and staring toward the house. Switching the audio feed back over, she listened as Tim tried multiple times to ask him what was wrong. Then, he simply walked toward the house, ignoring Tim's pleas as he ran after Bobby. That was at one hour and forty-nine minutes into the feed.

Exactly two hours and one minute into the feed, all hell broke loose.

Chad and Aaron entered the basement, so fascinated by the EMP activity they never heard the heavy oak door upstairs open and slam. Tim's body then flew across the camera two field, landing in a crumpled heap at the foot of the couch. Blood immediately pooled under his head. Sheila never saw his assailant.

The thick floors muffled all sound from the foyer. The two investigators in the basement went on unhindered by the knowledge that their friend was dead. On the audio, the basement door squeaked open and closed. The sound obviously caught their attention.

"What was that?" Aaron asked.

"Basement door," Chad said, holding up the EMP reader. Sheila could see even across the distance that it was going wild. Then a blur across the camera knocked it askew. Three sets of feet moved back and forth. One throaty gurgle and a scream later, Aaron's body hit the floor, his head twisted so that his dead, frightened eyes stared into the camera, a thin trickle of blood running from his nose.

Sheila screamed into her hands and reached over to snatch the van doors shut. Something was definitely wrong, and it was still loose on the grounds. In her rush to secure herself, she missed the body being dragged away. All she saw when she looked back was a single set of sneakered feet passing through the camera's line of sight and retreating up the stairs.

Tim's body was gone as well, the only indication he had ever even been there a pool of blood seeping into the thick Persian rug. All other furniture looked dusty and untouched, covered by sheets that didn't so much as flutter with a draft. On the second floor, Buddy and Martin moved gingerly out of view of the only clear camera from the floor, sticking close as the sounds of disembodied footsteps and laughter echoed around them. Breaking glass sounded through the headphones, and she realized when she looked out the back window of the van that one of the upstairs windows was, in fact, broken. She heard the sound of the other man dying, but it was obviously in a room without a camera. His screams echoed in her head long after the hissing silence resumed.

Screeching, Sheila slammed the stop button. Curling her arms around herself, she buried her face into her knees to fight down the nausea crawling back up her throat. Tears streamed down her face, but she hardly noticed. Her whole body shivered and jolted, but she couldn't stop it. Alarms were going off in her head, telling her to get out. It was not safe.

As she turned to exit the van, her hand caught the corner of one of the journals. It slipped from the metal desk and thumped to the floor of the van, falling open several pages forward from where she'd read. Even in a state of panic, she noticed the transition in handwriting, and it deeply unsettled her.

November 18, 1994

Paranormal activity calmer. Demonologist a fraud. No imp. No people on stairs. Horses are skittish after stroke and had to be put down. Hearing small voice, but doctor says is normal.

This was not Elias Gaston. It might have looked like him when it was written, but the consciousness was not his. The difference in the writing jolted her memories of the last few times she visited him. He looked the same, yet different. Something more than just a stroke was wrong with him. And the horses... they had been fine. They were frightened of him, yes, but never of her. Elias never would have put those horses down without a valid reason—he loved them.

And in her mind, *skittish* was not a valid reason. With numb fingers, she turned the pages, noticing the majority of the book was blank. Entries tapered off significantly after November of 1994. The last entry was dated two years and one day before he died.

March 28, 1995

so hungry existence not fulfilled silence

It made no sense, and only reinforced the feeling that Elias Gaston's downfall had very little to do with his "stroke." She glanced back at the monitors, still eerily unmoving and quiet. He spoke of a demon... the very word chilled her to the bone. Sheila was sure then that when Elias Gaston's body died, it was not his consciousness inside.

God, she wanted to leave; to get back in her car, drive to Junction City, and pretend like she'd never seen any of this. She could do it, too... the keys were still in the ignition, and there was nobody to stop her.

But if she left… the knowledge she'd deserted Bobby would haunt her forever. She would always remember she ran away when her family – the only family she really had left, no matter how distant – needed her the most.

A small whimper escaped her throat, followed by a racking sob. She didn't want to do this, but she couldn't live with herself if she didn't. Sheila knew the only way she could hope to figure out what happened was to keep watching. With shaking fingers, she punched the play button and scanned the feed forward.

Sometime later, the basement camera jostled and then righted on its tripod. The feed focused and she recognized Bobby's face… but something about him wasn't right. His features looked stretched, his eyes hollow and dead.

"Bobby?" Chad's voice filled her headphones. He sounded terrified. "Are you down here?"

"Yeah," Bobby replied. Even his voice didn't sound like she remembered. It had that same spooky, unloving quality that Elias' writing carried, by which his voice had been overwhelmed those last few years. "Just fixing the camera."

"Leave it!" Chad shouted. "We need to get the hell out of here!" His voice was high and thready. "You were right… there's something bad in here."

"No," Bobby replied, baring his teeth in a horrific caricature of what she could only assume was supposed to be a smile. "I was wrong."

"Are you nuts? The guys are all dead!"

"Yeah," he said again. For a split second it looked like his skin warbled over his bones – vibrated as if trying to escape from his skull. Sheila shrank into herself further, drawing her knees up in the chair again. The transformation was unearthly, and his grandfather's words sprang to her mind. "I think we should go upstairs now."

Flashing one final, deathly smile for the camera, he turned and followed Chad up the stairs. His teeth looked sharper, his eyes dim and cruel. His fingers curled into hooks at his side.

Somewhere in the house, the sound of a body hitting the floor echoed off the walls. Thin, distant, female laughter followed it, growing louder as Chad's body slumped down the basement stairs, landing in a broken heap.

The next time Bobby appeared was in the master bedroom. Following his grandfather's footsteps, he padded around the bed, pulled the covers back, and lay down. It wasn't right. She knew his face, but he was a stranger. A lump gathered in her throat. Bobby shuffled around the bed as if he'd had a stroke, his eyes dead and soulless.

Then, at 2:06 AM, Bobby sat up, looked around as if he had no idea where he was, and ran. When he ran, he looked like the healthy young man she'd met only hours before. And it was then she knew he'd met the same fate as his grandfather.

"Well, hello again."

Sheila screamed. She'd been watching the tape so intently she never heard the van door open. Bobby, a lunatic grin on his lips, leaned against the open door.

"Bobby!" she gasped. "What's going on?" He didn't answer; only looked at her with those dead eyes. "Bobby?"

He shook his head. "Bobby's gone." The voice was not his. She didn't have time to scream again as he lunged for her.

Several hours later, the abandoned camera played back footage of two police officers in the basement. At the foot of the stairs, Bobby Gaston's form materialized. Then he walked past the camera's field, toward the officers. Two shots were fired. One officer flew backwards, hitting the wall with fatal, spine-cracking force. The other backed into view, jaw working like a loose hinge. Bobby stepped forward and placed his hands on either side of the man's head. Then, he turned to smile at the camera as he twisted the officer's head around on his shoulders and dropped him to the floor, dead.

He laughed in a voice not his own.

THREE

WHEN I WOKE UP, I had a splitting headache. Large patches of my memory were missing from the last two days, threads of my conscience telling me they were filled with darkness. I didn't doubt it... who the hell knew what I had done?

Flashes of history blinked behind my eyes like snapshots from some B-grade movie. Blood. Bodies. Screams of terror. Broken glass. A bed. Sheila's tits. And more blood. I crawled out of the bed and went to the bathroom, noting my nakedness and the thin trails of dried bodily fluids crisscrossing my belly and legs. I looked like a war victim, covered in blood and semen, cuts and bruises.

The motel I was in wasn't much, I noticed as I left the bathroom and picked up my jeans, but it was clean. Sheila lay on the bed next to where I'd woken up, face down and naked. There was no blood, but I didn't think she was alive. I wasn't sure, and I didn't want to find out.

In the back of my head I heard sickly laughter. The voice was familiar and female — my grandmother's voice, I noted with a hint of sadness — but the thing laughing at me had never been human. My gut instinct was to throw my hands over my ears and wait until it went away, but that wasn't going to happen.

The laughter grew in pitch until the sound of it was deafening, rattling off the walls of my brain, and I was helpless to back away. My vision narrowed as if I were looking down a long, dark hallway toward my own eyes. That sick feeling of inevitability settled in around me again, and I felt myself losing control one more time.

I had the feeling that, after this time, I wouldn't ever be me again.

A set of keys jangled in my hand, and I knew they belonged to an orange Camaro that would be sitting right outside. I couldn't hear Sheila breathing, but I hoped she was. In the mirror, I could see myself reflected back, surrounded by something that wasn't at all me.

Then, I remembered everything.

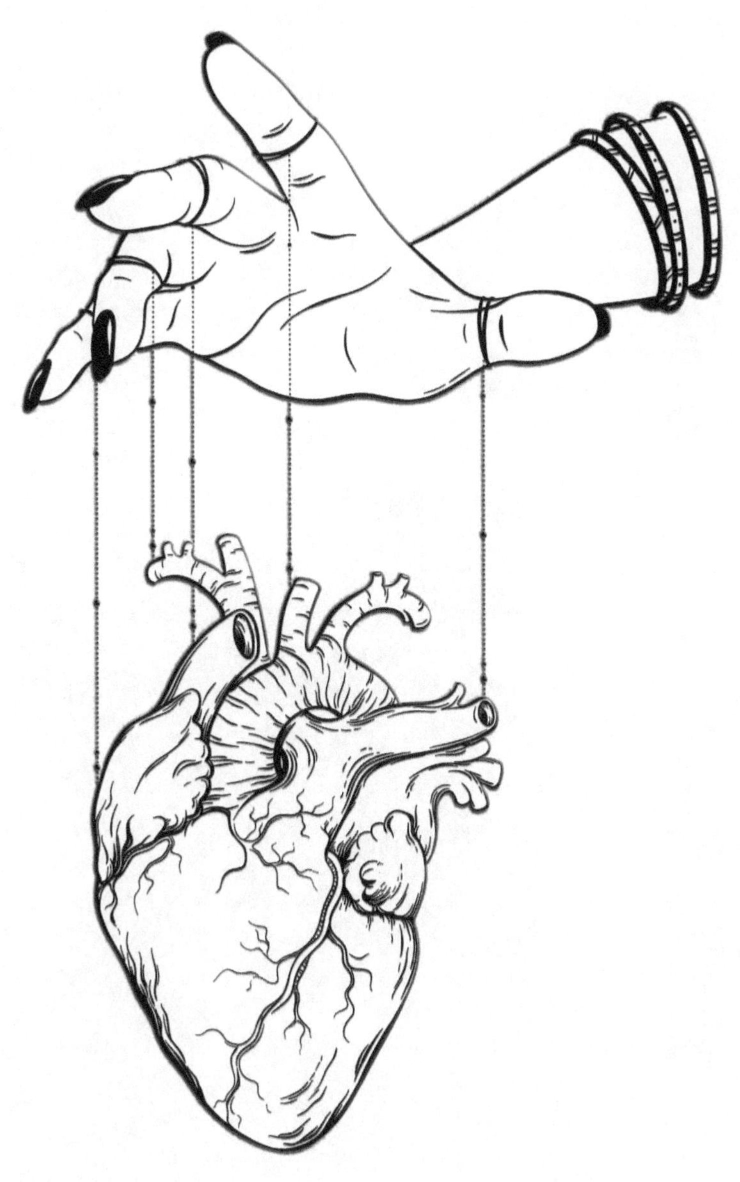

Wolfy

THE LITTLE BLONDE BIMBO'S GUTS TASTED PRETTY good. Not a lot of meat on her, but I'm partial to the liver anyway so it was a lot less work. Hers was pretty well saturated too. Tasted like vodka and cranberry juice. There were other parts on her that were tender and mighty tasty as well, but we don't talk about those. I mean yeah, I'd rather eat a brunette any day, but when it's that time of the month, I'm not very picky.

For me, not her. Anywho, back to Little Red Riding Whore…

She came skipping down the road with her red cape flapping along in the breeze. I know, I know…it's cliché for the wolf to go after the girl in the red getup. I did that one time before and almost lost my head to some wayward do-gooder with an axe. You'd think I would have learned my lesson.

But this girl…man, she was just slobberin' for it. Bitch had to be a hooker. *Had* to be. The poor excuse for a skirt barely covered her ass. Her stockings were torn to hell and back and that slip of fabric over her tits? It was an insult to shirts everywhere. I very highly doubt she was on the way to Grandma's house for a picnic. Unless said picnic involved copious amounts of blow.

And it sure as shit wasn't cookies filling that little red bag of hers. Still, she was clean enough and smelled pretty, and there were no discernible diseases. And, damn it, I was hungry.

I romped my way down the side of the road just out of her line of sight, and when she stopped to adjust the buckle at the top of her bright red hooker boots (are we seeing a theme emerge yet?), I pounced. Took her down with a spine-popping bite to the throat and laid her out in the tall grass. Then I ripped her guts wide open and had a fine meal. Then the moon started to set. The fangs and fur retracted, leaving my naked ass surrounded by Blondie's guts.

That's right beotches. I is a werewolf. Grade-A Moon-Mad Meat, baby. I follow the canine way of thinking, except that I generally don't piss on the things I can't eat or fuck. And let me tell you, I certainly ain't afraid to eat a bitch either. It's why I'm so well suited to my lupine syndrome.

Wow. Serious mental detour there. Back to the point.

After dinner I found myself picking blonde out of my teeth as I walked naked and blood-soaked down the highway. I left my clothes at home, not thinking that I'd shift again before I got back. No such luck. The wolf in me is a seriously selfish bastard and left me hanging. Now the tricky part would be getting home without being seen. These back roads were mostly deserted, but it was still a considerable walk. If I'd been able to stay in wolf form the three miles back would have gone by a lot faster, but the sated beast didn't give a shit about me. To make matters worse, it started to rain.

At least the rain washed most of the blood away.

By the time I got home, I was starving. Eating blondes is sort of like having Chinese. Half an hour after dinner, a brother is hungry again. So I did what any self-respecting bachelor would do. I put on pants and hit up the all-night diner in town. When I opened the door, the dubious aromas of pork fat, axle grease and body odor crawled out to greet me.

Classy.

Like a good single man I went in anyway. The Department of Health and Environmental Control's giant "C" sticker on the door didn't faze me at all. Inside was cheap food, beer, and no rain. And the no rain part was the most important in my book, and apparently I wasn't the only one who felt that way. The place was slammed. My stomach rumbled loudly as I took the only unoccupied booth in the place and lit a cigarette. The waitress wasn't thrilled with my presence, nor was I with hers. I was irritable and the raw human flesh sloshing around my insides wasn't playing so nice, so I did the only thing I could think of:

"I'll have three eggs over medium with sausage — well done — hash browns, toast, and a side of bacon. Make that a double order on the bacon. Oh, and a beer."

The waitress gave an impatient sigh and stormed off. I briefly considered eating her, but she was really skinny. And a redhead. They're chewy, so what little meat I might find wouldn't be worth the search.

The food came before the beer, which pissed me off because I was thirsty. Before I ever took a bite I made loud coughing sounds which brought the cook running with a glass of water and an apology. I drank the water, then the beer. Then I ordered another one while I tucked into my eighth meal of the day.

Somewhere around the third sausage patty and my fourth belch, a trio of overweight cops sat down next to me. They ordered coffee and cake – again, another nasty cliché — and started to discuss police business in voices much too loud for the diner. See, that's how small-town gossip spreads. It's the cops.

I attempted to ignore the chatter as I started in on that lovely plate of poor, unsuspecting bacon. It was damn good bacon, too. There's something to be said for a dirty grill in a small-town diner—and that something is bacon. Fucking awesome bacon at that. The other thing to say about small-town diners is that they never stay quiet long.

In a valiant attempt to ignore the Long Pig Special at the next table, I envisioned them sizzling on the grill in the back. The thought wasn't nearly as appetizing as the greasy pork on my plate because at the moment I was human. If wolfy-boy came out to play, that might be a different story. As I contemplated the smell of burning cop-fat, one of the oinkers said something that brought my attention back around to them.

"...dead on the highway..."

"...guts ripped open and eaten..."

The hair across my neck stood on end. They found Little Red Riding Whore already. Shit. Of course Little Piggies One, Two, and Three would have an easier time winning the Miss USA Pageant than catching me, but they didn't know that. Still, I had serious problems with authority, so I shoveled the rest of my food in my face, downed the second beer, and wrapped the remainder of my bacon in a napkin for the trip home. Too bad I didn't realize there was a bloody handprint on my t-shirt until I went to bed.

Which was exactly why Little Piggy Number One showed up on my doorstep at eight o'clock the next morning and woke me from a sound sleep. That pissed me off so when I answered the door, I did it bare-assed naked and with a scowl on my face. At nearly six-feet-eight-inches, I'm a big guy, and this Little Piggy wasn't much bigger than a minute. Unless we're measuring waist-size.

"Charles Black?" he asked. He looked terrified. I didn't smile even though I wanted to.

"Yeah?"

"I need to ask you a few questions."

Great. "Like what?"

"Can I come in?"

"Theoretically, yes."

He looked shocked. I still didn't smile. "May I?

My face hurt from my forced stoicism. This might prove to be fun after all. I stepped back, still naked, and greatly enjoyed his sudden hesitation. I knew from the look in his eyes that he'd already convicted me of murder. And I was a hell of a lot bigger than him.

"Either come in or I'm going back to bed."

He came in, damn it. I took a seat in my recliner. No offer of a drink or a snack. Yeah, my Mama raised me with manners. Didn't mean I always used them. I left him to figure out how to sit down on the sofa.

"What do you want to know?" I prompted after several minutes of boring silence.

"Could you — er — would you mind greatly putting on some pants?"

Actually, I did. I minded greatly. But I wasn't about to tell Bacon McOinker that. The pudgy little fart looked like he was going to cry, so I spared him the sight of my nudity and went to put on pants. Hell, I couldn't blame the poor soul. If I'd seen me standing naked in a doorway I would probably be a little intimidated too. He looked decidedly less frightened when I returned, and I immediately felt the need to rectify that. I poured myself a glass of whiskey.

"You were going to ask me something?" I prompted as I came to stand directly behind him. Poor Little Piggy actually squealed. I smirked.

"About your activities last night…"

"What of them?"

"Were you in Madigan's Diner at 11:45 last night?"

Idiot. He knew damn well I was. How many people in Cook County are nearly seven feet tall?

"Nope." I drained the glass to hide my smile.

"You were seen leaving the diner with blood on your clothes."

Uh-huh.

"Nope. Wasn't me. I was here most of the night."

"Doing what?"

"Some chick named Candy." I said it with a straight face. It derailed him.

"Is she still here?"

"Hell no," I snorted. He blinked at me. "Tricks don't sleep in my bed."

"How can I get in touch with her?"

I shrugged. "Don't know."

"You mean you had… relations… with a stranger?"

"If by 'relations' you mean 'fucked seven ways from Sunday and bounced out the door like a basketball' then yep."

"Oh. Was she blonde?"

"Why do you ask?"

He hesitated. "There was… an incident… not far from here last night." Ah, and so he began the interesting, if not moderately tedious I-can't-tell-you-anything-but-I'm-going-to-tell-you-everything dance.

"You mean the girl with her guts ripped out?" He paled and nodded. I picked a cigarette out of the pack on the table and stuck it between my lips. "Yeah," I mumbled as I lit the butt, "heard about that."

"How?"

"Leak in the department," I replied. "Jared Champlin. Good buddy. Called to warn me to lock my doors." I took a long drag and blew the smoke directly at him. He coughed and waved a stumpy hand in front of his face. "Got a bad habit of forgetting way out here." I got up and crossed the room, the cigarette stuck out of my mouth. In one swift movement I poured and knocked back a second glass of whiskey without ever dislodging my smoke. "And to answer your question: No. Candy is a goth chick with a blue mohawk."

Little Piggy swallowed hard as he rose and started for the door.

"Thank you for your time."

Five minutes later, my phone rang.

"Good morning, Jared," I said by way of introduction.

"Goddamn it, Charlie! You have to stop with the name dropping! You're going to get my ass fired!" I remained silent. He sighed. "I don't mind covering your ass when you wolf out, but damn it!"

"Thanks, buddy. I owe you one."

"More than one, jackass. He's suspicious, you know."

"I know."

"Charlie…" He said my name as a warning.

"Jared?"

"Don't."

"Yep." I hung up the phone and jerked the cord out of the back for good measure. Then I went outside and pulled the deer carcass from the refrigerator under my shed and threw it in the back of my truck.

Then I tossed it at the Little Piggy's cruiser and made his murder look like an accident. On the way home I realized something. This time I might have fucked up just a little bit. Little Red Riding Whore's guts weren't worth this shit.

Four hours later, Jared showed up at my house.

"Goddamn it, Charlie…"

"You like that phrase." I handed him a beer. He growled and snatched it up as he followed me inside. He still had his uniform on.

"I'd hate to think you had anything to do with it."

"It's not like I keep dead deer in my refrigerator."

He groaned. Then he drained the bottle. "Damn it, Charlie." I gave him another one.

"Alright, I got sloppy. Just keep the pigs off my ass and I won't do it again."

He wandered around the room, steadily sucking at the longneck in his hand. Jared and I, we go way back. We grew up together. Oh, and he's the only person in the world that knows about my affliction. I saved his life once, so he saves my ass all the time. But that one act of kindness doesn't make me a good guy. I'm okay with that.

So, Jared scolded me some more. Then he drank two more beers. After that he took off his badge. And he had another beer. He didn't ask any more questions and I didn't offer any other information. However, I did figure out several creative ways to dispose of the uniformed long pigs waiting in the wings.

I had two whole days to forget about Little Red Riding Whore before Little Piggy Number Two showed up. When he did, he came in with guns blazing. Figuratively. Big guy, kinda ugly. Still not as big as me, though. He scowled a lot too.

"We know where you were and what you were doing," he said and scowled some more. Intimidation. Admirable, but it wasn't about to work on me.

"Care to tell me what point in time we're discussing?" I asked. "I've been to lots of places and done lots of things."

"You know what I'm talking about."

"Do I?"

The conversation went on like this for another ten minutes or so. The more pissed off he got, the harder I had to fight not to laugh. The meathead turned the color of burnt pepperoni. I half expected him to stroke out on my living room floor. Would have saved me a world of trouble if he had, too, 'cause this big sumbitch did not seem to want to go easily.

When he finally got angry enough to leave, I gave him a three minute head-start. Then I jumped in my truck, sadly if I do say so because I knew it would be the last time I'd drive her, and took a short cut around. There's this intersection a few miles out that's a bit of a death trap. It's got a stop sign laid down next to the road under blackberry bushes. People tend to fly through it going way too fast. This guy would be going way too fast. If I could just position my old truck…

BINGO.

Right on schedule, Little Piggy Number Two blew through the intersection at breakneck speed and slammed into the bed of my truck. I spun a few times, but his cruiser flipped twice and landed top-down in the ditch. The way that car was crunched down I just knew he was dead.

No such luck.

Fucker was still alive when I got to the car. Dazed, but still breathing. So I reached through the shattered windshield and snapped his meaty neck. Then I went back to my truck, picked my cell phone up off the passenger's side floorboard, and dialed 911.

Naturally the location of the accident piqued Jared's interest. When he arrived, I was balanced on a stretcher with a paramedic taping up the cut on my head. Little Piggy Number Two was in a black bag on the side of the road. I got a really dirty look from my buddy, but he didn't say anything. Nothing he could say, either. This one was a complete accident.

Mostly.

But they didn't need to know that.

"Not my fault, Jared," I said as the paramedics went to load the body.

"I very highly doubt that, Charlie."

"He was going too damn fast. He ran the stop sign and hit me."

"Funny coincidence." Jared stared at me. He was so calm he almost looked maniacal. I didn't like that look. Yeah, Jared saw through me. However, in the eyes of the law I was the victim and my assailant was dead.

Woo-hoo! New truck for me, courtesy of the police department.

That left me with one last problem: Little Piggy Number Three.

On the scene, pissed off, and way too damned suspicious. He didn't say anything as the paramedics loaded me into the ambulance with the body bag. If it were *that time of the month*, I'd have tucked in and had a fine meal.

But I behaved myself and let them cart me off to the hospital. Four hours later, they let me go and Jared took me home, yelling all the way without stopping to take a breath. I took a nap. He punched me in the arm to wake me up.

"Goddamn it, Charlie!"

"You keep saying that," I replied and shot him my best shit-eating grin.

"You keep killing people."

"No shit, Sherlock."

"Why?" he asked. Wow, what a stupid question.

"They won't leave me alone."

"You ate a woman," he said.

"Not consciously! I was a wolf at the time!" That's a pretty damned good defense, too. It's not like I can control the wolf.

"It isn't the first time."

"Uh, hello? Werewolf!" Did I seriously have to remind him?

"Irrelevant. Stop it."

"Tell them to leave me alone."

Jared scowled. "I'll do my best to clear you but I make no promises."

Good enough. Too bad it didn't work.

About a week after the accident, Little Piggy Number Three showed up with a stack of forms and even more questions. I signed the papers and put him off touting a migraine—left over from the accident, of course—and took his card. He wanted me to call and make an appointment. Yeah, right. But I said okay and slammed the door in his face.

Then I went back to watching porn.

Not really, but it sounded pretty good at the time. I actually sat back down in my recliner and finished off a TV dinner while contemplating thirty different ways to wipe out the cop. Yeah, Jared would have my hide for it, but at that point I'd rather take an ass-chewing from a friend than be trapped in a prison cell on a full moon. That wouldn't work out very well for anyone.

So another week passed, putting me that much closer to the full moon, and Little Piggy Number Three showed up to antagonize me again. This time he came armed with a search warrant.

Oh, yeah, I was *so* freaking scared. Too bad sarcasm doesn't translate to text otherwise I'd snort.

So I let him in.

"Would you mind stepping outside?" he asked. I rolled my eyes at him.

"Tell you what," I replied, "It's hot out there so I'm not sitting outside. But I am going to sit right here in my recliner and finish watching this episode of Jerry Springer. Feel free to look anywhere. Just clean up your mess afterwards, 'kay?"

"That's against protocol."

"Dude, I'm twice your size. Do you really want to try to wrestle me outside?" He paled four shades. He knew as well as I did that he didn't want to piss me off. Smart boy... sort of.

So I sat down and turned up the sound. He dug around for a few minutes and found nothing of any interest. Apparently in small southern towns all killers are supposed to keep trophies for easy identification when the police come searching, but not this wolf. The more he dug, the more frustrated he became.

At one point he came out of my bathroom with an antique bowie knife and wanted to know why it was in there. I told him I kept weapons in every room in case some psychopath decided to break into my house and attack me. He didn't believe me, but he didn't ask any other questions.

He did leave with a bag of my stuff, though. I assumed he was taking it for DNA profiling or some other bogus cop shit. My first instinct was to eat him, but I behaved myself and let him leave. Instead I called Jared.

"Make sure that bag of shit disappears," I told him when he answered.

"Not my area, Charlie."

"Dude. You either have to get rid of it or I'm going to eat him."

Jared hesitated. Then he sighed. "Goddamn it, Charlie." I had him on that one. "I'll do my best to get my hands on it but I can't promise anything."

"Would you rather I become a headline on the *New York Times* when I wolf out in a four-by-nine cell and eat an entire prison full of people?" He didn't answer. Didn't say much else after that, as a matter of fact. "Look, I know I'm asking a lot and I know I fucked up big-time on this one. If I need to leave town I will. Just stop him from profiling my stuff and we'll be good. Oh, and I want my damned knife back."

There was a long, awkward pause. Jared sighed. "I'll do what I can. Just don't kill him." I hung up the phone without answering. I promised nothing and he knew it. Yeah, I'd leave if I had to, but I really didn't want to do that. I liked my home—I'd lived in the house my whole life, so I wasn't thrilled with the idea of deserting it now. In fact, I refused to leave home for something as trivial as a hooker in bright red boots.

I assumed Jared held up his end of this not-so-square deal because I didn't hear anything from anybody. Good thing too, because the closer it came to that full moon, the more irritable I became. I probably would have snapped someone's neck just for setting foot on my porch. Justin would be proud of me for staying locked up in my house, mainly because it meant I wouldn't cause him any more trouble.

When I finally wolfed out and took to the woods I made sure to steer clear of the main roads. I kept to myself and only ate a few small animals. Of course, being a werewolf is sort of like being Dr. Jekyll and Mr. Hyde because part of me tried to keep my nose clean while the other half wanted to go all Incredible Hulk and bust up in the police station to beat the you-know-what out of Little Piggy Number Three. But I didn't.

I just looked up his information in the telephone book, then very calmly walked up to his front door in his nice suburban neighborhood, knocked, and put a .38 slug right between his pudgy little eyes when he answered. Yes, it was messy. Yes, it was completely uncalled for. Yes, Jared jumped my ass for it. But there was no way in hell I was letting him keep on with any sort of suspicion. The advantage I had was that he was home alone and nobody saw a thing. Convenient, wasn't it?

So in the end everything worked out just peachy. The three Little Piggies stopped bothering me for various reasons. The coroner ruled Little Red Riding Whore's death accidental—an animal attack. Jared got off my back and eventually returned my stuff. And I got to stay home in my corner of the woods on the outskirts of Cook County.

Look, I never said I was a good guy, okay? I'm a monster, and I'm perfectly okay with that. I'm the bad guy. I'm the thing that goes bump in the night. I'm the creature with teeth and fur. I'm perfectly happy being me. So what if I ate some farmer's stock of pigs one time? And who cares about the grandmother I chewed up when I was a kid? The old biddy didn't taste very good, and she sure as hell wasn't useful for very much, either. That woman was one step away from a padded room in a nursing home. As far as I could tell I did her and her pathetic family a favor by saving them the cost of room and board.

Whatever. I don't see what the big deal about eating people is anyway.

Skippin' Stones

SKIPPIN' STONES DOWN BY THE CRICK...

That was where any momma could find her little boy on a Saturday afternoon in Rock Mountain, Tennessee. We would line up, one by one in even spaces all up and down the loamy crick-bed, searchin' for the best, shiniest river-rocks to thump across the surface of that little offshoot of the Tennessee River. Sometimes we would all huddle up together and compare stones before havin' a contest to see who could skip the farthest, or who could drag the most jumps outta our rocks. There weren't no television or nothin' like that, so us kids had to entertain ourselves. Skippin' stones meant we got to throw things without getting' in trouble.

Me, I always liked the little, flat ones. Perfectly round, and light-colored. Sometimes I picked up ones with veins of dark sumthin-or-other runnin' through 'em, but most of the time I went for the white or light gray ones. Call it superstition, but those light colors always did me good. I still believe it, too, 'cause the day I met the Devil, I was skippin' rocks with dark streaks in 'em.

Me an' Jimmy Tanner was out by the crick one afternoon when we was six and Jimmy's momma came lookin' for him, mad as a wet hen and armed with her favorite whippin' stick.

"Get yo'self back to that house right his minute, Jimmy-boy!" she screeched, wavin' her hands around like her tail was on fire. That skinny little stick wobbled around in the air, but we knowed better than to think it would break. Them green wood switches she picked would bend into all sortsa knots before they'd up and break. "Yo' daddy is gonna ring yo' neck for what you done gone and did!"

The boy took off runnin' like his tail was gonna be on fire…and it prob'ly was, too, cause his momma really liked her whippin' sticks. She caught me 'cross the knees one time for smartin' off to her. I never did it again, I tell you what.

After Jimmy run off and left me standin' knee-deep in the cool water with my shoes up on a sunny rock, I bent down and picked up somethin' outta the water. It was a stone; the flattest, shiniest one I ever seen. It was bright white, but it had a streak of sparkly black runnin' right down its middle.

I'm gonna have your soul, Mickey.

I felt the voice, like a cold chill of goosebumps up my back and my arms. It sounded like the wind, like nature had found her voice and wasn't too happy with me.

You can't run, and you can't hide, Mickey. I'm gonna take your soul straight to Hell.

"Who's there?" I called out. Now, don't get me wrong…I was scared. So scared I didn't notice the warm trickle down the inside of my right leg 'til long after I'd gone screamin' home and crawled up cryin' in my momma's arms.

You know who I am, Mickey. Don't play dumb.

"Now you listen to me, you dirty ol' Devil!" I screamed. I know I sound a lot braver than I was, but when you're eight years old, you ain't got the good sense God gave a wet paper bag. "You gonna turn right back around and you is gonna go straight back to Heck!" I couldn't say Hell yet. Momma woulda washed my mouth out for sure. It didn't matter. The Devil knew what I was talking about.

Tell me, Mickey… what's it like to be afraid of something you can't see?

"I don't wanna see you! I want you to leave me alone!" I turned right around and I ran all the way home, leavin' my shoes sittin' on that rock. I got a whoopin' like you wouldn't believe for it, too. She wanted my Daddy to send me back down to the crick to get 'em cause they costed a whole fifteen dollars and eighty-three cents, but it was already getting' dark and my Daddy said no he weren't gonna make me do it 'cause I might get hurt.

The next day I went back down by the crick. I told Momma I was goin' to get my shoes, but I was really goin' with Jimmy an' our friend Timmy Barnes to skip some more stones. My shoes was still sittin' there waitin' on me, an' that was when I realized I'd done gone and made a mess of myself for nothin'. There wasn't nobody waitin' to take my soul.

After awhile Timmy went home, and not long after that Jimmy's momma came and got him, still squealin' her head off over something Jimmy gone and did now. I shoulda gone home when them boys left me, but I was feelin' brave. I wanted to prove that I could be a big boy, so I stuck my hands down in the water and pulled up a handful of stones.

In the middle of those stones was another solid white one with a sparkly, black vein. It mighta been the same one I picked up yest'day, cause I don't remember if I dropped it or not.

I have your shoes, Mickey.

I stopped to listen to that voice in the wind again then I decided then to do the big-boy thing and ignore it. I still had the stone in my hand, and I focused on its smooth, cold surface. My stubby little fingers slipped over it, finding the perfect hold. Pulling my arm back, I slung that rock as hard as I could, twistin' it out to the side and letting go with my thumb on top, just like my Daddy taught me to do.

It bounced all the way across the crick, then turned in midair and bounced right back to me.

I turned around and started to run, but then I saw him standin' on the bank, right next to my shoes. He was a tall, thin man, and he looked like every other tall, thin man that ever walked this planet. But it was the middle of the summer and that darned ol' Devil wore a suit and tie, and leaned on a fancy walkin' stick. My top half was sweatin' like a pig, so I knew it was H-A-W-T — HOT.

But that Devil, he didn't sweat. He didn't breathe heavy. He just stood there and smiled at me. If I hadn't knowed that was the Devil lookin' at me, I woulda thought he was somebody's brother. His hair was the color of sunshine and he had big, blue eyes. Only…in the middle of those eyes, I could see the fire just a-burnin'. And it weren't no fire I never wanted to see again.

Come on, Mickey… come and get your shoes.

Uh-uh…no way was I gonna leave the water and let that monster get near me. And I sure as heck wasn't gonna go home without my shoes two days in a row. My Momma would have my hide for sure.

I was just a kid and all, but I was pretty darn sure that if he got his hands on me, my goose was cooked. So I stood there, that shiny stone clutched in my hand – how did it get there, I wondered—staring into the eyes of the Almighty's nemesis.

"What do you want with me?" I asked. I'd already pissed myself again. I was scared out of my gourd, but I was stuck. If I set foot on land, he was gonna get me.

I want your soul, Mickey.

"Yeah, you already said that," I said. I'd heard his voice, clear as day…but his mouth didn't move. What he said came from somewhere else, and I didn't like that. "Why do you keep sayin' my name?"

Does it bother you, Mickey?

Yeah, it bothered me, but I weren't about to let him know it. Sure, I knowed somethin' was wrong, but I shoulda knowed it didn't have jack-all to do with that stone, but I was naught but eight years old that day. I know now that I didn't know no better then 'cause that stone disappeared into my pocket by my own hand. It mighta been that minute that I really got lost, 'cause after my hands was free, I hitched up my pants to wade outta that crick. I weren't really scared no more, 'cause I weren't really thinkin' so much about what I was doin'.

"I ain't gon' letchoo kill me, you mean ol' Devil!" I shouted while my feet carried me right on up to stand in front a' him. That man that wasn't a man looked down at me with a slick, nasty smile, an' then he laid his cold, slimy hand on the toppa my head.

"Oh, Mickey," he said outta his mouth and I realized I liked that sound even less than the wind-voice, "I have no intention of killing you." My head started to tickle and tingle, like he was suckin' my brain out with his fingers. His smile got real wide, and I got dizzy. "You are an innocent, Mickey," he told me. "But your family is not. Your mother sold you to me, Mickey. You and your brother."

"I ain't got no brother!" I squealed, and tried to jerk my head away. An' me pullin' away? Didn't work, 'cause he had a strong hold on my hair.

"Oh, yes you do, Mickey. She gave me your souls—both of them—because she wanted to be pretty." Maybe so, an' maybe she just went ahead and sold him outright. Didn't give him a chance to go bad like me.

"I don't believe you," I said, but those words didn't have much backbone. All my energy was drainin' outta the top of my head and into his hand. I stood there and stared up at that evil man, my pants wet with piss and crick-water and my feet still bare. My shoes was in his hand and tears and snot was runnin' down my face and I didn't know anything at all but that my Momma didn't love me enough to protect me from the Devil hisself.

A warm feeling spread out all over me, and all that fright disappeared when he took his hand offa my head. I felt so empty. I didn't like it, but weren't naught I could do about it. The Devil, he stuck my shoes in my hand and he smiled down at me again.

"Go home now, Mickey. Go on home and don't you tell your mother about any of this. Understand?"

I nodded, struck dumb, and with my shoes in my hands and piss drippin' from the leg of my rolled-up pants, I went home, just like he told me to. Only I stopped on the porch and looked up at the ratty ol' door. I stood there still feelin' all empty inside, knowin' for sure my Momma didn't love me enough to let me go to heaven, an' for an eight-year-old that kinda news could end the world.

For me it did.

That night I thought on it some more, and I stopped carin' about ev'rything. My grades wasn't the best in class anyways, but they got worse after that summer. They got so bad the school wouldn't take me back the followin' fall. Jimmy teed me off so I pushed him down into the crick. He skint his knees all up an' I didn't care. We stopped bein' friends 'cause I wouldn't 'pologize for it neither.

Weren't no need for me to be good no more. I weren't goin' to heaven.

When I turned twelve, I stole Bobby Dickey's bicycle an' I sold it for ten bucks. My Momma whooped me good for it, but it didn't hurt. I didn't feel mucha nothin' after that, 'specially when it came from her. She kilt my heart that day she let that Devil take my soul.

That's why I kilt her.

My Daddy done gon' an' died a year a'fore I done it, and I 'spect she mighta had sumthin' to do with that too, 'cause after he was gone she had lots money an' a diff'rent man comin' over to the house every night. She tol' me it was a heart attack or sumthin' like that, but her eyes was cold and dark and I just knew she was lyin' to me. I didn't know just how she was lyin', but I knew she was, an' I hated her for killin' my Daddy 'cause he was the only person in the world that still loved me. I don't think he ever knew about that deal she made with the Devil neither, 'cause I don't think he woulda let the Devil take my soul.

The night I kilt the evil old biddy was the night that drunk fool named Bradley throwed me down the stairs. I bounced off the bottom step and it broke. Pieces of the rotten old wood crunched against the bones in my arm and sliced me wide open from my elbow nearabouts to my shoulder. I started cryin' and she came runnin' out the door in her housecoat and slippers with a cigarette in her mouth. I tried to tell her what he done gone and did to me, but she didn't care. She tol' me I deserved it, too, for bein' such a stupid little S-H-I-T.

So I was standin' knee-deep in the snow, bleedin' all over the place, cryin' with snot runnin' down my face and piss pourin' down my legs, beggin' my momma to carry me to the doctor and get stitched up and she said no 'cause she had to get dressed to go somewhere and she was tired.

That was the final straw. I got tired of takin' a back seat to her trash and her men. She didn't love me…I knowed that for years. So I picked up the snow shovel an' when she turned around in her slippers and shuffled back up the steps, I bashed her skull flat. She fell face-first to the porch with Bradley screamin' at me goin' "what did you do Mickey, what did you do" and I reached up and smashed her head in again. Then hit him – not so hard to kill him but hard enough to hurt him good. Then I blamed that a-hole she called a boyfriend and told the police he done tried to kill me too and showed 'em the scrapes on my legs and that big, nasty cut up my arm. He went to jail for murder an' I went to the hospital for the first time since I was born. Then I got carried over to a home for boys and stayed 'til I turned eighteen. Nobody wanted to 'dopt a screwed up kid like me from a murdered-up family. My Momma and Daddy was both dead an' I saw one of 'em die… nope, nobody wanted poor little Mickey Landis. Maybe they all knowed sumthin' was wrong with me. Maybe they all took one good look at me and saw I didn't have no soul.

After I got throwed outta that home for bein' too old I took up with two other boys that got throwed out for bein' too old too an' we made a livin' rippin' off old folks in the parks. Made a right good racket too. We stole wallets and jewelry and pretty much everything else we could get our hands on, and we pawned it all for cash. It worked out great 'til that little snot named Jason went an' got hisself caught with drugs and turned us all in. When the cops showed up at our house Chris went all quiet and said okay, but not me. I ran, and they chased me. I weren't about to wind up in the can. Kilt a cop to get away, too.

It took two weeks for 'em to catch up with me. They chased me, but I ran faster. Kilt eight more people, too. Weren't like I had a chance at getting' into heaven noways.

That part started just outside Birmingham. I tucked my thumb out an' hitched a ride with an old man wearing thick glasses and a bad wig. He took me into Shreveport and bought me dinner, and then when we got back in the car the radio said I was a runaway copkiller. The old fart thought it might be a good idea to be a boy scout and turn me in, so I reached over and elbowed his nose just about clean off his face. The car ran off the road and he stomped the brakes. When he throwed it in park, I pummeled him until he didn't have no face left, then took his wallet and tossed him out the passenger door into the gulley. I drove off with his car and didn't never look back.

That old man was the first. After him I ditched the car in a parking garage in Dallas. After him I tucked out my thumb again for round two. My thumb carried me across the country and every time I took wallets an' cars an' left the owners dead in ditches. I did all those things people talk 'bout doin' on the television. I always knowed I'd get caught, but I didn't never consider what would happen to me 'til I got to the last one.

That girl—she weren't much older than me truth be told—she tol' me I had to do sumthin' good for her so she'd carry me around. I stayed with her the longest, robbin' houses and stealin' stuff outta people's unlocked cars. She kissed me all the time and hugged on me like I was her boyfriend or sumthin'. She even took my rock out of my pocket. Said it was purty. Then she crawled up in my lap in that dirty hotel room and asked me to stick her.

Laid her three times that night 'cause she asked me to. She liked it too, 'cause she wanted to do it again, but I knowed some bad things was about to go down. The news people on the radios were findin' my bodies and getting' closer. I had to get out fast and I didn't want this sweet little thing to go down too, but I didn't have time to fool wit' her anymore. I cried when I did it, with snot runnin' down my face and all just like the night I kilt my momma, but I cut that girl's throat in her sleep. Left her dead in the motel an' took her car.

By the time I got to California I had just about ev'ry cop in the world on my tail.

Nineteen years old. That's how old I was when I got busted. An' that white stone wit' the black streaks o' sparkly stuff was still in my pocket when they booked me. I carried it ev'rywhere with me until the cops took it from me.

But you know what? It always showed up again. I was in my hand durin' all nine o' my killin' trials, and in my hand for every single sentencin'. That rock's been in my hand every day for the last eleven years while I been sittin' in this little five-by-nine cell all by myself. An' I'm gonna tell you somethin' else, too. That rock, it's gonna be in my hand tomorrow mornin' when they strap me to that table an' stop my heart beatin'.

I deserve to die. I know that, an' that's why I ain't never let all those law people fight my penalty. Keepin' me alive like a caged animal weren't gonna solve nobody's problems, 'cause all them people I done kilt weren't gonna just not be dead anymore. I might as well join 'em. I ain't skeert. I did what I did 'cause there weren't gonna be no consequences for me. See, I got nothin' left to lose, 'cause my Momma already gave it all away.

The audio turned to a high, rasping hiss, then clicked off. The young man sat motionless, staring at the cassette player in frightened disbelief. He ran a sweaty hand through his hair and swallowed hard against the lump in his throat. The tape had come in the mail that morning, addressed to Cooper L. Chisolm of Memphis, Tennessee from the Texas Department of Criminal Justice. At first he didn't know why. He couldn't remember ever meeting this Mickey Landis. The tape came with no documentation save a hand-scrawled sticker on its face.

Michael Wayne Landis—final statement to reporter Austin Greene.

How could a parent do something so cruel to her child, he wondered, but he didn't have to wonder too hard. He'd been given away as an infant. At twenty-nine hours old his mother signed over her rights to him and let the State of Tennessee take him away forever.

Cooper paused, his forehead knitted in confusion and rewound the tape to the start. He punched the "play" button and sat back, his breath held tight and his teeth clenched in anticipation.

"Skippin' stones down by the crick… That was where any momma could find her little boy on a Saturday afternoon in Rock Mountain, Tennessee," that emotionless voice repeated, and a chill ran up his spine. Rock Mountain, Tennessee wasn't but twenty-five minutes from Memphis.

He wasn't sure why, but the longer he stared at the machine, the faster the gears in his head turned. One by one the tumblers of his mind clicked into place and the fog that followed him day to day began to lift. While he and this stranger had the same beginnings, Cooper realized he wasn't as unfortunate as he would like to think.

He always wondered why things worked out the way they did. His infancy and childhood in the State's care likely saved him from a much worse fate than the one he survived. He could have ended up as one of Mickey's victims. Worse, if he'd stayed with his real parents, he could have been just like Mickey. Maybe being that adopted kid kept him from suffering on a much grander scale.

They'd never met, at least not that Cooper could remember, but something about this man still seemed so familiar…and it felt so wrong. The haunting sound of the dead man's words rang eerily in his ears, tickling at some long-forgotten memory. Some part of him that begged to be set free. That unknown sense of need pulled him, tugged him toward the one and only thing that could answer all of his questions. Leaving the box and the old cassette player on the table, he stumbled to his bedroom on shaky legs to retrieve a box of papers he hadn't bothered open in years. When he returned to the table, Cooper pulled the lid loose and rifled through the papers, pulling out the oldest ones scattered along the bottom. He pushed the box to the side, inadvertently knocking it to the floor as something caught his attention.

There atop the cassette player, was a smooth, white stone with a sparkling black vein running straight through its center. The box lid fell from his limp hand and bounced once on the table. The papers sifted down from his other hand as it went slack as well, spilling the contents of his life across the pressboard tabletop and the grungy linoleum floor. Cooper didn't need to look at it anymore because the name that rang a faint bell half an hour ago screamed through his head in a way that declared its ownership of him as well.

Yet there it was all the same, lying at the top of the mess—a birth certificate. Old, tattered and faded, it confirmed his fears.

Cooper Lee Landis.

Cooper realized one other thing as the sick lump formed in his throat: that he'd thrown that very same stone away eleven years ago, on the day he was adopted out of that horrible state-run home by John and Betty Chisolm. The day he went from being a throw-away second child to having a stable home and a loving family.

But there it sat, unassuming yet menacing, silent yet speaking volumes and though it seemed silly, as he picked the stone up Cooper found he was afraid to turn around.

The Cock Doth Crow

THE OLD ROOSTER LET GO A WARBLING CRY INTO THE pre-dawn hours, the distant and lonely sound echoing off the tattered barn and over the pasture, bringing about the low of the cattle and the annoyed cry of the old barn-cat. Back toward the farmhouse, a leaning, dilapidated structure consisting of creaky floorboards and drafty rafters, a candle-flame flickered.

An aging farmer by the name of Duncan Hearst tottered onto his porch, and from the candle-flame flickered to life a hand-rolled cigarette, which the old codger clutched between his withered lips. He drew a shallow breath around the years of pollutants and the growing infection of emphysema, then let out a shaking, choking death-rattle of a cough. The dog sleeping on the porch whimpered and scuttled under the ancient rocking chair, its tail curled around its paws for protection.

"Duncan, you old fool!" the rackety woman's voice screeched through the open door, "You get in here this instant and stop it with that nasty cigarette!"

"Coming, Martha," he croaked, and took a final drag from the thing before flicking it over the porch-railing and scuttling back inside.

Duncan and Martha lived two miles from another soul, mainly because Duncan was such a horrid old coot that their neighbors had sold their farms off to be away from him. Even their two daughters were grown and gone, and the whole slew of grandchildren Martha so desperately wanted to love never, ever came to visit.

Duncan was nearly sixty years old by Martha's count, which meant that she was close on to fifty-five herself. In their parish, they would have been considered among royalty for their ages, yet they were the outcasts, and she a pariah for her sweet doting on the undeserving wretch she called a husband. But she had pledged 'until death do us part' all that many years ago, and until death did they part, she would continue to be true to him.

The old cock fluttered down from the fence in a torrent of feathers, then strutted toward the henhouse while Martha stood over the hearth, desperately wishing for the modern conveniences in which Duncan did not believe. To have electricity, and a working oven that did not involve the chopping of firewood four times daily… running water in the house that did not require the cranking of an old well reel… Martha sighed wistfully as she gloved her hand in a tattered old pot holder and reached for the handle of the cast-iron skillet lying on the embers.

Hacking out a cough from lungs that sounded full of phlegm and infection, Duncan dragged himself into the house and seated himself at the table. "Where is my breakfast, woman?" he snapped, pounding his fist on the table. "At least get me my coffee if you plan to make me wait!"

Martha drew in a breath and held it for a three-count while she carefully placed the heated skillet on the prepared towels and cracked three eggs onto its smooth, black surface. While the eggs sizzled in the pan, she pulled the kettle from the fire and poured two mugs of strong, black coffee.

"Here's your coffee, Duncan," she said, her words clipped from frustration, and turned back to flip the eggs. While the pan was still hot she threw in four slabs of salted ham, careful to keep the fatty edges from popping into the eggs. Mingling the flavors of Duncan's breakfast certainly would not do, she thought with a sneer.

When the old fool's breakfast was on a plate, she placed it gingerly on the table in front of him. After thirty years of marriage, she had grown to expect no compliment, or even a thank-you… but when his lip curled and he glared at the eggs as if they were poisoned, she felt her patience wearing thin.

"Before you even think about insulting that breakfast, Duncan Hearst, you just remember how many ways you have deprived me! If you for one second think I will stand here and allow you to insult my cooking, you've got another thing coming. Now keep that smart trap of yours shut and eat your breakfast." Martha smothered a smug smile as Duncan's jaw flapped like a loose hinge. Before she lost her composure, she turned and strode from the kitchen. She did not stop until she was out the back door and well toward the barn with the morning's milk pail. On the way out, she thought she heard the snick of a fork against a plate, but she wasn't about to go back and check.

If anyone had asked her what had come over her in talking to her husband that way, Martha could have only shrugged. She could easily tell a questioning party that she had grown weary of his insults and general lack of support, but that was only part of it, she mused as she pulled the stool up to Daisy's side. To be perfectly honest, she hated the old fool, and had since their youngest daughter, Lila Mae, had gone away to school and not come home again.

Her hatred flared brightly as starbursts behind her eyes as she sat down beside the cow and began her morning's work. First the milk, then the eggs, then she would feed the animals before returning to the house to knead the day's bread for baking. Duncan required fresh bread each day; he would never eat the remainder from the previous day. Martha would feed yesterday's loaf to the chickens. It was Thursday, which meant she would boil up another chicken from their shrinking collection. She would take the hand ax to its throat and rip out its feathers from the tail up.

The aging woman rose with her frothy milk pail and sat it in the window to separate before taking up her egg basket and heading for the henhouse. The cock strutted back and forth, back and forth, displaying his vibrant plumage for the biddies inside who, if they were at all like Martha, wouldn't concern themselves with his show.

She let the chickens loose and collected the morning's eggs—only six for the day; Duncan would be less than pleased—then returned for her milk pail.

When she returned to the house, Duncan had taken up his post in the rocking chair on the front porch. He sucked at one of his scant-made cigarettes, mostly paper and wood shavings to save on the cost of tobacco, and set about his list of the day's complaints. The ham was not cooked properly. The eggs were too few. He would be damned if he'd eat day-old loaf. On the complaints continued.

When Martha went to the back garden to collect the chicken for dinner, Duncan took it upon himself to follow her. His complaints echoed through her head, pinging shards of pain against the base of her skull. The old bastard was never happy...never. And she hated him. Yet his tirade continued, the poor fool unaware of his own misstep until the moment the ax blade meant for the fat hen wedged itself into the joint where his neck and shoulder met.

Martha jerked the blade free and swung again, severing Duncan's windpipe and esophagus. Blood spurted and oozed from the wound with each frantic beat of his heart, spraying the yellowing grass with a deep crimson coat. The third strike of the blade severed his spinal cord. His head, separated from his neck safe a thin strip of skin and his still in-tact jugular vein, lolled forward. His face bounced against his chest, leaving reddened lip prints on his dirty, white shirt.

The body collapsed to its knees then fell forward, trapping Duncan's miserable face between chest and dirt. Blood pooled from the raw, jagged wound, crawling across the dingy ground like fingers through pudding.

Martha dropped the bloody ax to the ground beside her late husband and, with a smile, hoisted her skirt and turned for the house. She needed a change of clothes and her hair needed freshening. A visit to her daughters was long overdue, and it was far past time the babies met their maw-maw.

The old rooster let go a warbling cry into the pre-dawn hours, the distant and lonely sound echoing off the tattered barn and over the pasture, bringing about the low of the cattle and the annoyed cry of the old barn-cat. Back toward the farmhouse, nothing happened.

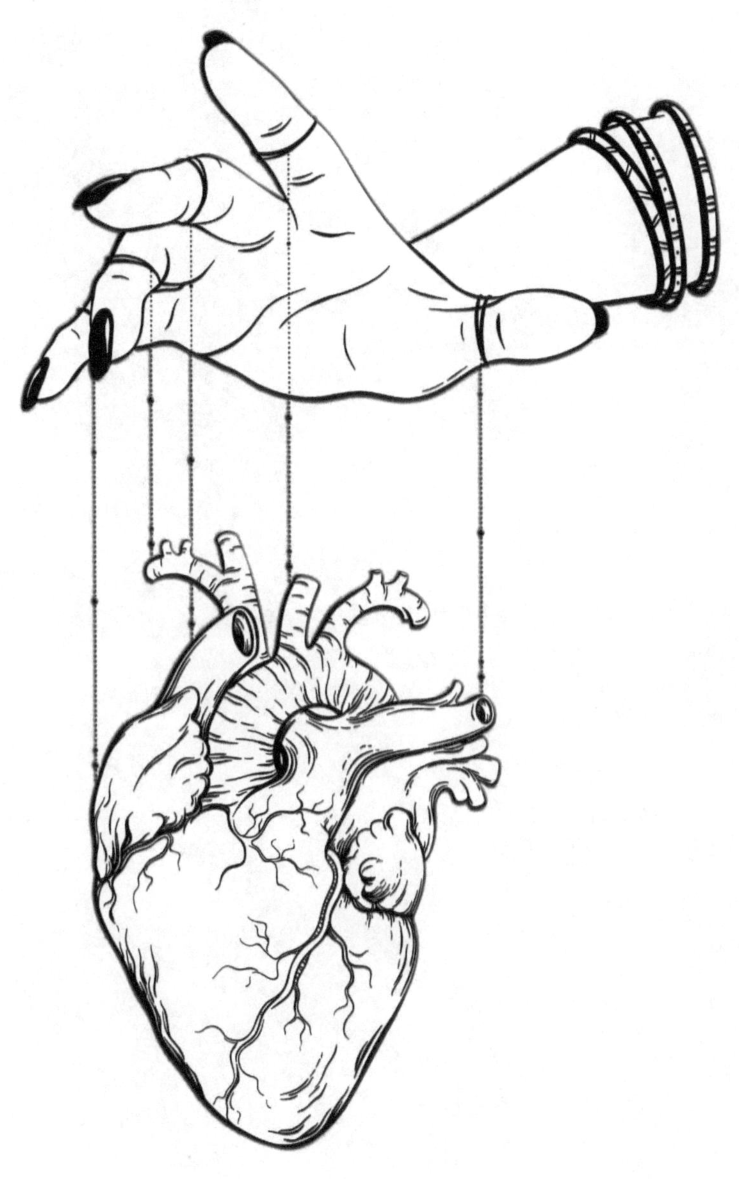

Downing Street

FROM THE FRONT IT APPEARED NO DIFFERENT THAN any other house on the 200-block of Downing Street—a well-kept two story monument standing as a proud testament to pre-1900s architecture. Festive decorations adorned the front porch while spooky blow-up caricatures lined the steps like undead marching soldiers. Even a pumpkin graced the front lawn, hiding inside it a peeping Frankenstein. Orange and black lights blinked along the trim of the wide porch day and night without fail. Hidden in the front hedges was a motion sensor that exuded an eerie laugh each time someone passed by. Many people paused to gaze at the spectacle. Some took pictures, but nobody ever stopped. Just because it was six days after Halloween with no change in scenery didn't mean the still-standing decorations were that unusual.

No, it just meant that the owners of the house were dead.

If the passersby were to look closely they would have noticed that the broken door jamb was real, and that the dark trail marring the bright-white boards of the steps was, in fact, blood, and it led across the threshold where it soaked into the running in thick, sticky pools. If they were to push open the ruined door they would notice other things out of place—a broken crystal goblet and an overturned bottle of scotch to start. The trail would continue through the house into the kitchen where a once-beautiful blonde woman lay, face up in a pool of blood that had long-since oozed from the angry gash across her throat. Her body had begun to bloat and decay, releasing the putrid stench of death into air once fragranced by the delicate scent of gardenias. Even the flowers lay dead on the table, wilted from weeks of thirst.

From there bloody footprints would lead upstairs where her husband lay sprawled on the landing, almost completely disemboweled. Decomposing intestines would be strung along the banister much like the lights out front. His eyes would still be open, staring sightlessly ahead.

But nobody would witness these gruesome sights. Nobody would stop. Nobody would care.

At least, not until Christmas.

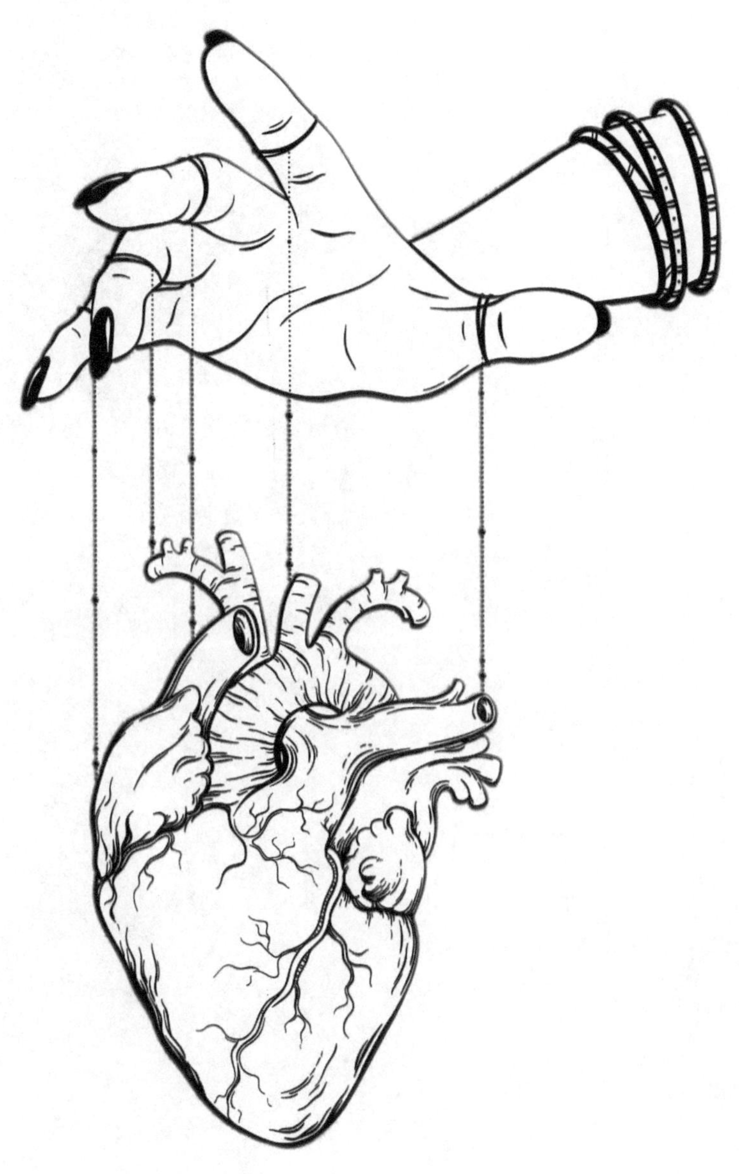

A Lonely Heart

IT WAS THE "TALENT AGENT" TAG THAT DID IT. Within fifteen minutes of the post going live, the disposable cell phone erupted in a cacophony of buzzes and chimes. Every woman in Los Angeles wanted to date an agent. It didn't matter what the agent looked like, so long as he had that "in" to the entertainment underworld. But it also meant superficial love. It wouldn't be real, no matter how long he searched. He'd felt that real love once... but it was long gone.

None of that mattered anymore. The falseness was part of the Hollywood glamour. They might be ugly on the inside, but he could find pretty things about them. Every woman, no matter her inner workings, had pretty parts. Some were perfect, even. Some could almost make up for...

No.

Scratch picked up the phone, his gnarled, arthritic fingers aching as he touched the tips to the small, smooth screen. Photo after photo flickered past, each one a prettier little waif than the next, but none of them quite measuring up to the epitome of beauty he once had the good fortune to touch.

"I can fix it," he said, his fingertips slithering over her porcelain cheek. A tiny tear slipped over her long eyelashes and trailed down her face. Rather than mar her beauty, the salty droplet added a new sheen to her already glowing skin. He loved this woman completely, desperately. She reached up and took his hand, squeezing his fingers in hers.

"Do you really think so?" she asked. Her voice was sweet and delicate, like sunshine on dew-covered leaves. Hope flickered in her wide, blue eyes and his heart stuttered against his ribs. To see her smile melted his bones.

"I know I can, Beth. I can fix it, and then we can be together forever."

"I would like that," she replied, and pressed her ruby-red lips to his.

They called him Scratch because of his obsessive-compulsive tic. He constantly scratched at his right elbow when he was nervous. Everyone in Los Angeles County had a nickname; anyone who had been there any length of time, at least. Scratch grew up there, a pillar of intellect among the artistic and artificial. A surgeon by trade, he'd developed the nickname as a youth in grammar school. Nervous energy bubbled in him constantly; the feelings he would later come to understand as longing.

His professors at University had little faith in his ability to wield a scalpel thanks to the constant scratching, but he'd proven them wrong.

"Scratchy fingers make steady hands," Beth had said of his hands as she'd put them on her hips and pulled him onto the dance floor. He missed her, but now was not the time to think of her lost beauty. They would be together again soon enough, if he could only complete his final task.

A pretty, black-haired girl named Kendra sent a photo showing off her greatest...assets. Pert and perky with rose-colored nipples, she had quite a bit of talent. Scratch appreciated her candor, yet she did not possess the qualities for which he searched. He skipped to the next photo, then a third. The girls were comely little things, but not right. Pretty hair, slender necks... he'd seen them before. He'd touched them before, held perfection in his very hands and had it whisked away.

Abby, Tina, Carly, Jeannie... all perfectly lovely girls with plenty of potential, but none had *it*. None of them had that unnamed, changeable quality he so desperately needed. Every single one wanted to be an actress. Everyone thought she had what it took to be the next Hollywood Sweetheart. Photo after photo tumbled across his field of vision, the names blurring into another until the letters became unreadable nonsense, pictograms of some long-lost code. Scratch sighed in frustration and tossed the phone to the table. His experiment seemed suddenly to have gone awry.

Then, blessedly, the phone chimed and his unspoken prayer was answered. The face of a demure young woman greeted his questing gaze. Sky blue eyes and ruby-red lips twinkled up at him from the small, glass screen. Her cheekbones held round curves that seemed to glow with an inner light. This one had potential.

The message said her name was Brandi Buckingham and she was twenty-two years old. Almost perfect. Scratch pecked out a message to introduce himself and hit the send button. Thirty seconds passed and the phone tinkled again, signaling a new message. Brandi had replied.

Free 2nite. Dinner?

Scratch's heart thumped a bit harder. After all this time, he still craved the nearness, the twinkle in innocent blue eyes.

Spago. 7pm. Reservation made.

He'd made the reservation weeks ago in anticipation of this evening. At the time Scratch had thought himself a little too optimistic, but the gamble, it appeared, would pay off. He stretched his fingers, aching by now from the exertion of typing on the tiny screen, and squinted at the last message he'd sent. A minute ticked by, then two, then three. Scratch, disgusted, laid the telephone down and staggered to his feet to use the lavatory.

He stood in front of the bright-white toilet and waited, growing more irritable with each passing second. Both his bladder and his phone had betrayed him. Then the light, tinkling chime echoed through the quiet house. It repeated once then fell quiet. The tension in his shoulders eased, and Scratch finished his business. Something that vaguely resembled excitement coursed through him as he turned and toddled back toward the living room. He was old; older than he wanted to admit. The years had really done a number on him. He remembered fondly the days when he would bound down the hallway, filled with the exuberance of youth, and wished once more for the heyday of his life.

OMG! Can't believe it! Pick me up!

He smiled and laid the phone on the end table, where it continued to tweet and buzz for over an hour. He could once have juggled two dozen beautiful women with this ruse...but not anymore. Now in his golden years, Scratch lived vicariously through grainy black-and-white films showcasing dearly departed friends and doe-eyed crushes. Though none of them ever quite lived up to the magic that was his first love.

"Why do they call you Scratch?" she asked as they stared at each other over a bottle of wine.

He immediately stopped the nervous scratching of his right elbow. Beth giggled and cast her ice-blue gaze toward the floor in a coy display of flirtation. They were sequestered in Siberia, but neither seemed to mind. The dark corner of Romanoff's might be a horrid punishment for Hollywood's finest, but it suited him just fine. This way he could be alone with her, the most beautiful woman he'd ever seen.

"Oh, I see," she continued, "it's because of the scratching, right?"

"So I've been told," he replied. Scratch couldn't take his eyes off her. Beth sighed. "How long have you been in Hollywood?" he prodded when she didn't step up to carry the conversation.

"About four months," she said after a small hesitation. "I never thought it would be so hard to find work."

"I can't imagine the camera not loving you, Beth. I know my eyes do." The compliment brought rose-blooms of color to the apples of her cheeks. Perfect, white teeth peeked out from behind her red lips, and her perfectly-styled hair bounced against her shoulders as she glanced away again.

"I wish everyone loved me the way you do, Scratch," Beth said with a sad smile. His heart skipped a beat. He did love her, more than she could ever know.

Scratch straightened his bowtie and rang the doorbell to the small studio apartment. Loud, unhappy voices seeped through the cracks in the door, alerting him to the notion that his presence wasn't exactly welcome. Stark silence followed and the door swung inward, the same girl from the photo materializing before him. Her hair and makeup were immaculate, even if her lips turned down at the sight of him and her expression appeared more harried than happy.

"I'm early," Scratch said, "I apologize."

"It's no problem," Brandi replied and tugged the door closed. Her voice carried a tiny spark of British Isles flavor, though the enthusiasm he'd seen in her earlier words had begun to fade. Scratch smiled. She was quite the exotic one.

"Shall we?" He extended his arm and she slipped her hand around his elbow.

"Spago..." she said dreamily as he led her down the walk to his car. "How on Earth did you get a reservation there?"

"I'm there quite frequently," he lied. He'd never been there before except to drive past once during a detour. Brandi's eyes grew wide as they stepped off the sidewalk and up to the door of his vehicle, a sleek, titanium-grey Lotus.

"This car, this dinner... I feel like I just won the date lottery!" she squealed as he helped her into the passenger's seat. A giggle greeted him as he slammed the door on her, the sound more closely resembling a grating cluck. Scratch cringed as he rounded the car. This vapid, little bubblehead had no clue when it came to her true shallowness. This girl embodied every problem from which present-day Hollywood suffered. He'd bet dollars to doughnuts she'd lick his balls if he asked. After all, she thought of this date as an audition.

Scratch didn't have to be a psychic to know it. She carried herself as Hollywood trash would – slinky dress, sleazy shoes, and whore-paint slathered across her pretty skin. It was such a waste. In his day, women flaunted natural beauty and carried themselves with grace and integrity. Back then they didn't sleep their way to the top. At least, not in his starry-eyed recollections, they didn't.

Brandi talked incessantly as he drove them to dinner. She never once looked his way, confirming his suspicion that she held no interest in all at him as a person. She never asked about him, never even bothered to ask his name. She told him her entire life's history, all twenty-two years of it, and made absolutely certain she accentuated her "natural acting talent" by discussing dog food commercials and her limited stint on the community theatre stage back in her hometown of wherever-the-hell-it-was. Scratch tuned her out, more concerned with the damage the makeup she wore was doing to her skin. It needed to come off as soon as possible.

"*Do you really think you can fix me?*" *she asked, then returned to chewing her lip. Scratch smoothed her hair back from her face and kissed her left temple.*

"*I'm a doctor, Beth. I fix people.*" *She rose from the bed, wrapping the top blanket around her body in a sweet display of modesty. Scratch shifted under the sheet, his body already reacting to her nearness and the sweet, supple curve of her waist. So long as she existed as she was born, their lovemaking would never be complete. He enjoyed her company and body no less for it, yet he longed to become one with her.*

Beth paced at the foot of his king bed, worrying her lip. She clutched at the blanket and her shoulders shrank in on themselves, as if she were ashamed of who and what she was. It pained his heart. "Do you think my…problem…" she hesitated on the word, knowing it couldn't begin to encompass the severity of the deformity from which she suffered, "is what keeps me from finding work?"

Scratch snorted. "Of course not, babe. Ain't a camera in this world has seen the parts of you I've seen. It's likely nobody knows about it at all."

"Then maybe it's just me."

"I doubt that's true either," he replied. "It's a tough market these days, what with close to two hundred pictures released in the last year alone!" Scratch took a moment to admire her beauty before holding out his hands to her. "You are a goddess among mortals, Beth. Now come and let me hold you."

Beth crossed the room, a tiny smile curling the corners of her lips upward, and sank into his embrace. "I love you, Scratch."

"Love you back, babe."

"Do you really think I'll make it?" she asked, turning her wide, blue eyes up to meet his gaze.

"I can see it now," Scratch answered, pausing to kiss the tip of her nose. "You'll be the belle of the ball, darling. Picture it," he raised his hands as if showcasing a billboard, "One Night Only, Hollywood's Sweetheart, Beth Short!"

Brandi more or less disgusted him, her ignorance and self-importance becoming increasingly evident with each passing second. She talked her way through dinner, gasping in surprise as even minor celebrities showed their faces inside the doors of Hollywood's current hot spot. Scratch told himself it was for the greater good; that this girl, however empty inside, would be the final piece of his grand puzzle.

Scratch paid for dinner without question, as the girl never once looked in the direction of the waiter when he brought the check. She chose instead to finish the last of the very expensive bottle of wine. Her cheeks already held a drunken flush but she soldiered on, draining every drop from the bottle, then the bottom of her glass. When they rose from the dark booth, Brandi stumbled into him, nearly knocking him into the producer and his wife at the next table. He miraculously righted himself and his drunken date before a major catastrophe occurred, and carefully guided her out into the dark California night. Scratch considered calling off the plan and taking her back to her grimy, little apartment as he accepted his key fob from the valet and helped the pathetic girl into the low car. However, when he pulled the car onto the freeway, she leaned over and laid her palm against the inside of his right thigh.

"Is it party time yet?" she asked, her words slurred together into one continuous sound.

"What exactly do you propose?" Scratch kept his gaze focused on the road and the oddly heavy traffic. She giggled again, that horrid, grating sound that set his teeth on edge. Her hand crept higher.

"I was thinking maybe we could go back to your place."

Scratch nodded. *Of course.* It always started with the overly ambitious touching and the request to go home. The alcohol not only lowered inhibitions; it made these girls shameless. As disgusting as it might have been, it made his job so much easier. When they were willing, they screamed less. With his project so near completion, he couldn't risk the screaming now. He'd come too far, invested too much of his life to give it all up for some stupid little waif who would sell her soul for a bit part on the back side of the silver screen.

He turned the Lotus abruptly, slinging the car off the main road and onto a residential street. It was then that he dared to glance at her. She stared out the passenger's side window, her head cocked at a strange angle to accommodate for her long reach toward his crotch. Her slow-moving hand reached his target, and a look of disgust passed across her face. Brandi—if that was even her real name—intended to do this not because she wanted the old man beside her, but because she thought doing so would get her somewhere in the film industry. Her hand slithered over his manhood, eliciting the natural male response such touches brought. Scratch found no satisfaction in the touch, even if his body enjoyed it.

Stupid whore, he thought as he slipped the car into his driveway and tucked it neatly into his garage. She took her hand back as the motion sensor in the garage's interior detected the car and lit up the space. She cleared her throat and let herself out of the car before he could get around to help her, which suited him just fine. He chose instead to unlock the door and guide her inside.

Brandi looked around as they moved from connecting breezeway to the foyer and beyond, her mouth hanging open as she wandered into the great room of Scratch's house. When she turned and looked at him – it was only the third time she had—her face lit up and she bounced on the balls of her feet.

"This place is gorgeous! Give me the grand tour!" She ran over and slipped her arm through his. Scratch couldn't help the small thrill of victory bubbling in his belly as he led her down the hallway toward the back of the house. The bathrooms, the bedrooms, his private study, all on the first floor, amazed her to the point of near hysteria. When he took her upstairs into the spacious, private theater, she nearly came apart at the seams. "Can we watch a movie?" she asked, tugging on his arm. Her excited actions hurt his old bones, yet he said nothing. His lower half still ached from her earlier ministrations as well.

"Perhaps later," he replied, guiding her toward the door. "I have something to show you first."

"Will I enjoy it?" she asked, the wonder of youth evident in her voice. Scratch chuckled.

"Oh, it's to die for."

The clinic was dark save the incandescent lights in the musty storage room. It carried the sterile smell of antiseptic, coated with the noxious scent of old metal. Scratch loaded tools into his briefcase then moved to the wall of medical supplies: gauze, bandages, tinctures and cleaning tonics… everything he might need to perform the surgery he'd promised himself would allow him to realize his greatest dream.

Beth waited in his living room, likely pacing the floor if he knew her, while he retrieved his supplies. She would be in knots by the time he arrived home, anxious to volunteer her body for the procedure. The surgery, at least what he could find on it, was still in experimental stages with varying degrees of success. There was no guarantee he could actually fix her problem, but come hell or high water, he was going to try.

The aging Chevrolet whined as Scratch turned the key and begged it to life. After three attempts, it complied. After finding first gear on the nearly-stripped column, he coerced the car into motion and started for home, his hands shaking from a sudden bout of nerves.

The nervous attack came neither from robbing his place of employment to perform illegal surgery nor the procedure itself, but instead from the small, velvet-lined box in his left breast pocket.

The basement wasn't original to the house. Scratch had it dug out and finished it in the 80's so he could have a place to work. He explained this to Brandi as they entered his bedroom. She cared less for the history and more for the golden era film antiques adorning every available surface, but she was at least courteous enough to nod and feign interest. A small, grainy photograph on his nightstand caught her attention.

"Hey... I know that woman," she said, rushing to pick up the frame. Scratch's breath caught in his lungs as she fondled the photograph. "Isn't that the Black Dahlia? Why do you have a picture of..." Realization dawned as Brandi looked up at him. Her eyes lit up as she pieced together the truth. "You knew her, didn't you?"

Scratch nodded. "I did."

"Do you know what happened to her?"

Of course.

It was always the first question. *What happened to her? Were you there? Was it you?*

"Come with me," he said, and held out his elbow. Brandi placed the photo back on his nightstand and took his arm. Scratch led her across the room to the hidden panel behind his bookshelf. Her eyes widened in surprise and for the first time a glimmer of fear skittered across her face.

She thought him a killer.

"Beth's death was a tragic loss for this world," he said. "She was the light of my life, the only person in this world I've ever truly loved."

The panel opened onto an expansive bathroom, and Brandi relaxed against his side. A small, frantic giggle escaped her, as if she were realizing for the first time how silly she seemed. She entered, looking at the tiny details in the architecture — the molding, floor tiles, and even the swirling plaster on the walls.

"You scared me," she said, pressing her hand to her chest. "For a minute I thought you were opening up the door to some kind of torture dungeon or something!" The grating giggle came again, and Scratch pushed the panel closed.

"How do you know I didn't?" he asked. Fear blitzed through her features, and the alcohol-induced dream-state immediately cleared from her eyes. When she looked up at him again, she did so with complete lucidity.

"W-what do you mean?"

"You're a beautiful girl, Brandi," he replied, pressing into her personal space. She backed up, a tiny shriek escaping her lips as her shoulders came in contact with the wall, "but you really should learn not to enter the houses of strangers."

"Y-you're n-not a s-s-stranger," she stammered.

"Oh, but I am." He drew his fingers down her porcelain cheek, feeling the tremble beneath. "You selfish, stupid little girl. You never even bothered to ask my name." She started to speak but he pressed his hand to her mouth. "You may have her skin, but you will never hold a candle to my Beth."

Her flesh was soft despite the caked on makeup, still supple and resilient beneath his fingertips. The frightened girl didn't dare move as he caressed her face. Excitement pulsed through him for the first time since the initial message. His palm came to rest against the side of her throat, and with gentle pressure Scratch guided her toward the sink where he began the delicate task of preparing her.

With a warm washcloth he cleaned her face; careful, almost reverent strokes removing the mess of oil and pigment. Beneath the façade he revealed beautiful, bone-white flesh. Scratch couldn't help himself as he leaned in and pressed his lips to her forehead. His body had long-since betrayed him, as evidenced by the near painful tightness in his slacks. But it wasn't Brandi he wanted; rather what she represented.

At last, his dream...

Beth lay on the cold, metal table, nude save the pair of white sheets draped over her form. Her slender fingers tapped a nervous rhythm against its surface while she chewed at her bottom lip. Scratch took his time arranging his tools. For his beautiful lover, everything was to be perfect. He lined up the scalpels and swabs, laid out syringes and a cauterizing machine, then placed beside the basin the velvet box. Plastic sheeting covered the floor beneath the table. It crinkled under his feet as he worked, preparing her arm for the intravenous needle which would deliver the anesthetic.

Gooseflesh rippled along her arm when he moved the sheet away. Beth cringed at the sight of the needle, turning her face into her opposite shoulder. She feared them, yet they were unavoidable if the procedure was to continue. Scratch bent and kissed the back of her wrist before balancing the thick shaft against her arm and driving it into her flesh. She cried out in pain, tears springing to her eyes. The sound twisted in his heart; he couldn't bear the thought of hurting his beloved yet he knew more pain followed. Worse pain.

After taping the needle to her arm, Scratch smoothed her hair back and kissed her forehead. He stared up at him, fear evident in her big, blue eyes. He hated himself for putting it there and for a moment considered backing out of this, however noble his cause may be.

"I'm going to put you under now," he said, and lifted the syringe of anesthetic from his work table, "and when you wake, you will be whole."

Beth swallowed and forced a smile to her lips. "I love you," she said.

"I love you, too."

Scratch regulated the flow of the IV fluids then introduced the new drug to the line. Beth cringed; it burned as it entered her vein. Then her muscles relaxed and her eyes fell closed. Her whole body went limp. Scratch took a deep breath and folded the lower blanket upward toward her chest.

Blood poured from the first incision; it always did. The slither of crimson liquid dripped into the sink beneath her head, but slowed to a trickle as the scalpel widened the cut. The girl never moved, even as the tip of the blade dug into muscle and scraped bone. Normally Scratch would have been more careful with his cuts, but he could scarcely contain this new excitement. Then the tip of the scalpel nicked a vein. The girl's heart rate tripled and her breathing became shallow. Scratch never veered from his course; her life was of no consequence to him now.

"I never meant to hurt her, you know," he said as he continued his work. "I promised my Beth I would repair the damage nature had done to her. She was perfect in every way but one." He lifted the scalpel and used a damp towel to clear away streaks of blood from her skin. It wouldn't do to let it stain. "We were going to be together forever, but Beth...she was convinced she wasn't a real woman. I wanted her to know she was, and how much I loved her even with her imperfections."

Brandi's heart rate dropped, her pulse growing weaker with each passing second. The color drained from her face, turning her porcelain skin bone-white. Scratch paid no mind; soon enough the blood would stop flowing, her heartbeat would cease, and her lungs would expel their final breath. The girl was expendable, a thing to be used in his plans. The next cut was harder, her skin growing elastic as the first stage of death set in.

He raised the makeshift stirrups higher and twisted the table-lamp toward her groin. Scratch cleared his throat and reached for the table, his normally steady hand shaking under the weight of his task. He prepared her body by shaving her smooth, and coating her skin in a thin layer of iodine. Then his work truly began.

The retractor laid her bare to his view and with a fine scalpel he sliced into the blue-tinted membrane. Blood poured from the wound, as he expected, though when he peeled back the fine layer of skin he discovered not the fully-formed channel he expected, but a wall of soft, bloody tissue.

Scratch pressed gauze into the incision to draw the blood away. Behind the gauze he discovered no trace of a standard female's inner-workings. The discovery was troublesome; rather than simply open her womanhood, he would have to create it. It would be much more invasive than he'd planned, which meant a longer recovery. If he were honest with himself, he would admit this surgery was out of his league. Yet it was for Beth, for her to have a chance at living a normal life.

Scratch made a vertical incision on her lower abdomen and pressed his hand inside only to find what he'd feared: Beth was lacking the majority of her feminine organs. Ovaries and a partially-formed uterus…but nothing else.

She would be devastated when she woke, as becoming a mother was part of what made a woman a woman in her eyes. Yet her ability to bear children was the least of her worries. A proper union could not be achieved with such deficiencies. Using his fingers he estimated the thickness of the fleshy wall to an inch and a half—surprisingly shallow for such an odd deformity. Blood pooled around his wrist where it disappeared into her body cavity, and her body began to convulse. He'd not severed an artery, yet she was losing much more blood than he liked.

Removing his hand from her abdomen, Scratch ripped away his gloves and ran through the house to retrieve an item. He re-entered his makeshift operating room as quickly as he'd left it, shoving his hands into a fresh pair of gloves and preparing for the next stage of surgery. He quickly manufactured a tether out of surgical thread and a lead fishing weight. The convulsions stopped, but her pulse fluttered under his fingers. The physical trauma on her body was more than he'd anticipated, causing more pain than the anesthesia could numb. He had to work fast.

Scratch threaded his tether through a surgical needle, then gingerly worked his left hand back into her pelvic area to receive the needle as it pushed through the wall. He drew the thread through, tugging at the weight to stretch the channel. His anticipation spiked as she began to make tiny noises of pain and he pulled too hard. The weight came through the flesh-wall with a sucking pop, and blood poured out between her splayed legs. Panic set in and he pulled his hands free, reaching for the cauterizing wand. The convulsions began again as he fumbled with the knobs on the machine. His fingers betrayed him, shaking and bouncing as he fought for the right settings. Meanwhile the lifeblood of his love poured across the surgical table and dripped to the floor.

The machine finally ready, he pressed the wand inside and turned the switch. A sharp, metallic buzz started, and the scent of burning flesh filled the room as he blindly twisted and turned the mechanism against her interior wounds. Small tendrils of smoke wafted upward from both openings in her body. Her breathing grew shallow and ragged, slowing with each passing second, but the bleeding refused to slow. Panicked, he dropped the wand to the floor and ran for the cabinets on the far wall. Scratch produced a utility candle which he lit and placed on his utility table. In his haste he slung his tools outward, the scalpels flying toward Beth's body. Yet he paid no mind as he grappled for and secured the speculum. Scratch held it over the flame as he counted to twenty, then pressed it to the wounds his antique machine failed to repair. Her interior flesh sizzled against the heated metal. He refused to register the true amount of blood loss as he removed the tool and pressed his fingers inside to check – a permanent opening had been created, torn and burned through the wall of skin and muscle which had previously stood in the way. Her inner muscles gave no resistance. It wasn't his best work, but it would suffice to allow their long-anticipated union once she healed.

"You're whole now, Beth," he said as he moved to clean the blood from her body. He then stitched up the incision in her belly, relieved the convulsions and tense movements had stopped. Though when he reached up to touch her face he realized her skin had gone abnormally cold. She had no pulse. No breath. "Beth?" he asked, shaking her shoulders. Her head lolled to one side, her eyes half-mast. Her skin, the color of bone china, had gone paler, lost its light. Her cold lips had turned to rubber.

Beth Short was dead.

Scratch stared at her lifeless body, his brain refusing to acknowledge his failure. He couldn't fail. Her life, their future… all of it depended on him.

"Beth?" he said again, his voice hollow and tinny to his own ears. He shook her shoulder. "Beth, honey? Wake up, now." When the shaking didn't work, he pressed his bloody fingers against her carotid artery and felt… nothing.

He could bring her back. He knew he could do it. She wasn't that dead, was she?"

There were techniques, new methods of prolonging life. He'd read those journals and papers, perused the catalogs of medical equipment in the hospital offices. He knew they existed but…

By the time I get her to the hospital, she really *will* be dead, *he thought.*

He checked her pulse again to be sure. But he couldn't be sure because his own pulse beat so erratically throughout his body.

"Come on, honey," he begged, taking her by the shoulders and pulling her into a sitting position. Her body was limp,

unmoving. He laid her back down gently and began to pace the floor.

Scratch carried the metal tray upstairs, his quarry balanced in a bath of distilled water. He'd disposed of the dead girl's body, tossing her off a bridge outside of town. It was always cleaner when the evidence could be washed away. He'd made a terrible mistake once before and had nearly been caught. Luckily the police never thought the question the doddering old man down the street.

She would wash up soon enough, but he no longer cared. All that mattered was the final piece of his long-standing puzzle, which he carried into the guest room.

He'd succeeded in creating her womanhood, yet he'd failed to take into account the trauma such a procedure would have on the rest of her. His beloved Beth was gone. There was no way to bring her back.

He sat by her side, holding her hand while wandering through the hallways of his mind. Thirst ravaged him, yet he refused to leave her alone on this cold table. He couldn't believe she was dead. Gone. Ripped from his arms as a web from a spider. There was no pooling of blood on the backs of her arms and legs. Her skin did not carry a purple tint. He washed and dried her body to be certain, gently scrubbing the places on her body he'd inadvertently injured when knocking his tools from his table. Tiny lacerations marked her torso and her neck, but worst of all was the realization that her smile was gone from her face. He wanted her to smile.

Scratch lifted a bloody scalpel and wiped the blade clean. It was okay. He would give her a smile which would never fade. Gently, and with loving affection, he sliced through the corners of her mouth, pleased as her jaw fell open and the wide, artificial grin made her happy once more. Certainly, she would wake now... she was happy.

Perhaps, he thought, she needs some fresh air.

His lover lay on the bed, an angel in her sleeping death. Where her true body had long-since wasted away to nothing—damn those vultures for taking her away before he could return to collect her – this new body was a testament to his patience and his memory. Created from the stock of six donors, his reborn Beth lay in wait, a patchwork of carefully-measured limbs and sutures. She was to be whole once more this night, pure and clean and perfect. With this final piece, they would be together once more, and their love complete. It was all there – muscle tone, bone structure, the gentle swell of her hips, her wild, black hair tamed into perfect ringlets...all but one piece, which he carried in his hands.

Careful not to spill the water, Scratch placed the tray on the bed and gently lifted her head to place a towel beneath. It would not do to disturb their marital bed with dirty water. A needle and fine surgical thread sat at her left hand, patiently waiting as he dipped his fingers into the chilled water and lifted the beautiful facade from the tray. This time he was slow and methodical, moving the skin to line up perfectly with the features beneath. The lips, the nose, the eyelids... each piece would match perfectly when he finished his gentle ministrations. What had moments before been a faceless mannequin transformed before his eyes.

Scratch took up the threaded needle and, with the tiniest sutures he could manage so not to disturb her beauty, consigned the dead girl's face to his lover's possession. Anticipation built as he wiped away the last of the water and carefully centered the skin over her cheekbones. With a final flourish, he produced the small, velvet box, its edges worn smooth after six and a half decades of waiting. From inside he produced a small diamond solitaire, the perfect stone catching the light of the bedside lamp and lighting a fire of color inside it.

Scratch lifted her hand and kissed her knuckles. Then he slipped the ring onto the fourth finger of her left hand, sealing their pact. She was perfect. At long last, his beautiful Black Dahlia was his once more. And this time, he would never let her go.

Rock n' Roll Angel

MOTHERFUCKER.

Máire Connolly pushed her shirttail down into her skirt as the steel door slammed closed behind her. The sound of metal rattling against metal echoed back and forth from the alley walls, ringing in her ears as the sick feeling of finality settled like a lump in her stomach. She'd been mistreated. Used. Had.

Debauched.

"Son of a bitch."

All by a man that she would have willingly followed to the ends of the earth. The stupid son of a bitch couldn't be bothered to look past the end of his own dick to see what he had in his bed, to see that she would have been faithfully his, forever.

Fuck that.

Adjusting her clothes, Máire brushed her hair back from her cheeks and started out of the alley, her boot heels clicking loudly against the tattered asphalt. At the head of the alley stood a group of scantily-clad women, their hair jacked to Jesus with hairspray and cigarettes dangling from their perfectly manicured hands. The tallest of the group, a blonde with heavy makeup, turned and sneered at Máire as she passed. Obviously, this woman had once been in much the same position. Only she looked like the type to weather such a storm without a scratch.

Máire wasn't like those women. She wasn't a groupie. She would never be two-bit whore who would sleep with a man just because he knew his way around a guitar. She wasn't capable of that sort of evil… at least she hadn't been, until tonight. And tonight was supposed to be different. She was supposed to be expressing unending love and devotion.

She loved Steven Cave. Truly loved him from the first moment she heard his voice. She'd given herself to him in spirit four years ago, and in the flesh tonight. She'd been his diamond in the rough, his prize, his ultimate woman.

But no more. The sorry son of a bitch used her and threw her to the side like an old shoe. She wasn't entirely certain he ever even looked at her except to shove his dick between her legs, take four weak strokes, and pull out in time to come all over her belly. He couldn't even be bothered to hand her a towel before stumbling out of the room. As she'd dabbed at the mess with a paper napkin, his bulldogs appeared, grabbed her by the arms, and hauled her out into the cold. No "hello", no "thank you"…a quick, passionless fuck, and not even a "fuck you" to go with it.

Máire had never in her life felt so cheap. She hated it – wouldn't stand for that sort of abuse. If he'd been so rough with her, she could only imagine how many hundreds of women had suffered her same fate. As she turned the corner and started toward her apartment, the sky opened up. Rain fell in pounding sheets, drenching her clothes and soaking her to the bone in a matter of seconds. It seemed a fitting end – nature's shower, sent to wash away the ills she'd suffered.

A bark of male laughter caught her attention when a white limousine screeched to a stop in front of the gentlemen's club at the end of the block. Instead of opening the door, the owner of the laughter came slithering out of the open sun roof, his leather pants sliding down his hips as he fell over the top of the vehicle and stumbled to the sidewalk. Sickness built in her stomach, roiled through her body with maniac force as she watched Steven Cave trip into the building, followed by his two bodyguards and several of his band mates.

She hated him…absolutely hated him. Twenty-four hours ago, she would not have thought him capable of what he'd done. His lyrics sounded so heartfelt, so deep and sincere…too bad he was nothing but a shell. A façade covering a heartless, soulless beast.

If only there was a way to make him pay for what he'd done…to make him regret all of the women he'd destroyed. But people like Steven did not feel remorse. They felt nothing, she was willing to bet, because only a man who felt nothing could so heartlessly use and toss away a woman the way he had.

Máire was not a violent person, quite the opposite in fact. She had always been the meek little wallflower, content to stand back and let everyone else do the bullying and the talking and the threatening. But something about him, something about Steven Cave, turned her into an absolute beast. From the moment she found out the band had scheduled their homecoming show right down the street from her little apartment, she knew she had to go. She wanted him with a ferociousness that rivaled Mother Nature in its intensity, and she set out after him. She had to have him. There was no other way.

Now, after all was said and done, the only thing on her mind was revenge.

Máire stood in front of the floor-length mirror on her bathroom door and slowly disrobed. She started with her shirt; a white, button-down number with rolled sleeves. The tie she'd worn earlier was long gone, thrown carelessly over a chair as she entered her apartment. One by one she slipped the buttons from their holes, pulling the shirt wide to reveal the lacy black bra underneath and her more than ample breasts threatening to spill from the neckline of the garment. She then tossed the shirt across the room where it landed with a soggy *squish* and reached for her skirt; a knee-length blue plaid number with red pinstripes. As the zipper buzzed open, she let the fabric go, and it puddled at her feet.

She took a step back and kicked it to the side, sending it sailing across the room to land on her discarded shirt. Next she popped the clips on her garter belt and yanked it away. Máire looked into the mirror at herself. Her matching black underwear and thigh-high fishnets were a good complement to her pale skin and dark hair. In her opinion, she had nice curves, not too much, but just enough to tempt a man's eyes. The boots she wore stretched her calf muscles nicely, giving her legs a long, athletic look. Gathering her wet hair into her hands, she pulled it up to the top of her head where it spilled in messy waves around her face. She watched the flex of her pectoral muscles as she raised her arms, focused on the quiver of her breasts as those muscles moved.

What the hell was so wrong with her that he hadn't even bothered to look her in the eyes? He hadn't asked her name. Hadn't paused but long enough to pull out his dick and shove her panties to the side. She didn't even get a chance to truly understand what had happened before he was done and gone.

"Sorry-ass motherfucker." Máire rolled her eyes. "Bastard doesn't know what he's missing." Looking beyond her reflection in the mirror, she caught sight of the poster on her wall. Her lip curled in a sneer as she turned and stalked across the room. With an angry screech, she reached up and ripped it from the wall, yanking and crumbling and tearing the waxy paper. Disgusted, she threw it to the floor and stalked away, entering the bathroom and slamming the door so hard the mirror hanging on its face rattled in its frame.

She gripped the counter, and as the frustration seeped away, Máire felt a new hollowness replacing her other emotions. Goddamn it… it wasn't fair! How could he do that? She was a good person!

Apparently, good girls were not what bad boys like Steven wanted.

Silent tears coursed down her cheeks as she reached down and unbuckled first one, then the other boot, and eventually rolled away her stockings. Máire started the shower, turning the hot water up as high as she could possibly stand it, and then stripped out of her underwear, the one part of her ensemble that still smelled of him, and stepped into the hot spray. It burned a bit, but the hammer of water on her skin felt good. The tension began to melt away, and as the calming scent of her lavender shampoo filled the steamy room, she found it just a little bit easier to begin letting go.

But when she pulled open the bathroom door and started toward her bed, Máire caught sight of his crumpled face on the ruined poster, and her heart gave a painful little tug. Bastard or not, she still couldn't stop loving him.

The Paper Doll Lounge, by day, looked like any other bar in the world. Soft lighting occupied the tracks and recesses in the ceiling. The two bar tops were long and clean, made of a dark wood and lined with chrome. Matching tables littered the floor, and the barstools and chairs all suffered from the same garish upholstery. The biggest difference that Máire could see was the series of steel poles drilled through the centers of tables and the stage on the far wall with three poles, one at the end of a long catwalk.

She tucked her black hair, with its new blonde highlights, behind her ears and crossed her arms over her chest.

"Miss Connolly," a sleazy voice said, startling her. Máire turned, resisting the urge to shudder at the sight of the greasy little man coming toward her. He leered at her with obvious appreciation, but his ogling did little to reassure her that she had made the best decision.

She'd called up and quit her cushy office job this morning, telling her boss that she no longer felt the need to be a well-paid medical research assistant, then stopped by the salon for a makeover, and hit the shoe store down the street for a pair of three-inch stiletto sandals before walking through *The Paper Doll's* front door.

"I'm Máire Connolly," she replied, taking the hand he extended. His skin felt as greasy as it looked. "I would like a job." The little man whistled low in his throat and sized her up again.

"You're gorgeous," he said. "I'll give you that. But the big question is, can you dance?" Hell if she knew…Máire had never a day in her life danced in front of an audience.

"Can I audition?"

"Hop up there, girly, and let's see what you can do."

Máire swallowed hard and turned to face the stage. She hadn't expected to do this so soon… but then again, what had she been thinking coming in here at all?

Did she honestly think she'd just be given a job without having to dance first? Of course she knew better… she just hadn't wanted to think about any of this. Very aware of the sound of her heels clicking across the floor and the stale scent of baby oil and lubricant in the cross-breeze, Máire reached up and pulled herself onto the stage.

"What sort of music you like, honey?" the sleazy little man asked. Only one thing came to mind.

"Rock 'N' Roll," she replied. "Something hard and sexy." He raised one hand and waved it around in an odd manner, and a moment later she heard the speakers in the place buzz to life.

Máire knew the song from the very first note. She reached out for the pole, her skirt riding high up her thighs as she set her feet apart and threw her head forward, letting her hair fall in a thick curtain in front of her. Steven's sultry voice filled the room in a long, moaning wail.

It was a sign. *Rock 'N' Roll Angel* was the song that first entranced her, made her fall so hard for him. It seemed a fitting beginning to her new career.

Máire closed her eyes and let the music flow through her. She imagined Steven sitting atop one of the barstools, a beer in one hand and a look of boredom on his face. Then she began to move. She twisted and turned, dipped and writhed, tangled her body around the pole and laid out on the floor, all the while imagining taking control of his attention, drawing him in as he had done to her.

The song came to an end, leaving her spent and weak on the floor of the stage, one hand still wrapped securely around the pole. Distantly, she heard what sounded like applause. With her heart racing in her chest, Máire sat up and pressed her back to the pole for support, staring in shock as the little man came toward her with a smile on his face, an unlit cigar clenched between his teeth, clapping his hands.

"You've got the moves, baby," he said and leaned on the edge of the stage. "Just remember, when you're onstage tonight, you do have to take your clothes off."

"Tonight?" she said, her voice a high-pitched squeak. "You mean I got the job?"

"Consider it a trial run." He looked her up and down, his gaze lingering on her cleavage. "Impress the boys, and you might get a regular spot in the rotation." Before last night, Máire would have hugged the little runt, but today, she simply smiled and stepped down from the stage.

"What time do I start?"

"Eight-thirty."

"See you then." This sexy vixen that seemed to have possessed her gave him a sly wink as she walked past him and out the door.

Adrenaline raced through Máire's veins as she listened to the thump of the music, muted by the hoots and cheers of the men in the bar. From the sounds they made, the show was a good one. Máire turned around and paced back across the small room, the tassels on her costume swinging with each movement. Why the hell did she think she could do this? She would be taking the stage after an obviously seasoned performer. She didn't know what she was doing. This was going to go horribly.

Especially if Steven was out there. If he was anywhere in her line of sight, she would freeze up. She would wither and die… even though she desperately wanted to see him again; wanted him to see her as something more than just a thing to be used and abused.

A thing to be used and abused… the thought stopped her in her tracks. After one night with him, she had become everything he believed her to be. She was no longer an upstanding medical professional. She was an exotic dancer now. A stripper. A whore without the sex.

The song ended, and the cheers crescendoed into a roar of clapping hands and stomping feet. The girl, naked save for a sparkling silver thong, came running through the back, giggling as she clutched fistfuls of one and five dollar bills to her bare, swinging breasts.

On the stage, Máire heard the muffled voice of the announcer, and the drumroll of the song she'd chosen began to thump. Her heart leapt into her throat, and cold hands landed against her shoulders.

"Go on, honey," the smooth, female voice said, "that's your cue. Knock 'em dead." Máire found herself propelled forward, shoved through the curtain as her feet stumbled to catch up with the rest of her hurtling body. The first of the poles came into view as the high wail of a guitar filled the building. She grasped at the cold, metal pole and spun around it, using it to catch her balance and find her footing.

A round of cheers rose as she spun to the ground, her skirt flaring so that her rear end met with the cool wood of the stage. She held the pole for several breaths, then slowly rolled her head back as the music began to build, and crawled up, hugging the cold metal to her body.

The music took control, and she began to move, to swing and sway and dance. The gloves she wore were the first things to go, their slick texture made it too hard to hold on to the poles and rails as she turned herself lose. Flinging the items into the crowd, she watched with a smile as men reached to pull them from the air.

Máire scanned her audience as she continued to dance, looking for that familiar, swarthy face. It was nowhere to be seen, even as her halter's zipper began to fall, and the article landed somewhere behind her.

The more clothes she lost, the more money she found at her feet. The more men reached for her, wishing to tuck it down into her bra or into the strings riding above her skirt. She let them, not caring when they lingered on her skin or touched her in places they shouldn't touch.

She didn't even care about the money. All she cared about was the devastating knowledge that Steven Cave was not part of her audience. Even as she stood nearly naked on the stage, clad only in her a thong and heels, her breasts swaying as sweat ran down her glitter-covered body, she could only see the night as a failure regardless of the money scattered around her feet, tucked into the garter on her leg, and crushed in her closed fists.

She didn't care that she was a success in the eyes of the club. She wasn't even concerned when the greasy little man from earlier that day took the money she'd collected and handed less than half of it back to her. He muttered something about it being payment for the costume, then handed her a schedule.

Máire scarcely noticed his presence at all. All she wanted was to curl up and cry. Steven hadn't seen her dance. He hadn't been in the bar. He didn't know what she could do.

Her life continued on this way for an unknown number of days. She slept all day then spent all night swinging around the pole with her bare body exposed for the members of the elite little club. Her costumes and the music changed, but the audience never did. Máire continued to twine herself around that pole, remove her clothes, and take unreasonably small cuts of the money she worked to earn, but none of it mattered. The longer she went without seeing him, the more desperate she became. She had to let him know…

Then one night, sometime later, Máire walked into the back room of the bar to find all the girls absolutely abuzz with the news.

Steven Cave was in the audience.

Máire zipped into action, ripping pieces and parts of her newest costume from her bag. Sliding the silky garments on, she checked all of her seams and laced up the new white corset. As she laced up the new boots she'd bought that morning, the sound tech appeared in the doorway. She hadn't bothered to learn his name. It wasn't important so long as he did as she asked.

"Song, Máire?" he asked as she strapped a pair of feathery wings over her shoulders. She turned and balanced a gold-plated halo on top of her pigtails. Máire smiled.

"My first song," she said. The man floundered, his mouth flopping up and down like a broken hinge.

"But…but he's in the audience."

"I know," Máire replied with a giggle. "I'm sure I'll do it justice."

Máire stood in the center of the stage. Every light in the building was out, save the small runner lights by the bar. Her heart pounded; the sound echoing in her ears as she focused on taking deep, even breaths. Her fingers clutched the cool, metal pole, still slick from the previous dancer's oiled-up body. The crowd roiled beyond the edge of the stage where she could just make out fine silhouettes.

Then, by the bar, she spotted the one silhouette she would never, ever forget. The long, full hair flowed over his shoulders, smoothed down over the top of his head by what she knew would be a black and white bandanna. His right arm moved, lifting his glass to his lips, she assumed.

It was time.

"Good evening, Gentlemen," a sultry voice said through the speakers. It was answered by a round of cheers. "I see you boys have been very, very patient tonight, and as they say, good things come to those who wait." The words were nearly drowned out by the cheers and catcalls of the drunken men around her. Máire smiled. "It's eleven o'clock… time to get this party started. Presenting…" the room fell silent, "the Paper Doll Lounge's very own *Rock 'N' Roll Angel!*"

The first note struck, and the crowd went wild. With the second note, the lights flared, and she lifted her head, immediately finding Steven by the bar and pinning him with her stare. The men around her threw money at her, but this dance was not for them.

This dance was private.

Máire locked her gaze around his, holding him captive with her eyes as she danced. Once or twice his vision strayed away from her face to take in the newly revealed parts of her body; her shapely arms, the bare skin of her belly, the deep crease between her breasts, and finally, the deep rosettes of her nipples as the lacy bra slipped down her body. She still wore her wings and the thin strip of fabric covering her sex, and the knee-high, white leather boots.

Without the hindrance of her clothing, Máire twisted and spun, turned and writhed, wrapped her fingers around the pole and caressed it with her body the way she would have done him had he given her the opportunity. As she danced for him, ignoring the fingers slipping dollar bills into her panties and garters, Máire let the rage from that very first night flood her senses, lead her in this hypnotic spell of seduction, and finally drain away as the music stopped, the lights went down, and she came to rest on her knees. The greasy, grimy hands that touched her meant nothing. From across the room in the dim light of the bar lamps, she could still see Steven Cave's face, see by the smile of appreciation that she had accomplished exactly what she set out to do.

After her dance, she stepped up to the bar for a drink with only her wings and boots on, and he turned to admire her. He even offered to buy her drink himself.

Máire, still fueled by her anger and loving hatred, smiled coyly at him, refused his offer, and walked away. As much as it pained her to leave her Adonis sitting on that stool, she had to take that gamble. To get what she wanted, she had to make herself not only irresistible but untouchable.

It really was amazing the things a person could order online Máire thought as she confirmed her latest shipment and handed the gadget back to the postal worker across the counter. To have such odd items drop-shipped to a decoy post office box made it even easier. The collection she had amassed in the last month was quite astounding, but when the time came for her to use her new wares, she would be well prepared.

He was at the bar the next night, and every night thereafter for a week. Máire knew his tour was finished, but she never imagined he would come back so often. It was obvious from the way he stared at her that he did not remember using her and tossing her away. All she saw when she looked into his eyes now was admiration and that deep, pulsing desire that she had once felt for him.

She danced again and again for him, every single night, watching with gleeful satisfaction as he moved closer to the stage with each performance. Every single night he attempted to engage her, and every night she walked away.

On the last night of the week and her last night of work for three days, a Saturday, she came onto the stage to find him sitting in the very front row, his elbows resting on the edge of the platform. He looked worried, as if the anticipation were eating him alive.

She smiled because she had him right where she wanted him.

When she danced tonight, she paid him no attention. Tonight she danced for the other men in the bar, the ones waving money at her; all the men whom she had neglected in hatching her wicked little plan. They gave her money; tucked it against her breasts, into the strings clinging to the flesh above her ass, her garters, each of them taking the time to caress her skin and use explorative motions to touch her again and again. Still he sat motionless in his chair, eyes fixed on her body as she swung her head from side to side and crawled on all fours around to the men, offering tiny touches and encouragement of her own.

Then she left the stage, and the gentle calm of finality settled around her. Máire would never have to dance again after tonight—never share her body with another man because the one she wanted was going to be hers.

Rather than dress, she picked one of the sheer, silky robes from the racks backstage and draped it around her shoulders. Her spindle-thin high heels clicked across the tile like bullets on a tin target, their sound disappearing in the din of the bar as she entered the main room. Weaving her way through the crowd, Máire moved to Steven's side, and without a word took his hand in hers, pulling his attention away from the stage.

Soundlessly, he rose and followed her as she led him to one of the small, private rooms near the back of the building.

Once alone, she turned and shoved him down into the armless chair, then stood before him with her hands on her hips. The robe draped in just the right way, exposing the bare curves of her breasts without giving away all of her secrets. Her skin sparkled in the dim light, the thin sheen of shimmer powder and residual glitter from the floor accenting the peaks and valleys of her body in such a way that the rock star stared at her with unabashed hunger.

"Dance for me," he said, his voice little more than a weak croak. "To my song." Máire nodded, turning her back on him long enough to access the hidden panel in the wall and select her song.

A moment later, that sexy guitar riff filled the room, filled her. She twisted her fingers into her hair, pulling it away from her neck, and began to move. She had very few clothes to remove, and the robe provided just enough cover when she turned back to bring him forward, his elbows resting on his knees as he watched.

She moved forward with a slow, sultry sway, placing one hand in the center of his chest and pushing him backwards as she straddled his knees, bending and dipping her body over him in movements that suggested every single thing she wanted from him, suggested all the things she had once dreamed of.

Too bad he crushed those dreams months ago. At least he had not figured out who she was yet. Chances were he would not remember her from that first encounter. Now, Máire knew, Steven Cave would never, ever forget her.

He brought his hands up to her sides to touch her, but she quickly slapped them away. If he touched her now, all bets were off. Taking his wrists in her hands, Máire held his arms above his head as she continued to undulate her body over him, her core vibrating with need. She wanted him to touch her, to take her, break her, and make her whole again. And he would…soon enough.

The song came to an end, and as soon as she released his hands, he captured her and pulled her hard onto his lap. He pressed his nose to her throat and inhaled as his hands traveled the length of her spine. Against her sex, she could feel his cock, hard and ready, pulsing in anticipation.

"I want you," he whispered into her ear. "Tonight. Right now."

The thrill of victory coursed through her body. Máire gently disentangled herself from his grasp and rose, once again taking his hand.

"Let's have a drink first," she said. He nodded and rose, unceremoniously making adjustments to the new tightness in his jeans. Then she led him back to the bar where they were given drinks. She only had one more step before her plan would be complete, and he would be hers. When he turned away from his beer, she reached into her hair where the small pill case was hidden and removed a single white pill. Dropping it into his drink, she stirred the foaming head with her finger and wiped it on a bar napkin just as he turned back. Oblivious to her ruse, Steven lifted the glass to his lips and took a long, deep swallow of the cold, frothy brew.

The smile that crossed his face was one she would have melted over just a few months ago. But now? No. She had become too strong to fall for his charms. It was his turn to fall for hers.

Steven picked up his glass again and took a sip. Máire did the same, using her neatly manicured fingertips to hold his glass at his mouth until it was empty. She lowered her own at the same time, and when he wobbled slightly on his stool, she smiled.

"How many have you had tonight?" she asked, leaning over so the curve of her breasts showed above the neckline of the robe. "Too many it seems."

"Not enough to quit," he replied, his speech slightly slurred. "I am going to fuck you tonight."

Normally, Máire would have been offended by such a brash and vulgar statement, but between his overexcited state and the little pill she fed him without his knowledge, that he could still speak at all amazed her.

"How about you have another beer…you sit yourself right here and enjoy it, and let me get my things." She leaned over, placing her hand high up on his thigh, her thumb dancing in small circles, dangerously close to the hardened bulge in his too-tight jeans. "Then how about you let me take you home?"

"Your place or mine?" he asked with a sleazy smile.

"Mine. That way you're free to go when you've had enough." Máire trailed her hand across his cheek and over his shoulder as she walked away. When she glanced back over her shoulder, he held a new glass of beer, yet still watched her with that glazed, lustful expression. If she never remembered another thing, Máire knew she would always remember the way he looked at her just in that moment.

Having to carry nearly the full weight of Steven Cave up two flights of stairs to her apartment was rough on her back and her knees, what with those spiky stiletto heels, but once he was through the door, the lights in his eyes seemed to flicker on again. With dim recognition, she could see that he knew he was going to get what he wanted all along.

Steven stumbled a bit, and she let his weight slump forward, pitching him onto the couch. She turned to walk away when he grabbed her hand and pulled her down to straddle his lap. Her knees landed on either side of his hips, and he tangled one hand into her hair. Even with the drugs in his system, he was much stronger than he looked. God, she wanted this… she had wanted it for so long, and now it was finally her turn to have him.

Her heart hammered against her ribcage, and her pulse fluttered at the base of her throat. When she swallowed, she could feel every tiny fiber of each muscle contracting and sliding, moving in tandem with his hands as they roamed across her back. The feel of his skin moving along hers was divine, so much better than she ever could have imagined it. Steven pulled her forward, and she allowed herself only the slightest inhalation of his skin before he closed his mouth over hers. A thrill raced through her body, and she molded against him, her breasts pressing flat against his chest as he tilted her head and tangled his tongue around hers. This was not how she intended the evening to start, but now that he was kissing her; the love of her life, the man of her dreams, the most scornful beast ever to cross her path, she was helpless to stop him.

While she reveled in the taste and feel of him, Máire let Steven bring his hands around to her belly, then drift up her body. She leaned away from him just enough to give his fingers room to work free the buttons on her shirt. Pushing the fabric away, her breasts spilled into his hands, full and heavy and aching for his touch. She whimpered, just the slightest of sounds, but he heard it and smiled against her lips.

The soft chuckle in his throat broke her concentration enough to allow Máire to push him back and stand up. As much as she wanted this, wanted him, it had to be done just the right way. He reached for her again, but this time she sidestepped him, her blouse hanging from her elbows, and took one of his outstretched hands.

"Come with me," she said with a sultry purr and towed him from the couch. He stumbled a bit, then turned his head and followed her as she led him into her bedroom. He appeared so intent on her that he never noticed the décor; the framed photos and posters of him, the CD booklets, the guitar picks and various other band paraphernalia scattered near her bed.

Máire turned, placing a hand against his chest, and brushed a soft kiss across his lips before pushing him down to the bed. He landed with a grunt and a thump as she reached toward the dresser and picked up the remote for her CD player. As planned, she pushed the play button, and that same familiar wail filled the room.

Their song.

"I've never fucked to my own song before," he said. Máire chuckled.

First time for everything.

She turned back to him, looking at him as he lounged across her bed like an oversexed alley cat. She loved him. She hated him. He was still the most beautiful thing she had ever seen with the voice of an angel. "Get over here and fuck me."

Dropping her shirt to the floor, Máire laid her arms by her sides and crossed the room, stopping just in front of him and raising one foot. She placed the toe of her shoe against his chest, and he immediately reached up to caress her leg.

"Strip," she said, her tone firm and demanding. She lifted her foot just enough for him to pull the fabric between it and his body. A sleazy, lopsided smirk appeared on his face, and Steven pulled his t-shirt over his head. He stretched back, wincing as the heel of her shoe slid down the center of his now bare chest and landed against his thigh. Using his arms, he hauled himself back and stretched his hands over his head.

"You can do the rest," he replied. The cheeky little bastard… Máire rolled her eyes and closed the distance before him, placing one knee between his outstretched legs and the other to the side of him. Slowly, she crawled up his body, her skirt riding up her thighs as she drew her fingertips over the smooth, chiseled ripples of muscle that made up his chest, scraped them through his shaggy hair then dragged them up his arms. The tiny click that followed brought a panicked look to Steven's eyes. He tugged at his wrists, the fear and uncertainty in his eyes delicious as he realized a moment too late that she had locked them into place with a pair of handcuffs hanging from the metal headboard.

"Relax, baby," she purred against his ear, using her tongue to trace the cuff, "I'll make you feel better than anyone ever has before." With his hands tightly secured, Máire took her time moving down his body, touching and teasing, drawing her fingernails across his nipples and listening to the harsh intake of breath that followed. She traced the lines of his body, smiling as he absently picked up the tune of the song and began to sing along. Her already racing heart kicked into overdrive, and she looked up at him to find him staring back at her. As the chorus of the song filled the room, his voice rose in volume, blocking out the sound of the recorded one.

Máire shook herself out of this daydream; she knew this would never be real. She knew the words were not for her. She knew she was not the woman of whom he sang in the recording. No matter how much she wished she could be that girl, she was not. This, here and now, was what they had, and she needed to make the most of it, regardless of the beautiful fairy tale he painted before her.

She jerked open the button on his jeans and dragged the zipper down, then paused. He raised his hips expectantly, but she only backed away and crossed the room.

"Where you going, babe?" he asked, sounding a bit

frustrated. Máire picked up the remote for the CD player and set the album to repeat. They were going to be here for awhile.

"Nowhere," she replied, turning back to him with a slight swing to her hips. He lifted his head and watched as she swayed from side to side, letting the music flow through her. "We're going to be here for a very long time."

With each twist, each swing, she moved closer and closer, enjoying the sound of his voice in her bedroom. It was like a living thing with its own consciousness and presence as it wrapped around her and drew her back to him.

She laid her hands on his thighs and slipped them higher, catching the waistband of his jeans and slowly towing the clothing down his body to reveal a pair of black boxer-briefs. He lay before her, golden skin and messy hair, a work of art in human form. Beneath the thin layer of cotton lay the object of her desire, hard and pulsing. The difference this time was that he was the one lying prone, and she would take her pleasure from him.

"Come on, baby," he urged, raising his hips toward her, "you know you want me."

"Oh, I want you," she said, and gingerly cupped her palm over the hard length of his cock. His body jerked under her hand, "and I will have you in time."

"Whatcha waitin' for?"

"I'm going to enjoy you," she said, giving the pulsing member a light squeeze. Steven grunted and rocked his hips up against her hand. She pulled away, leaving him only with a sharp, stinging swat that drew a shriek from his throat and brought tears to his eyes. He tried to pull away, but having his arms pinned above his head severely limited his movement.

Reaching out, Máire soothed the spot with her palm, stroking his cock through the thin fabric until he moaned. His hips pumped up and down in time with her caresses. She could tell he was getting close when she pulled away and hooked her fingers under the fabric. She wanted to see him.

She stripped the remaining fabric away and sat back on her heels, marveling at the way the soft lamplight reflected over the planes of his body, marking the droplets of sweat that she had produced with her ministrations. Or was that from the drugs? Either way, it didn't matter.

Máire bent and drew her tongue up the center of his body, from his navel to his lips, collecting the salty dew and mingling it with the taste of his saliva as her tongue dipped between his lips. Steven returned her kiss hungrily, his body arching and twisting beneath her in search of contact. He tasted like sin, the rich mingling of alcohol and desire swirling on her tongue with each intimate touch. She spread her still-clothed body atop his, enjoying the feel of his hardness nudging against her belly. Again, he thrust his hips against her, grunting and moaning with the friction her body created. He could no longer talk now that she had control of his mouth, but even her questing hands and the feel of his slick skin under her palms couldn't quell the urge rising inside her. She had to have him. Would have him. With her skirt bunched around her waist, it was easy to taunt him, to blind him with need. He grunted and surged upward, but she easily lifted her body away from him.

"Don't tease me, baby," he said with a groan. Máire giggled and lowered her body back to his, sliding her slick core along his cock until she had him whimpering in agony. Bending low to lick at his lips, she lifted her hips and sank her body down on him, burying him to the hilt in her heat. He surged upward again, the strength of his body enough to lift her completely from the mattress.

The CD player clicked, and that familiar guitar riff tore through the air. A fragile laugh broke free of his throat. For one flawless second she sat atop him, reveling in the feel of his body beneath her, inside her, and of the sound of his enamored groans of delight. When she began to move, it was with a mindlessness she had never known. The delicious friction of the seek-and-retreat between their bodies pushed her higher and higher, moved her closer to sublime pleasure. The idea that it was Steven Cave giving her such pleasure nearly pushed her over the edge right then and there. But no, she could not give in so easily. There was too much yet to be done.

Try as she might, Máire could not hold back the orgasm that broke over her, bending her spine backwards with the force of the pleasure. Still, she continued to move, draping her body over Steven's as she reached beneath her pillow and wrapped her fingers around the cool leather she found there. Under her, Steven's movements were sharp and stuttered; he was losing control. She tightened her hand and brought the blade out from beneath the pillow.

A heady mixture of anxiety and anticipation raced through her veins as he began to unwind. Then the moment she felt it, felt his body rise and the deep, hot pulse of his climax deep within her, she bent to kiss his lips and brought the tip of the blade down, slicing through the skin covering his ribcage. He bucked beneath her, screaming even as his body betrayed the agony and continued to pulse again and again.

A high-pitched, broken laugh echoed through the room as she dragged the sharp weapon down the length of his sternum, watching the thin rivulets of blood run over his flawless skin. Red blossoms pooled under him, staining the pristine white sheets a deep crimson. She smiled. Using the tip of the knife, Máire wedged it into the wound, working free skin from muscle, and still atop him with his softening cock buried within her sex. She used her neatly manicured fingertips to lift apart the layers of his body, reveling in the sick squelching sounds that accompanied her ministrations. His mouth was open in a pained, soundless scream. His chest bowed upward as if offering his skin in sacrifice. Máire, still laughing, brought the weapon down his body all the way to the point where their bodies connected, then sliced from side to side his chest and his belly. As the blood pooled in the crevices of his body, she began to peel back his skin, exposing layers of fascia and bloody muscle.

What would have been a scream slowly died into a low, gurgling growl as the trauma to his body sent him into shock. Under her, he went slack, and he stopped responding, even as she made new, smaller cuts and pulled more skin away. Steven scarcely moved as she pushed her bloody fingers into the meat of his chest and with her arm buried to the elbow inside his body, began to loosen the skin of his right arm from muscle. Between her legs, she could still feel his rapid, shallow pulse moving through his flaccid cock.

Finally, covered in his blood, she lifted herself away from his dying body, mourning the loss of his filling warmth, and bent to retrieve a box of supplies. Steven's breath came in slow, shallow pants as she opened the box and retrieved two glass jars and a large needle. With manic glee, she unscrewed the cap on the first bottle, recoiling slightly at the smell of formaldehyde that filled the room. She glanced at his face and took in the glazed look of terror she found there as she submerged the tip of the needle and filled the well. With his semen dribbling down the inside of her left leg, Máire set the bottle to the side then drove the needle into the muscles of his skinned abdomen, in the approximate location of his liver. She pumped half of the contents of the needle under his skin, then removed it and plunged it through his breastbone and into his heart.

As the embalming fluid began to fill the chambers of his heart, the displaced blood appeared at his mouth, running down his face as he gave one last heaving and gurgling gasp, and fell still and silent.

"Serves you right, you bastard," Máire muttered, yet even as she laid the needle to the side and considered how she would remove his hulking frame from her bed, she felt the pang of loss tear through her still-beating heart.

Steven Cave… was dead. And she killed him. A small thrill of victory ran through her, followed quickly by a deep, aching sadness. He may no longer be alive, but no matter how she attempted to consider a world without him, each outcome was emptier and lonelier than the next.

There was only one option left: to continue with her original plan.

Without the natural movement of the living human body, Máire very quickly removed his skin, taking special care with his face and the more important parts of his anatomy. Splitting the skin along his scalp, she gently slipped her fingers between the tissue and bone, having to stop only long enough to slice away the thin connections of his inner lip and eye tissue in order to remove the shell of his body from the rest of his meat. Once done, she carried it into the bathroom and carefully washed and dried it before folding it into the cooler she had stashed there. As she layered the hide, she packed it thick with salt and ice, then closed the cooler and placed a small padlock on it.

Returning to her bedroom, she looked at the skinless body, then at the ruined bed beneath it. Tears began to roll down her cheeks when she glanced around at the photos and posters lining her bedroom walls. She missed him, but if all worked according to her plan, she would have him back very soon. Permanently this time.

One month later…

Máire opened the deep freezers she'd purchased with the money made in her time as a dancer. The large plastic-wrapped mass at the bottom, the only occupant of the freezer in fact, would take time to defrost, even though she had unplugged the appliance nearly two days prior. If she left the top open, hopefully it would be ready by the time she finished tanning the hide currently draped over her shower curtain rod.

The neighbors had only complained of the smell for the first hour, then she had learned that a pair of air purifiers could easily remove the odor of any tanning chemicals. She hated that she was going to have to ruin another set of bed sheets, but the process was almost complete. Now was not the time to stop.

The disappearance of Steven Cave never made the news. According to the website, it would be another month at least before he was scheduled to go back into the studio, so his band mates would not consider him missing until long after she was done.

Máire had continued to dance for two more weeks, until she made enough money to sustain her for a decent length of time and pay for the new carpet, bed, and paint for her bedroom. With the cash she found scattered across Steven's pockets, an astounding fifteen thousand dollars, she was easily able to locate a house for sale nine hours away and place a down payment on the rent-to-own contract. The credit card in his pocket bought her a whole house full of new furniture, drop-shipped to the address on his driver's license. His neighbors never questioned, even when she took the keys from his pocket and went into his home to search for the rest of his cash. As it stood, she could live comfortably for at least another five years. The thought filled her with manic glee.

Máire cut open the plastic around the partially mummified body and left it to thaw, then returned to the bathroom to finish the task at hand.

Three weeks later…

A soft smile christened her face as she laid the tanned skin across the plastic lining her bed. This would be the hard part, lining it up just so. The frame, laden with embalming chemicals and the weight of death, was heavier than she remembered as she dragged it through her apartment and heaved it up onto the bed. The limbs were stiff and did not move well. Hopefully it would loosen up as he warmed to room temperature.

Starting with the head, she lined the stripped skull up with its covering. The skin, she discovered, had suffered quite a bit of shrinkage. No matter… it would stretch when she began to stitch it closed. The arms were next, though bending the joints to fit the fingers into their original coverings was much tougher than she thought it would be.

The fingernails were a bit longer, too; further proof that they continued to grow after death.

Piece by piece, inch by inch, Máire fitted skin to form, careful not to stretch or tear it as she laid the bits and pieces of Steven Cave back together again.

When she rose to retrieve her needles and thread, she paused long enough to turn on the stereo. His rich, angelic voice filled the room while she knelt beside his almost-finished form and threaded the first needle with flesh-colored suture. The preserved skin only gave a moment's hesitation before the sharp point pierced it. With the slow, methodical patience of a madman, Máire put her idol back together again.

When she finished, she sat back on her heels to inspect her handiwork. He lay cold and still, silent and unmoving, but the wounds were minimal, the skin a perfect tan that fit over muscle and bone with flawless form.

Then the guitar sang out, the first notes tearing through the quiet. Máire bent and pressed her warm lips to his cold ones while she maneuvered her body over him. Finally, after all this time, all this planning, Steven Cave, her *Rock 'N' Roll Angel*, was all hers. She laid a hand over her belly and bent to kiss his lips again.

"I'm glad I decided to keep you," she told him as she slowly started to move. "I've got a surprise for you." She paused, her breath leaving her body in a moan as she took her love into herself once more. "That's right, baby," she continued, as if answering a question when she was able to breathe again, "you're gonna be a daddy."

EASY AS PIE

ENOUGH IS ENOUGH.

"Yes, it is."

Callie brought the cleaver down through the center of the meaty joint. Bone and cartilage separated from one another with a sickening pop and the sharp blade clunked against the butcher-block counter, sinking deep into a previous divot. She raised her arm and with her dirty sleeve wiped sweat and blood from her face. Jerking the knife out of the counter, she hauled it over her head and brought it back down on the next joint, easily severing the flesh and crunching into the bone. The pieces of meat fell apart, and she picked up the larger of the two. With a fillet knife, she separated skin from muscle then split it apart. The bone came away easily, the squelching vacuum-suck ringing in her ears long after she'd moved on to the remaining chunks of meat lying on her counter. Her shoulders ached from the constant up-down motion.

Butchery is hard work, isn't it?

"Yes, it is," she said again and dabbed at her face with her sleeve once more. Of course, the last time she butchered this sort of meat, she was a lot younger. Thirteen years younger, to be more specific. There was a big difference between beating up bone at nineteen and trying it again at thirty-two.

Callie flipped a switch on the side of her industrial stand mixer. The grinder attached to its face came alive, easily turning the chunks of raw meat into hamburger. As it filled the bowl beneath the machine, she turned toward the mirror on the back wall of the darkened shop and picked up a towel.

She looked awful. But then again, she supposed that after forty-seven hours without sleep, thirty-two of which included steady butchery work, anyone would look awful. Callie ran the towel under cold water and used it to wipe her face. When she reached her right eye, she gingerly patted away the caked blood and strings of shredded meat. The mirror on the wall above the sink showed a grisly sight. Under the layer of grime, her skin glowed deep, harsh purple. Surrounding the bright, blue eye was a sickly green ring. She screamed, a desperate, frustrated sound, and flung the towel across the room. It hit the wall with a meaty squish and landed in a lump on the floor. It left a thin, pink trail down the freshly-painted wall, but she didn't care…it would come off with a little bleach and some elbow grease. The sight of the pink-and-white mess filled her with a manic sort of glee. After ten years, she thought that part of her was gone. Apparently not.

Overhead the naked fluorescent light bulb flickered garishly, reminding her that her kitchen — her safe haven – hadn't been spared as a casualty of war. Perhaps it was that trauma, the destruction of her inner sanctum, which started her down this maniacal new path.

New? The tiny voice in her mind whispered. *What's new about you and slaughter?*

Callie covered her ears with her hands and shook her head sharply to dislodge the voice. She hated that voice. Hated herself, if she were truly honest.

She picked up the bowl of ground meat and sniffed

it once. It stank of blood and of raw, dead flesh. The tiniest sizzle of guilt trickled through her mind as she turned around and upended it into the hot skillet on the stove. The guilt didn't last long, though… when it came to cooking, guilt never really hung around. The meat popped and sizzled happily, and as she added her special seasoning blend, Callie began to hum. Cooking made her happy. It was the very reason why she opened the bakery in the first place. This little shop—the one thing in this world that truly belonged to her—was her sanctuary.

Turning away from the stove, Callie picked up a different bowl, this one filled with chocolate chips. She drizzled over the top a few drops of corn syrup, then pulled a measuring cup from the microwave and poured heavy cream into the bowl. Picking up her whisk, she scraped and stirred until the ganache was smooth and creamy. The aromas of chocolate and cooking meat battled for dominance, causing her nose to twitch. The juxtaposition of sweet and salty made her smile. The little voice inside giggled with manic glee.

She reached behind herself to stir the meat then returned to her chocolate. Callie took a cookie sheet from the cabinet and lined it with parchment. A small plate sat beside the sink, the meaty bits atop it still steaming from their recent stay in a pot of boiling water. She upended the contents into the bowl of chocolate and stirred them well.

Had it coming…had it coming…

"Won't do that again, will you Matt?" she said aloud. Her voice echoed around the empty kitchen, disturbing the quiet stillness. Callie paused… she was so happy here. This bakery and its industrial, all-steel kitchen truly was her refuge, her home away from home, her quiet in the storm.

But even this place couldn't protect her. The door with the board over it in the storefront stood as a hard, harsh reminder of that fact. When he couldn't get the door open, he'd broken it down. She loved Matt, she truly did, which is why she'd taken so much of his shit over the last four years. But lately as his drinking increased, so did his anger, and tonight…

He deserved it… the bastard had it coming. You know he did…

Tonight was the final straw. He pushed the wrong buttons, and Callie? She made him pay.

Placing the bowl of chocolate to the side, Callie turned back to her pan and spooned the meat into the prepared, paper-lined bowl. Pouring the majority of the grease into a coffee tin, she returned the dregs to the flame and began to throw in other ingredients. Soon she had a beautifully colored, though slightly soupy, gravy. Callie patted the meat dry, enjoying the fine, slightly gamey smell of it, and tipped it into the pan with the gravy.

Venison…tell them it's venison when they ask. She stirred it together and turned it down to simmer.

"I should have soaked it in water," she said aloud. "It would have smelled so much better afterward."

Callie came to the shop to get away. In four years Matt never once lifted his hand against her. Never before had she felt the need to defend herself against him. When he drank, he yelled.

He shouted. He insulted. But she ignored it because she knew it wasn't him, and the version of him that was sober was loving and caring and always apologetic would always resurface in the morning. Not that apologizing made him a good guy. It just made him worth forgiving because he always sounded so repentant. And Callie herself wouldn't be where she was if it hadn't been for second chances.

So she tripped over the rug and spilled a cup of water on the floor. She cleaned it up – most of it anyway. Leave it to Matt to get drunk and find the one bead of water left on the floor that she'd managed to miss while wiping up the mess and nursing a stubbed toe. He'd yelled at her up one side of the house and down the other for it, too. She went into the bedroom, as always, with her hands over her ears to block the screaming, both inside and out.

She couldn't let it out…couldn't let that voice take control. She might get lost. Bad things happened when she got lost.

But tonight Matt did more than yell. Tonight he followed her down the hall. When she told him to get out he threw the empty beer bottle at her and called her a cunt. And then he cocked his fist back and gave her that ugly purple and green shiner. The bastard even went so far as to hold her down and try to make her take him. Callie told the world she was not a violent person by nature and if asked she would swear the knee to his groin nearly did her in. If she told the story later, she would force herself not to cry and admit that she didn't have any other choice.

But Callie knew better. She felt it long before she took that swing. She had to get out, for his protection as much as her own. When Matt tumbled to the floor in a groaning heap, she ran for the door, leaving her shoes against the wall as she grabbed her keys. At least she said she was sorry before she left.

Callie picked up a pair of tongs and swirled her chocolate treats around the bowl. Then she lifted each one carefully and placed it on the prepared pan. Giggling sickly, she pulled out a container of almond slivers and laid one on the end of each, then took up a pastry bag and drizzled white chocolate across them. Her candy-coated fingers were so pretty!

"I'd call them lady fingers, but that's not entirely true," she said as she looked down at her latest confectionary creation. The sight made her want to simultaneously laugh and vomit.

Precious treats!

She shoved the pan away. At least she had the forethought to boil the fingers first and remove the skin and bones. In her rage she'd even replaced the real bones with some of those cute candy ones she had left over from last Halloween.

Callie went to her pantry and rifled through the shelves. This kitchen was stocked for pastry, not the creative culinary arts it witnessed tonight. She would have to improvise, just like last time. When she exited the closet, Callie carried a box of potato flakes, a bag of fresh carrots, and a bowl filled with various spice jars. This little experiment might not work, but she was more than willing to give it a go. The items she grabbed spilled across the last uncluttered counter in the kitchen, leaving just enough space for the stack of miniature pie tins. She took several layers of her signature puff pastry dough from the refrigerator and laid them across each of the tins, then punched them down into the proper shape. She poured a layer of potato flakes across the bottom of each, then chopped several carrots and sprinkled the pieces atop the dried potatoes. Last, Callie poured the meat and thin gravy over the tops, filling the shells almost to bursting. When she laid the new sheets of pastry over the tops and crimped the edges, she shuddered. It was wrong to do this.

It was also wrong of her to feel this way. Callie knew it was bad. She knew it was disgusting. She knew she should be locked up, and the warden should throw away the key. Still, it didn't stop her from shoving the pans into the oven to bake.

Good girl…take the bastard down.

Callie pretended the voice didn't exist and wiped her face with the back of her arm. Her kitchen was a wreck – blood, bits of meat, and strings of cooling chocolate covered every surface – the floor, the counters, the cabinet faces, the walls…and even the ceiling. The pies had a good long while to bake, the chocolates needed to set before she decorated them, and all that was left was the pile of bones in the sink.

Item by item, Callie put away her mess. She rinsed her bowls and utensils and neatly organized them into the dishwasher racks. She pulled out her mop and her bucket of cleaning products, and sprayed the entire kitchen with a fine layer of bleach-based cleaner. Then she began to scrub. Last time her sloppiness almost got her caught. Last time she didn't clean up after herself and her mess threatened to haunt her.

This time it was contained. And nobody would ever think to suspect sweet, angelic little Callie Clark of such dubious misdeeds. After six years, nobody bothered to suspect that Callie Clark wasn't even a real person.

She tossed bone after bone into the sink as she wiped the blood and bits of meat from the counter tops, giggling as it slithered down the cabinet facings and landed on the floor with sick, squishing sounds. The deep crimson fluid turned pink as the bleach and water thinned it out. The whole kitchen smelled like blood and death, thinly masked by the scent of baking puff pastry and cooling chocolate. Callie inhaled deeply and let loose a slow, contented sigh as she picked bits of meat and fat out of the soggy mixture on her floor and tossed them into a bucket. She pulled out a clean mop head and gave the floor one more once-over for good measure.

When the timer went off, the kitchen sparkled. Callie pulled the pans from the oven and set them on her cooling counter. They smelled good…like normal, tasty meat pies. She certainly wouldn't be eating them, but someone would. No one would be the wiser and once they were gone, Matt would be as well. Steam rose from the vent slits in the tops of the perfectly browned crusts. Yes, they would fit nicely into the pastry case out front.

Speaking of out front… she was going to have to contact the glass company and have the door repaired. She still couldn't believe Matt had gotten up off the floor and followed her. She'd been certain to lock the doors behind herself, but it didn't stop him. He barreled through the plate glass, destroying her awning and the door frame in the process. Of course he followed her! He was drunk, and if Callie learned anything over the years, it was that alcohol always dimmed a person's sense of self-preservation.

Bleeding and angry, Matt came through, kicking open the swinging door between her and the kitchen. Screaming, he flung her flour tin across the room, sending fine, white powder floating around to coat the floor, the counters, and her. The tin bounced off the metal cabinet face and flipped backwards, knocking the hand-blown glass cover from the light fixture. It crashed to the floor, spraying colored glass across the floors in a fine, tinkling mist. As it sang its way across the room, Matt raised his hand and he hit her again, this time with an open backhand to the cheek. Her face already hurt from the punch to the eye, and the sting of his hand added to the throb of her bruised eye socket tipped her over the edge. She spun around, her bare knees landing amid the shards of glass. The sharp, jagged slivers jabbed into her skin, tearing open the flesh along her legs. But the pain? It was irrelevant now.

"Get up, bitch," he snarled as he stood over her. In his left hand he held a beer bottle, and in his right hand he held a spatula. "Take your punishment like a big girl, Callie. Turn that pretty little bottom up here and take it, girl." He taunted her, waving the spatula over his head. When he lifted his booted foot and stomped on her bare ankle, she screamed. More glass dug into flesh and bone. Fireworks exploded in front of her eyes, colorful bursts of pain that threatened her very consciousness. Still dizzy from that last swing and the pain of his foot grinding against the bones in her leg, Callie scooted away from him, dragging her injured leg out from under his boot. "I said," Matt snarled, jerking her from the floor by her elbow, "accept your punishment, bitch!" The

pop of her shoulder nearly dislocating echoed across the kitchen, nearly drowning out the sound of his shrieks.

It started as a muffled susurrus, like wind through tall grass. Slowly it built, grew larger and stronger, became more defined. It nagged at her, chewed at her subconscious, laughed and taunted.

Do it, Callie, *it said.* Do it now or be his slave forever. *She covered her ears and shook her head, trying in vain to force the sound away.* You can't ignore me forever, you know.

Callie accepted her punishment as motivation. The second slap across the face curled her body close enough to the wall that she easily slipped a large knife from the magnetic strip there. As he shook her around and brought her back to face him, the knife came too, its sharp, sleek, serrated blade easily sliding deep into the flesh of his chest. It pierced his sternum with surgical precision. Matt paused and his eyes glazed over as he looked up at her.

"What the hell have you done?" he asked on a gasp, dropping her to her feet. Callie collapsed at the same time Matt did, but rather than lie motionless and shocked on the floor she snatched the blade away and brought it down again, just a little bit lower this time. He gasped, sucking air in as the knife sank into his gut. Callie heard a pop and a hiss, and the putrid stench of bile filled the kitchen where she pierced his stomach. Again and again she stabbed him, sending blood and ragged bits of flesh flying around the room. She stabbed, jerked, and stabbed again. Callie kept going until her arm gave out and the knife fell limply from her fingers. It clattered to the floor and landed in a pool of Matt's blood. She collapsed beside him, gasping for breath while her ruined knees bled into the puddle under his body. The wicked voice laughed.

Matt didn't move. Couldn't move. He was covered from head to toe in blood and slivers of his own ruined muscle. His breath was gone – both lungs punctured from the force of her blows. Blood bubbled out of his mouth and ran down his face. Trails of the viscous substance trickled from each wound – there had to be three dozen or more scattered about his chest. His eyes, wide and glassy, stared coolly up at the ceiling. They didn't move at all.

Callie looked over at the pile of bones… she'd disposed of the entrails down the sink – garbage disposals and trash compactors were powerful little things, she'd learned. All the squishy parts – the stomach, the eyeballs, the tongue and all those other weird little bits she didn't have a name for – they were little more than meat byproduct in the box under her sink now. All she had left to do was find a way to dispose of those bones and she would be done. Oh, and the brain sitting in a bowl in the big, industrial refrigerator in the corner.

Whatever happened from here on out, she had to do it quick. The sun, already on the rise, winked through the tops of the curtained windows. It was early yet, but the bakery would be opening soon. Her big stand mixer sat on the counter with the grinder attachment still latched onto the top. She had lots of attachments for that thing and she wondered…

Hurry up, bitch. They're going to catch you.

Callie jerked open the cabinet that contained her lesser-used appliances. All of the attachments for that mixer sat in a neat row across the bottom – she'd gotten them all in a bulk order when she bought the mixer. Most of what was down there had never been used. She carefully examined each item until she found what she was looking for – talk about getting lucky.

Callie all but skipped back across the kitchen with the grain mill in her hand. She began to whistle as she attached it to the front of the mixer and placed the flour tin beneath it. Matt ruined her flour stock in his rage, so it was only fitting that he replace it. She picked up the meat cleaver one more time and one by one chopped the bones down to small pieces. The ribs? Those were no problem. The pelvic bones, however, were another story. The cleaver, even as sharp as it was, stuck in the larger, denser bones.

"Stupid…stupid…stupid…man…" Callie grunted with each swing of the knife, breaking a sweat as she strained over the thick calcium creations. Her eye throbbed and her palms stung from the pressure of the knife's handle against her skin. The more she chopped, the angrier she became. Forget the guilt! Callie was pissed. "You deserve this, you know," she said to the pile of chopped bones on her counter. "You should have kept your hands to yourself, you asshole." She dropped the first of the bone slices into the top of the mill, but it was much too large to fit through the grain sifter. Plus, she realized, if she dropped them in marrow and all, the spongy mess might clog up the apparatus. From years of pastry making, Callie knew the price of flour was on the rise, and she didn't dare compromise the integrity of her fresh, free batch.

Matt's body was heavy. Callie had plenty of strength from years of the physical labor cooking entailed, but even her well-toned arms couldn't heft his dead bulk to the counter. She couldn't drag him, either, because every time she did his skin and clothes caught on the glass sprinkled across the floor. Every time she took a step, her bare feet found more of it as well. Grunting in frustration, Callie dropped his body back to the floor, ignoring the sick thump of his head cracking against the tile, and went for the broom. It left broad, wet streaks of blood all over the floor as she dragged it around but it served its purpose and cleared the glass from the floor. There would be more under his body but she could deal with that later. So long as she could walk around the kitchen, she could continue to work in peace.

With the floor sufficiently cleared, Callie contemplated her options. Matt was obviously too heavy to put in the dumpster – she wouldn't do that anyway because it was sloppy and too easily traced back to the shop. Sloppy landed her three nights in the Sonoma County Detention Center and a further six months in the Claxton Road Mental Heatlth Facility for a whole string of personality disorders she couldn't even name. She swore when she got out that she wasn't ever going back to a place like that, no matter how well-deserved the stay might be. Besides, that first one was for fun. This one was justified.

The son of a bitch deserved it, *she thought as she stripped off his clothes.*

She started with his shoes and socks, then his shirt, then his jeans which had to be cut away. She couldn't get rid of him in one piece, that much was for certain, No, she had to cut him up into more manageable pieces. Then she could figure out what to do with him.

Callie set her jaw in determined stubbornness as she jerked her biggest meat cleaver from the magnetic strip on the wall. She started at his joints, hacking deep into his hips and his shoulders, listening to the sick, wet squish-crunch as cartilage and tendon began to separate. One by one his limbs came loose and she hefted the hunks of meat up to the counter for easier access.

The torso, now that was another story. Callie easily severed his head then stopped to sharpen her knife. The first time wasn't nearly this much fun. Of course, the first time was just an experiment by a teenager. A sloppy display of psychosis that could have ended much worse had the judge not seen fit to fall into her "poor little neglected girl" ruse and send her to rehab. She wasn't really abused. She just wanted to kill that man. She hated him from the first time she met him – that night her piss-poor excuse for a mother brought him home as her "new daddy", and even her better judgment couldn't keep her from cutting his throat with a broken beer bottle she picked up out of the parking lot.

When the blade was ready again, she lifted his penis – a sad, small thing, she realized as it lay against the gaping wound that used to be his hip – then placed the knife just beneath his testicles and began to slice.

She briefly thought about keeping it, but that would be weird. Plus, souvenirs meant a trail, and there could be no trail.

The set of fondant tools she kept in the drawer by the sink worked well for scraping out the marrow, which she dropped into an old mixing bowl. She'd figure out something to do with that later.

She picked up the cleaver and chopped the bones down again and again until they would fit. They fell into pieces much easier without the gooey centers, and with each heavy *thwack* of the knife on the counter, a little more of her murderous rage melted away. She had her revenge and — her eyes trailed to the pan of Matt's chocolate-covered fingers with their new-and-improved candy centers — it was sweet.

Callie poured the bits of bone handful by handful into the top of the mill and turned it on. The machine made a harsh, dragging sound. It squealed loudly, and then a fine dusting of flour-like powder began to fall to the bottom of the bucket. She watched the last bits of Matt flutter down like snow, an innocent-looking ingredient for her next batch of cookies. The mountain grew and grew, and as it expanded her anger wilted into determined uncaring. Matt was gone. He deserved it and if she had to do it all over again, she would do the same thing. Callie poured the next handful of crushed bone into the machine.

"New marketing idea!" she said aloud and giggled. "I can go gluten free for a week!" Her laughter rang off the walls happily as the mill continued to churn out fine, white flour. The tin filled nicely as the pile of chopped bones shrank. When it was done, Callie leaned back against the counter and covered a large yawn with the back of her dusty hand.

No wonder she was exhausted! She lost an entire day in the shuffle and the girls would be in to open the shop for the Monday morning rush any minute now… the kitchen wasn't nearly as disastrous as it had been thanks to bleach and high-powered cleaners. The only sign that something was out of place was the bowl of bone marrow sitting on her counter.

The lock tumblers on the back door began to fall away. Jessie. Right on time, as always. Callie hurriedly tipped the bowl of marrow into the sink and turned on the disposal. Footsteps echoed up the back hallway as she rinsed out the bowl and shoved it into the dishwasher.

She was just laying the newly-detached grain mill in the washer rack as the young woman with the bouncy, blonde ponytail came skipping into the kitchen.

"Mornin' Callie!" she chirped as she pushed her purse into the lock-box beneath the microwave. Callie looked down at her bloody apron and quickly jerked it off. It landed in the linen hamper just as Jessie turned around. Her smile faded fast. "Oh, my goodness… look at your eye! What happened to you?"

Callie sighed as she pulled a clean apron from the back of the pantry door and looped it over her head. "Matt got drunk Saturday night."

"He hit you?" The blonde nineteen-year-old looked horrified and disgusted when Callie nodded. "I don't understand why you stay with him."

"He never hit me before," she said and picked up the hamper full of dirty, bloody material. "This weekend was bad. I left the house and came here at 9:30 Saturday night. He followed me and broke out the door. I've been here ever since."

Jessie gasped and her hand flew to her throat. Callie turned her back on her employee and disappeared down the hall into the laundry room where she hurriedly dumped the soiled rags and apron into the industrial washing machine. She added detergent and pushed the door closed, and when she turned around Jessie was standing in the doorway. Callie jumped.

Stab her!

She stifled a shocked cry. "Don't sneak up on me!"

"Sorry…" Jessie's voice hitched. Callie realized then that the girl was crying. "Please tell me you dumped him!"

"You could say that." She pushed her way out of the small room and went back into the kitchen where she picked up the trays of cooled meat pies. "I made sure he wouldn't hurt me anymore." She started into the shop, the sniffling Jessie on her heels. The pies on the tray smelled wonderful. They were cool and the crusts still crispy as she pushed them into the top rack of the pastry case. "I need you to run the front this morning, Jessie. I've got some things to take care of in the back." *Insurance claims, filing a police report, that brain hidden in the back of the refrigerator…*

The girl, stricken, paled by several shades. "But he broke the door, Callie! He'll come back!"

Callie slid the trays of pies onto the top shelf of the empty pastry case. "No, he won't," she said then turned and began to pull sheets of pastries – croissants, cookies, turnovers and everything in between from the steel storage cases. Rack by rack she lined the cases.

"You don't know that."

Callie stepped around the counter and headed for the door. She flipped the lock, propped the broken door open with a brick, and turned her "open" sign on. The first of her regulars, she saw, was already crossing the street and heading her way. The young man was long and lean. She'd admired him for months now but this morning, she saw him in a brand new light…and not a shining white one.

He looks tasty, doesn't he? You want him, don't you?

"Oh, yes." She took a deep breath of the cool, moist morning air and smiled. Matt's misdeeds and untimely end were already forgotten. "Yes, I do."

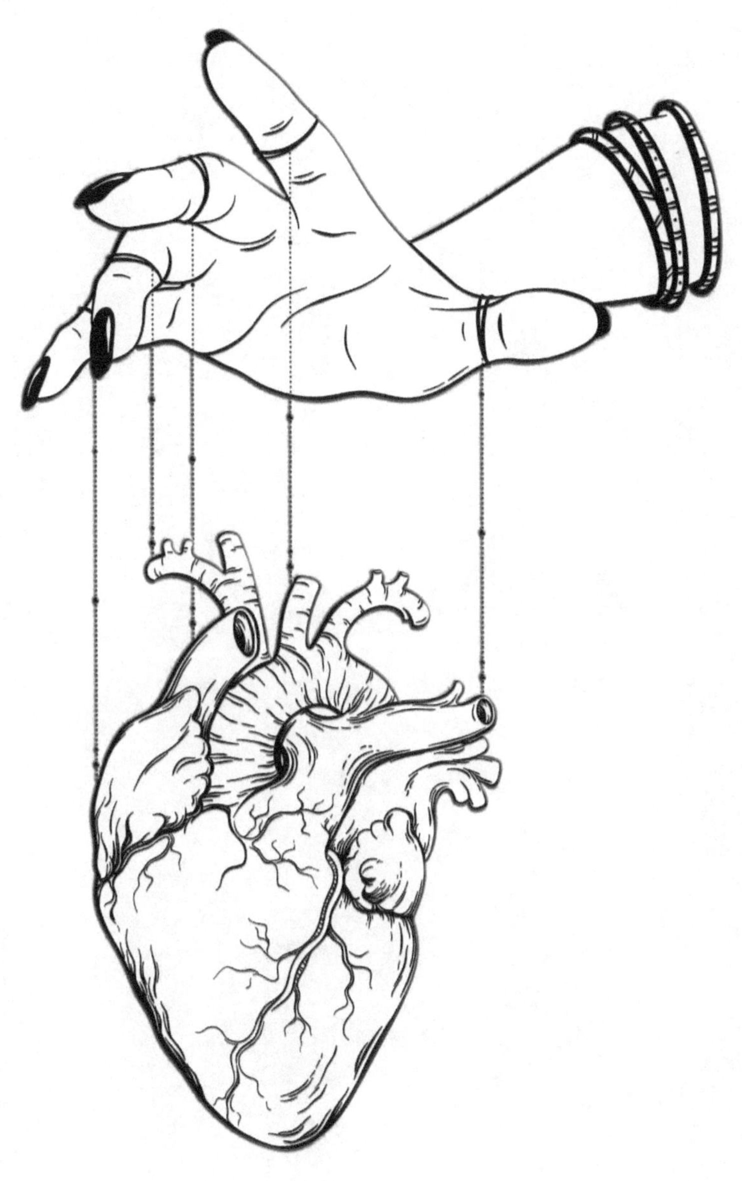

Angel with the Scabbed Wings

THE FIRST KILL WAS MESSY.

Blood went everywhere, and he was lucky he hadn't been killed on the scene with the way the girl screamed. He'd been so hungry that he couldn't stop when he needed to, even after the sound of footsteps rushed toward him, their owners ready to destroy the abomination he'd become.

After that night he learned. He learned to listen, to control the rage, to slow down and savor the end. He figured out that death was only a satisfying side effect of the hunt.

Stalking the prey was the best part—smelling the fear on those that would inflict harm on others, watching their eyes glaze over as they realized they had stumbled upon their deaths, taking that first sweet taste of human blood from each unwilling victim…

The bloodlust stirred just thinking about it.

Being immobile during daylight hours gave Vincent Iscariot plenty of time to plan his vengeance. He could scour newspapers for stories about potential victims, and being a vampire made it easy to break into police stations after hours and take reports. Criminals of all sorts ran loose because the police couldn't see things the way he saw them. They couldn't understand a murderer's mentality, so the do-gooders had no way to track the evil. Vincent was of the darkness now, one of those proverbial monsters under the bed that could spirit away bad children without a word. He knew how to hunt evil.

He had no taste for innocents anyway. Virgin blood was too sweet. He preferred the bitter tang of evil with his meal, like the dry finish on the finest of wines. Being a killer now, he understood why killers did what they did, and he enjoyed being one of them. He could have lied to himself and said that he only killed to save human life, but he knew better than that. The facts were simple: Vincent enjoyed the taste of human blood, and would not feel remorse for succumbing to his beastly nature.

He'd never had the pleasure of hunting a woman before. At least, not as game. In life, he'd rivaled Casanova as a lover. And now...he'd *become* death.

According to the police files, Sarah Anne Bennett murdered her husband and child, cut the throat of a neighbor who witnessed the crime, and fled Jacksonville. The grainy photograph of the happy family Vincent had taken from the file made him smile. Photography had come such a long way since he was human. The image was faded and grainy, but he could yet see the misery shining in her eyes. When he looked at the photograph he knew as well as she did that even then she was planning on leaving. The difference between them was that she had yet to figure out just how to go about it.

Sarah Anne passed by the alley where Vincent lurked, bringing him back to the present. Even without the photo he'd have known her anywhere. The flowery scent of her perfume did little to mask the stench of murder that lingered on her skin. That smell, something that would have once turned a man like Vincent away, acted as a drug these days. He stepped out of the alley and into the luminescent halo cast by the gaslight on the storefront and began to follow. Sarah Anne walked down the street unaware, bundled tightly beneath multiple layers of brocade and linen with scarves piled around her throat. Her hat was pulled low so that only her eyes were visible from the street. Even in this strange place where nobody knew her, the fear still consumed her. It tainted the air around her and left a strong trail for Vincent to follow.

He'd come with her from Jacksonville to Asheville, yet she had no inkling. He followed her now as she through the streets, silent and alone in the middle of the night. She never heard him; never sensed him. He made it a game, hunting her. She was easy prey, and he a seasoned predator.

Across the street, a group of drunks stumbling out of a closed down bar spotted her. The one who fancied himself a leader—or at least the drunkest—let loose a slurred obscenity followed by a wolf whistle as they started across the street. Sarah Anne picked up her skirts and bustled along, panic and alarm flavoring the air. Vincent faded back to watch from a shadowy nook between storefronts as the men encircled her, ripped away her hat, and flung her shawl out into the street. Before she could scream her mouth was covered and her arms behind her back.

Vincent smiled. Four-for-one tonight…his luck was up.

Stepping out of the shadows, he moved to her side and tapped the nearest man on the shoulder. He turned, shrugged at the boy, and ripped Sarah Anne's bodice open. She shrieked against the hand over her mouth as her flesh spilled into view.

"I think you should leave the lady be," Vincent said. They ignored him. "It would be wise to walk away, gentlemen."

"Fuck you, boy," one of the others spat. The smile on his lips turned to a cruel sneer. The tallest of her attackers swung his fist at Vincent. The vampire caught the blow in the palm of his hand and squeezed. The satisfying pop and crunch of bone and tendon made the venom run.

"I don't think so."

The man crumbled to the ground, holding his ruined hand with his mouth wrenched open in a silent scream. One of the others turned with a sneer, and took three steps toward Vincent.

"You shouldn'ta done that, kid."

"Why not?" Vincent asked. He stepped into the dim halo of the gas lamp and tipped his face up to the man. Even in the darkness, they could all see the bright scarlet irises glittering back at them. The next step faltered, but before the drunk man could turn to run Vincent leapt, fingers sinking in to the bone of his victim's shoulders, teeth breaking the delicate skin encasing his carotid artery. Little more than a gurgle escaped before the drunk man was limp and lifeless in Vincent's very capable hands. He was dead before the first drops of blood spattered the snowy sidewalk.

In the seconds it took to drain the first, the two watchers dropped the woman and turned to run, but Vincent was faster, knocking the legs out from beneath one with a swift kick and halting the other's escape by closing his long, cold fingers around the thick wrist and yanking. The arm snapped free of the socket, flesh tearing and spraying them all with a fine, red mist. Vincent held the severed arm in his right hand as the body collapsed to the street.

He dropped the drained body and the severed arm as he turned and stepped over the armless, screaming man. The third man's neck broke with a sick pop when Vincent laid his hands on either cheek. Sarah Anne cowered against the rain-slicked brick wall, quivering with fear. Vincent looked up at her, still clean and immaculately presented save a small line of blood trailing from the left corner of his bottom lip.

"Thank you," she said in a meek voice. "Thank you for saving me."

"Your gratitude is appreciated," Vincent replied, coming toward her, "if not misguided. You see, Sarah Anne, I have not come to rescue you."

Her eyes went wide and her mouth fell open into a perfectly round O. She stuttered and stumbled, searching for words as she slipped along the wall. The layers of her skirt caught on the rough building face as she tried to escape.

"W-what do you want from me?" she cried. Vincent closed the distance between himself and Sarah Anne, stopping four pace away. His head canted to the left and he smiled, a look he knew would frighten her even more. "You...you were my guardian angel, come to rescue me from the monsters."

"Oh, no, sweetness," he said, smile turning to a sneer. "I am the monster, come to make you pay for what you've done."

"But I'm innocent!" she cried.

"Innocent?" he asked, his voice went cold and hard. "I

think not, sweetheart."

"I've done nothing to deserve this!"

"Oh ho!" Vincent cheered, smiling at her brazen lie. "Explain to me exactly what a young woman is doing out alone after dark."

"I was on my way home!"

"Liar," he replied. "You, Sarah Anne, are attempting to escape the reach of the law. Have no fear, the police will never prosecute."

"No!" she sobbed, inching along the wall as far as her tangled skirt would allow. "I do not fear prosecution! Let me live, sir!"

"Why would the guilty not fear prosecution?" he asked calmly. Vincent crossed his arms over his chest and sniffed the air, taking in the increasingly strong scent of her terror.

"I maintain my innocence. Please, let me live! Let me live!"

"Innocence, Sarah Anne?" The smile faded. "Innocence is what died in your arms twenty-eight days ago. Your daughter begged for her life as she bled out in your lap, sitting in your bathtub." Sarah Anne's mouth fell open and she collapsed to her knees. Tears streamed over her round cheeks, dripping from her chin to soak into the fabric of her dress. "Setting fire to your home in the night does not absolve you of sin, woman." Vincent knelt in front of her and closed his long, cold fingers around the slender column of her throat. "Consider your death one more scab peeled from my wings, murderess."

She did not beg, did not plead for mercy as he pulled her forward and sank his teeth into the delicate flesh of her throat. The first splash of hot blood, rich with the flavors of sin and fear, hit the back of his throat, Vincent knew he'd done the right thing. Sarah Anne's body went limp in his grasp as her heart slowed and, with one final, weak flutter, stopped. He laid her gently against the ground and, with his thumbnail, slit open her throat to hide the bite mark. The last of her blood, already congealing, leaked from the wound to stain her collar and drip into the muddy snow beneath her.

"*Requiem Aeternam dona eis,*" Vincent said as he rose and wiped his mouth on his sleeve. "*Domine et lux perpetua luceat eis.*" He made the sign of the cross above her, then turned and walked away. "*Requiescant in pace. Amen.*"

WORLDS COLLIDE

THE SHERLOCK HOLMES CASE FILES

TUESDAY

"HOW CAN YOU POSSIBLY NOT NOT UNDERSTAND?"
he asked with an exasperated sigh. He raked his hands
through his hair as he turned in a complete circle. "The
angle of the fingerprints on her throat clearly indicates her
attacker is at least fifteen centimeters taller than she but
no more than twenty, putting him at approximately two
meters tall. Long, narrow fingertips indicate he is not only
tall but quite slender as well."

"And how exactly do you know this is a serial killing?"
the Detective Inspector asked.

Sherlock growled. "Why do I have to keep explaining
simple things to you?"

"Because not everyone in the world is a sociopath,
Holmes."

"The placement of the thumbs. He understands the use
of pressure points, as his thumbs were pressed firmly over
both the jugular vein and carotid artery. The only other
marks about her neck are those where his middle fingers
held her vertebrae still while his thumbs not only cut off
her circulation but crushed her windpipe as well. The
marks are small, which indicates a professional."

He turned and walked away, and I, unable to console
the embarrassed and angry inspector, followed in his
footsteps.

SUNDAY

It only occurred to me something might be wrong with Sherlock Holmes when he began to speak. He'd been silent for nearly a week, staring up at the ceiling from his place on the couch with a blank stare and a moroseness of person which led me to keep to my room. When he had such fits of despair, I always found it best not to engage him, because doing so meant suffering the wrath of his brilliantly demented mind.

This latest melancholy, I'd assumed, had come about after finding himself unable to secure the identity of the murderer in his most recent case. In my tenure as Sherlock Holmes' sole colleague and friend, I had never borne witness to such an unspeakably complicated case. This particular killer appeared to have committed the perfect crime; no clues, no footprints. Not a single fiber or fragment which could connect the series of mysterious deaths to any one perpetrator.

That, coupled with the gypsy fortune teller's revelation that he and I both had been reborn to this life from the last in quite the same forms we take now appeared to be his undoing. She'd stopped him on the street with "important information" and naturally Holmes had assumed it meant information relevant to his current case (as his is a particularly unwavering mind when on the hunt for a perpetrator). I had laughed her revelations off as absurd even as she ushered us into her gaudy establishment, yet the statement seemed to strike a chord with Sherlock. Perhaps it triggered something in his expansive, yet oddly relevant, knowledge base. I could only fathom a guess, however; Sherlock never spoke to me of his personal feelings. I often wondered if he had any at all.

"That is not possible," Sherlock said quite suddenly on a Sunday morning. I'd taken my morning tea and toast and had begun the return to my room when his voice rang out across the silence. I paused, waiting for the continuation of his statement, but it never came. It was followed only but a frustrated grunt, then silence. I simply shrugged off the comment as another of his delusions and returned to my room.

It was well into the morning when I dressed and returned to the sitting room. I had every intention of leaving 221B for a spot of lunch and perhaps to enjoy my Saturday by taking in a show with Mary. Sherlock still lay on the sofa, staring forlornly at the ceiling.

"*Rache*," he said.

"Bless you," I replied as I reached for my coat and scarf. Sherlock sat up and I paused mid-motion, curious to see what would come of it.

"I did not sneeze," he said, annoyance coating his words. "I said '*rache*'." He looked at me and I stared back, awaiting his explanation. This stalemate lasted nearly five minutes before he threw his hands into the air and groaned. "I don't know why I bother."

"I don't know why you bother either, Sherlock," I said and slipped my scarf around my neck. "If you'll excuse me, I shall leave you to your…whatever this is." I turned and strode for the door, though just as my hand reached the knob, Sherlock appeared before me, his palm flat against the edge of the wood, even with my line of vision.

"I had such high hopes for you, John," he said, without his usual anger or indignation. He sounded almost sad. "I never could understand my obsessive need to relive the past, couldn't see beyond the...the..." he beat the palm of his free hand against his forehead with each word, as if to accent the pain of his internal struggle.

"What are you on about, Sherlock?"

"Can't you see it?" he shrieked. His eyes held a new insanity I'd not before seen. "We have done this all before!"

"I don't follow."

"Of course not." Sherlock backed away and straightened the collar of his shirt. "As always, you see, but do not observe."

"Then by all means, "I replied tartly, "do tell me of your observations so I might enjoy the rest of my afternoon away from the dusty clutter of your books."

"Aha!" he exclaimed, reaching for his own hat and scarf. "A field trip is just the ticket to complete your lesson in observation." He pulled open the door. "Come, Watson."

Against my better judgment, I followed Sherlock Holmes down the stairs and out the door of 221B, however when he turned left, I made an abrupt right turn and immediately hailed a taxi. He was half-way down the block, still prattling on to himself, before he noticed I'd made my escape.

"Oh, John, I can't believe you abandoned him like that," Mary said, shaking her head as she lifted her teacup to her lips. I tried in vain to ignore the tingle of guilt along the back of my neck as she scolded me. It was true; I had abandoned my friend in a moment of annoyed selfishness. Truth be told, I was curious to know where he intended to take me and why. It was part of my own psychosis…I was horribly driven to follow Sherlock's insane adventures, wherever they may lead.

"He'll be okay," I replied weakly. Mary clicked her tongue and placed her cup back on its saucer.

"Of course he'll be okay, John. But these little adventures are his way of telling you he needs you." As if the guilt weren't already bad enough, the woman I loved knew exactly how to compound it until I couldn't live with myself.

"You didn't hear him, Mary! He was carrying on about reliving the past. I think it had something to do with that crazy fortune teller from last week."

"Then take him back to talk to her again," she said. I knew my expression wouldn't please her, but I couldn't stop the sour look from passing across my face. Rather than scold me again, Mary laughed. It did my heart good to hear the sound. "Would you feel better if I suggested it? He does seem to listen to me, you know."

"Heaven only knows why," I replied. "He doesn't listen to anyone else, whether the advice is good or not."

"John Watson, I think you just insulted me."

MONDAY

I never expected Sherlock Holmes to agree to going back for a second visit to Madame Felicia, yet at 6:00 PM sharp, I found myself standing between he and Mary, staring up at the garish sign.

Since our last visit, the gas lamps on either side of the door had gone out, presumably using up the supply from their hidden tanks, and the curtains in the window to the right of the door had begun to fray along the bottom edge. Sherlock turned to me with a put-upon look about his face.

"This is ridiculous," he said, and I half expected him to stamp his foot. "An utter waste of time." Chuckling, Mary bypassed me in favor of taking his arm and leading him up to the door.

"Come on, Sherlock," she persuaded, tugging at his elbow, "humor me. If you believe she has information you need, simply use your talents to uncover it."

"But..."

"No buts. Come on," Mary ordered, and pulled him up the step and inside. Just before the door fell closed behind them, I reached out and placed my hand against the jamb, affording me the opportunity to slip in behind them without turning the latch again.

The building was decorated in a gaudy, garish manner. Tapestries and scarves hung from every surface, and beads jangled against one another in the door frames, caught in the draft creeping in from the top of the stairs. I shivered against the chill and followed diligently along behind my fiancée and her unwilling yet oddly complacent victim. We were led to the same room as before: a tiny, cramped area with a round table and a glass orb on a rusty tin base. In this room, as with the rest of the space, brightly-colored scarves and linens decorated every surface, and cobweb-covered beads hung from the dusty sconces along the walls.

Mary guided Sherlock to a seat opposite Madame Felicia, then took the seat beside him, putting me between her and the fortune teller. From his very posture I could see how uncomfortable my flatmate had become, but I said nothing with the hope that Mary's foolhardy plan would remove this inconsolable frustration from his head.

I took my seat in stony silence, fighting the urge to curse as my fingers slid against the rough surface of the table, catching a rather large splinter in the process. Irritated by this happening, I jerked the offending plank of wood from the side of my hand and flicked it into the air, where it landed somewhere near the old gypsy's feet with a noticeable clatter. Mary glared at me across the table as I dabbed at my bloody hand with my handkerchief.

"You have returned," the withered woman said, her voice thick with Slavic inflection. Sherlock immediately leaned into the conversation, his whole attention focused on her.

"I need to know more," he said. "Tell me where I can find the killer."

"Sherlock," I growled in warning, but Mary laid her hand over top of mine, attempting to quiet the ire growing in me. From that point on I kept my mouth shut and listened.

"When past and present collide, only then shall you find what you seek," she said. "You are drawn to the unfamiliar, the unexplained, the impossible. It is not the answer to the question you crave, but the hunt itself."

While her words rang with absolute truth, I could not help but wonder what this game of smoke and mirrors was meant to disguise. Sherlock Holmes, however, appeared to not realize the ruse for what it was, which surprised me. I had never in my years of tracking his footsteps known him to miss a clue at all, much less such a broad one. Yet so enamored of her words was he that he let the comment pass without question. Instinct more than deduction told me this wizened old woman knew more than she'd chosen to share. I wanted to question, to subtly bring him back around to himself, but the constant pressure of Mary's hand on mine reminded me of my promise of silence.

The banter continued much in this fashion for the remaining forty minutes of our visit. Sherlock spiraled deeper into the gypsy woman's web of deceit and lies, willfully doing so, while she continued to duck his questions with vague, misleading answers. I fought valiantly to hold my tongue, and when finally released from the chair and thus my prison of silence, I exploded from the front door of the establishment, rounding on Sherlock in preparation for the rant of the ages, when his gleeful, manic expression stopped me cold.

A performance.

His entire belief of her tale was a lie.

TUESDAY

I arrived at 221-B after a supper with Mary to find Sherlock standing on the sofa. His violin hung limply from one hand, almost completely forgotten by its owner. The smell of burned tobacco hung in the air, thick enough to almost be visible.

"When past and present collide," he said to no one in particular.

"Are you suggesting we should build a time machine?"

As usual, I asked the question while not expecting an answer. To my surprise, Sherlock whooped with absolute glee as he leapt from the couch and darted toward me.

"Don't you see, John? The past has come *to* the present!" he shrieked as he grabbed my shoulders and spun me round twice. Dizzied and confused, I blinked repeatedly as I forced my vision to focus.

"I don't follow."

"Of course not!" he shouted, a manic smile reminiscent of a joyful puppy-slayer etched into the lines of his face. "It is absolutely brilliant! There is no other mind in this world which could solve such a riddle but mine!"

"Right," I replied. I hated to admit my own morbid curiosity, so I paused and waited the appropriate length of time to allow my companion to realize I would not speak again.

"The deceased, I have learned, follow the same lineage. While they appear to be of no relation today, they share a common ancestor, a Romani performer of Indian origin by the name of Šaban Badi. His wife, Ostelinda, worked as a fortune teller and tarot reader in a traveling carnival."

"We're talking about gypsies?"

"The Romani people are proud, John. Do not insult them by calling them 'gypsies.'"

"When did you become a champion for the rules?"

"When I discovered the blood feud between the Badi and Kopanari families."

I stared at him, hoping for an explanation to this but knowing I wouldn't get one. "Are you going to elaborate on that?"

Sherlock rolled his eyes in response and threw his hands into the air. "How do you not see these things?" he shouted, and set about tugging at his hair. Then it hit me; he was referring to Madame Felicia.

"The fortune teller?"

"Yes!"

"Madame Felicia? What does she have to do with any of this?"

"The killings started a week after her shop opened. I knew she was involved from the start, but I couldn't figure out *how*."

"So how is she involved?"

"The business license is in the name of a Mihai Kopanari."

"Her husband?"

"Brother."

"Oh." I watched him for several moments, contemplating the glee in his stare. His face split into a wide, toothy smile reminiscent of a shark. I never before realized just how many teeth Sherlock Holmes had. He waited for me just as I did him, and I quickly deduced that he would not continue with his story until prompted. "Do tell me, Sherlock, how this fortune teller is involved."

"Well you see," he began, inordinately pleased that I'd baited him so, "Felicia Kopanari is not tall or strong enough to facilitate such intimate killings. However, this brother, by all accounts, *is* of the perfect size to commit such heinous misdeeds."

"Have you seen him yourself?"

"Not yet," Sherlock replied, "which is irrelevant, Watson." I simply listened, knowing I could offer nothing but frustration to his monologue. "The family does have quite the history behind it, which leads me to believe these murders are as much for her benefit as his." He prattled on for some time more, discussing with himself the existential conundrum in which these two people found themselves, and I didn't bother trying to follow.

However, when he finally exhausted this line of reasoning, I made the same mistake I always make: I asked him another question.

"You mentioned a blood feud. What of it??"

His eyes lit up as if I'd handed him the biggest Christmas gift in the room. "That, my dear Watson, *is* the answer to this mystery!" He laid the violin to the side and came close to me, more lively and animated than I'd seen him in weeks. "The Badi family were performers, as you know. The Kopanari, however, were from strong Christian stock. The women tended towards midwifery and other healing arts while the men made their living predominantly as sin eaters."

"Sin eaters? As in the men who eat communion wafers from the chests of the dying?"

"Yes and no. Rumor has it this particular family was able to provide true absolution to the dying. My sources tell me the Kopanari man had the ability to literally draw the sins out of a dying body and consume them to sustain his own life."

My brain began to ache as I listened to this insane story. "So they really ate people's sins?"

"It would appear so."

"What do either of these families have to do with one another?"

"When Šaban Badi was mortally wounded during a performance, his Ostelinda and their children called in a member of the Kopanari family to perform the service."

"Let me guess," I interrupted, "he refused to do it."

"Oh, he performed the service," Sherlock countered, "but the sins on Šaban's conscience were numerous and overwhelmed the sin eater. He demanded higher payment or threatened the return of the sins to Šaban's now deceased body."

"What would it have done had he returned the sins?" I asked.

"I haven't the foggiest, though I imagine it would not have been good for the owner. If Christian dogma were to be believed, the return of the sins would have sent the soul immediately to Hell. The physical manifestation of the exchange, however…" he trailed off, sinking into his own sordid imagination. I shuddered to imagine what he might have concocted in that magnificently twisted brain of his.

As quickly as he vanished into his own mind, Sherlock returned, picking up his initial thought where I'd first interrupted. "Ostelinda made payment, but once the sin eater left, she placed a curse on him."

"A curse?"

"Yes, John. Ostelinda Badi cursed the Kopanari man to forever walk the earth, feeding on the most wretched of sins."

And with that, I'd heard enough to convince me he had officially gone totally off his head. "It's just a story, Sherlock?"

"So I thought when I first heard it."

"Then what made you believe it?

"I learned the cursed sin eater's name. As it turns out, our mysterious Madame Felicia's brother carries the same name: Mihai Kopanari."

I stared at him, unable to find words to respond. This story was so absolutely absurd yet Sherlock Holmes, the stoutest pragmatist I'd ever met, believed it with all his being. He danced around the room in an excited display of victory.

"So you see, the deaths are all connected!"

"I was under the impression you had already established this," I replied, unable to help myself.

"Yes," he answered flatly, "but now I have proof even those fools at Scotland Yard cannot deny!" With a great, whooping cry he exited the building, presumably to showcase his new victory in Detective Inspector Lestrade's office. And as I watched him hail a lorry from the upstairs window, I wondered if the next time I heard his name, it would be as part of an incarceration order at Bethlehem Royal Hospital and, having yet to remove my coat, followed the crazy person I called a friend.

I arrived shortly behind him to find that Lestrade had, in fact, threatened incarceration for Sherlock's ravings of an immortal gypsy killing young men and women for the benefit of eating their sins to stay alive. Upon my arrival I found him in the process of being forcibly evicted from the Scotland Yard offices after creatively insulting his only ally in law enforcement. From the look upon Lestrade's face, I imagine he'd done so with no small amount of satisfaction. Having not been believed, Sherlock then insisted we catch the murderer ourselves.

WEDNESDAY

Because of the previous evening's events, I found myself yet again in an uncomfortable situation thanks to the deductive reasoning of the brilliant madman beside me. He'd located three possible victims, all stemming from the Badi family, and based on whatever harebrained logic he'd used this time, determined which of the three would be the next target.

Sherlock Holmes approached stake-outs with the type of enthusiasm rarely found outside the psyche of a serial killer. I often wondered, just as many in Scotland Yard did, when he might tip the line from detective to perpetrator. The sooty industrial air permeating this section of the city threatened to choke me and the evening fog began to roll in. A thrill of anxiety coursed through me and the hair along my arms stood on end as an unusual silence descended on the city.

"Remind me why we're here," I said, tucking the lapels of my coat up around my throat.

"We are waiting."

"Obviously. For what again?"

"The victim."

Had he asked, I would certainly have argued my boredom, but the sweetness of anticipation kept me in lace. I wanted to see the action as much as Sherlock did, and that realization quite frightened me. Could I truly be as deranged as him?

Within the hour, a young man exited the flat across the street, turning his collar up to the chilly London wind, and started in the direction of Primrose Hill. As he turned the corner, we fell into step behind him, Sherlock with the focus and concentration of a bloodhound and I near delirious with excitement.

"Why would this young man be out alone so late at night?" I asked as we tracked his steps through a corner store and into the sprawling expanse of the park.

"He intends to meet a girl. The blood of the traveler runs thick in his veins, John. I very much doubt his family would approve of this one were he to bring her home for tea." Only Sherlock's keen sense and the yellow-green glow of gas light haloes in the thickening fog kept us from being spotted.

Grabbing me by the collar, he pulled me behind an old tree. He placed a hand over my mouth to stop my complaint as he motioned toward the sitting area at the top of the hill where the young man stood.

"Nicholas Cavill." This new voice startled me, and the appearance of its owner even more so. Sherlock's explanation left me expecting a young lady of somewhat ill repute, and no such woman materialized. The man who did come into my line of vision was unreasonably tall and slender, as if he'd been stretched upon a rack. The light of the nearly full moon cast wicked shadows across his already grotesquely contorted features, making his comically broad smile seem even wider, his large, protruding eyes heavier, and his long, spindly arms appear more like pincers than human appendages. The young man, Nicholas, froze in terror, allowing his assailant to close in on him. Just as Sherlock had predicted, those exaggeratedly large hands cradled the victim's neck, thumbs pressed into the jugular and carotid. "Confess your sins to me," he said, his words thick with a haunting, old-world accent.

Nicholas' jaw fell open and a mucousy gurgling sound issued forth in the place of words. The air around them began to shimmer. The eyes of both men lit with an inner fluorescence, and the breezy air trolling across the park turned deathly cold. Thin, wispy tendrils of white mist issued from Nicholas' mouth, nose, and eyes, twining around each other as they entered the open mouth of the large man and I realized as I watched that the mist was the corporeal embodiment of Nicholas' soul. With every passing second, the bigger man's skin tightened, the wrinkles leaving his face as the glow of youth returned to him.

I tore my gaze from the scene and looked at Sherlock, who watched not with the stoic disconnect of a scholar, but with the enthusiastic delight of a fellow assailant. Nicholas' skin grew pale and waxy under the assault, but Sherlock never once moved. I could not bear witness to this murder; could not, as a doctor, allow another life to be stolen in so horrific a manner.

I ripped my pistol from its holster beneath my arm and raced up the hill, slamming the butt of the gun into the base of the assailant's neck between his shoulders. He let out a pained cry and collapsed to his knees, dropping Nicholas in the process. The mist dissipated and the young man began to cough. He scrambled away, gagging and gasping for air, leaving me alone atop Primrose Hill with the serial killer Sherlock had been stalking for the last two weeks.

The monstrous man rose to his feet, the effects of my blow having already dissipated, and turned to face me. Without the menacing drape of moonlight his face became familiar, younger yet nearly identical to that of the old fortune teller. Dread seized my heart; Sherlock was right. Mihai Kopanari grinned down at me, his big hands reaching for me. I ducked his grasp and, threw my arm up for another blow. He caught my wrist mid-movement, wrenching my arm around until I lost my grip on my pistol. I took a swing with my left hand, hoping to land at least one blow but he moved faster, twisting and shoving me down the hill toward the center of London. I stumbled and tumbled to the bottom of the hill, the wind leaving my lungs with each hard new blow against the ground. He did not follow, but his laughter echoed across the still park, carried toward me on the wind.

I lay on the ground, unable to regain my breath or my footing. With each beat of my heart, my body grew heavier, more sluggish. It became nearly impossible to lift my feet or to order my arms beneath me and stand. I wanted to call out to Sherlock for help, unsure of the cause of this new fit, but found my tongue glued to the roof of my mouth. I had become paralyzed, frozen in place some unseen force. The laughter grew louder, but unable to rise or turn, I could not see why. Then his hands closed on my arms and lifted me as if I weighed no more than a bit of discarded trash. The harsh, maniac smile had returned to his face and as I looked up into his cruel, crazy eyes in the yellow-green halo of the street lamp, I knew my death stared back at me.

"My sister knew you would cause problems," he said, "so she took precautions." He chuckled as he lifted my arm and turned my palm over. A tiny scab rested where the sliver of wood had entered the side of my hand. "A single drop of blood is all it takes to give her complete control of mind, body, and soul" He ran a hand down the side of my face. "You gave her your life, and you gave it willingly. She owns you, John Watson." His cold fingers closed under my chin, lifting my head to expose my throat. "Now, confess your sins to me," he continued, and reached toward me with his other hand.

The air left my lungs as those long, slender fingers closed around my throat. My blood seemed to congeal in my veins, growing thick and sluggish with each labored beat of my heart. I could feel my life leaving me, the rush of vitality as it drained from my bones and brain. I was helpless to stop it, paralyzed by the old woman's spell.

It was the surprising left hook of Sherlock Holmes which saved my life. The blow connected with Mihai's cheek, loosening his hold on me and sending him sprawling to the dirty brick pavers. I fell backwards, and still paralyzed, landing hard and rolling into the legs of a metal park bench. From my awkward new position I watched the scene unfold: Sherlock taking up a fighter's stance, the murderer rising to his feet unfazed by the assault, Sherlock ducking the first swing of the bigger man's hand. Sherlock took a second swing, angling his arm upward so his bare fist connected with the hinge of Mihai's jaw.

With the crack of bone, Mihai spun around but remained on his feet, growling as he balled up his large fist and returned the blow. It connected with Sherlock's shoulder, eliciting little more than a grunt as the wiry detective turned again. Sherlock landed blow after blow, beating the gypsy to his knees. None of the four hits taken even made him flinch in against his furious rage. Blood trickled down Mihai's face from the gash above his left eye and from both his nose and the corner of his mouth, but even on his knees he continued to resist, to swing his giant fists and to reach for Sherlock's throat.

"Leave him be!" Madame Felicia shrieked, having appeared seemingly from nowhere. She stood above me, her gnarled, spindly fingers stretched toward me. My heart, still beating sluggishly, picked up its labored pace. My body responded to her presence in startling ways, anticipating every bit of pain and suffering I knew her capable of inflicting, though I couldn't rightly understand how she had been so easily able to control me.

I forced my focus back to Sherlock, who halted his assault, his attention focused on the old woman standing above me. His face remained stoic though even across the darkened park, I could see the fear standing in his eyes. Sherlock opened his hands, palms facing forward, and backed away from the big man.

"You will not harm him again," Madame Felicia ordered. "You will walk away and leave us be. The blood debt must be paid, and I will see it through!"

Sherlock remained calm and collected, not responding as the gypsy woman continued to stand over me, my very life force resting in the space between her outstretched hands. One change in her demeanor and I knew my life would end. Sherlock seemed to know it too, as he stood very still, any movement he made slow and deliberate.

"You caused me trouble one time before," she continued, moving in closer to me, taking a defensive position in front of me should he attempt to save me, "and I escaped you then. You will not change my path tonight, or any night, Mister Holmes."

"May I ask you a question?" Sherlock's voice was as calm as the rest of him; he'd returned to the morbid curiosity of the detached detective. The old woman cocked her head to the side. "What do you hope to gain from killing the Badi descendants?"

She laughed, a cold, harsh sound which sent ripples of disgust trailing down my frozen spine. The wind picked up again, howling through the trees near the bottom of the hill, and clouds began to suffocate the moon, darkening the empty park.

"The blood of the enemy shall absolve our sins. What was taken from us shall be returned with the taking of their sins."

Sherlock resisted the urge to laugh, yet the humor was apparent on his face. "You mean to tell me you think your curse will be broken if you destroy the entire family of Šaban Badi?"

"When the blood has been cleaned, only then will Mihai and I rest." As she spoke, I watched Mihai rise to his feet and come toward Sherlock. "You see, we have lived for *centuries*. Too long." I wanted to shout, to warn him of the impending attack yet I was still trapped in stasis. I struggled, but in vain. "My brother has taken the sins of thousands, and with each absolution of the Badi bloodline, our humanity returns, little by little. We do not kill unless it is necessary…" she paused as Mihai stretched his wiry hands toward Sherlock's throat, "but tonight, the threat of our undoing is just cause for a taking."

Mihai's hands slipped around Sherlock's throat as Madame Felicia began to laugh. My own ability to breathe ceased as my own fingers closed off my windpipe. I wanted to scream, to take a deep breath, anything to force air into my lungs, but I still could not move, held captive by this woman's will.

What happened next came so fast I scarcely had time to register before it was over. Mihai's fingers closed around Sherlock's throat as Sherlock produced his own revolver from beneath his coat. In one fluid movement he drew the butt of the weapon hard against his attacker's face, knocking him back to his knees, then spun and fired a single shot into the shoulder of the withered old woman standing above me. She screamed as she fell, stumbling over my outstretched legs to topple backwards into the grass. He turned and pointed the weapon between the big man's eyes, bringing his movements to a complete halt. Sherlock grabbed the Mihai and, without breaking a sweat, dragged him over to where I lay as Madame Felicia struggled back to the top of the hill. He threw the man down and pressed the barrel of the gun to the back of his head.

"Now you worthless piece of shit," he ordered, glaring hard at the old woman, "remove the curse and take your influence from him, or I shall see to it your debt is never fulfilled." She gasped for breath, her demeanor changing to that of a frail, injured woman. The hold on my throat eased, my hands falling back to the ground, and I choked in a shallow, ragged breath. Even the soot hanging in the air tasted sweet to me as the realization that I would survive this moment came over me.

"Please… please, my brother is all I have…"

"Then I suggest you do as I say. I will kill him."

"You can't kill him," she replied, the frailty in her voice faltering over anger.

"And why not?"

"You poor fool," the old woman said on a laugh, "death only comes to the cursed when the one who curses him allows it."

Sherlock's face split into a wide smile. "I may not be able to end his life, but I can certainly inflict enough physical damage with this cannon in my hand to make it quite impossible for him to feed. And I do imagine,"

Sherlock continued, forcing Mihai's head forward with the weapon, "his inability to steal lives would come as a great inconvenience for you."

"What makes you think such a thing?" she asked, and I heard it – that tiny sliver of uncertainty.

"Because as you are were not involved, then by your own admissions you cannot share in his curse. Blood is unique to each person, and that control only comes with a remnant of the physical being. I find it endearing, or would were I capable of such emotion, that your brother would do you the great honor of sharing in his eternal disease." The more he spoke, the paler her complexion became. "So by your very own admission it would mean the inability of your brother to feed himself properly would lead to your demise as you are still quite mortal and quite at his mercy. Now if you would be so kind, please remove your influence and control from the mind of Dr. Watson."

She hesitated, glancing back and forth between her brother and me. Sherlock again drove the barrel of the gun into the back of Mihai's head, thrusting him forward even farther. "Do it now!" he shouted, his voice echoing around the empty park. Overhead thunder rattled in the gathering clouds.

Moments later she crawled over to where I lay, bleeding profusely from her right shoulder, and laid her hands on me. She muttered something in another language, presumably her native tongue. Slowly the feeling returned to my limbs. My heartbeat returned to normal, if a little sluggish from the muscle's over-exertion, and exhaustion took hold. My whole body began to shake and as the flashing lights of Scotland Yard's finest buzzed into view below, I succumbed to the darkness closing in on me.

One week later

I rose from bed later than normal, prepared to take my toast and tea for the first time since the incident. The soreness in my throat had finally eased and my muscles were no longer frozen from the strain. Sherlock had brought me a newspaper two days after the incident, complaining of the lack of thanks from Scotland Yard in apprehending the Kopanari siblings and halting the murders. I'd simply nodded and allowed him to rant, as just the thought of speech made my throat ache.

I made my way slowly into the main room, expecting to find Sherlock lying on the couch in the throes of some fresh personal hell, but what I found surprised me. Sherlock and Mary stood at the window, talking quietly from behind a large bouquet of mixed flowers.

> *To Dr. John Watson,*
> *Thank you for your assistance. Get well soon.*
> *Regards,*
> *Detective Inspector Lestrade and Scotland Yard*

"It's disgusting," Sherlock said, loud enough for me to hear, "I solve the crime and *he* gets the flowers."

"He was also a victim," Mary reminded him, "And Detective Inspector Lestrade did thank you personally." Sherlock scoffed but didn't argue. It surprised me, and I didn't interfere. My tea and toast waited on the counter in the kitchen, and once I retrieved them and returned to the sitting room, I found Mary waiting for me with her arms open, Sherlock's attention turned to something else.

In the end, it turned out, Sherlock Holmes was right to believe at least a fraction of what Madame Felicia had said. The idea of revenge had stuck with him not as a hunch, but instead as a remnant of past lives, placed there by a careless criminal who believed herself above contemporary law.

We later learned of the siblings' separate incarceration and the eventual death of Madame Felicia – starvation, they claimed was the cause and Sherlock surmised – radically and quite inanely, I'd have said had this occurred two weeks sooner – it was due to the inability of her brother to pass on the lives he'd stolen to her. Mihai Kopanari could easily sustain his own life, yet as the years passed I would often wonder what would come of him when the guards learned of his immortality. This blood feud, however, was already wiped from Sherlock's immediate memory, as another mysterious murder had taken his attention. I found myself wondering if we would ever come across another case as interesting or extraordinary as this one. Another where past and present collide.

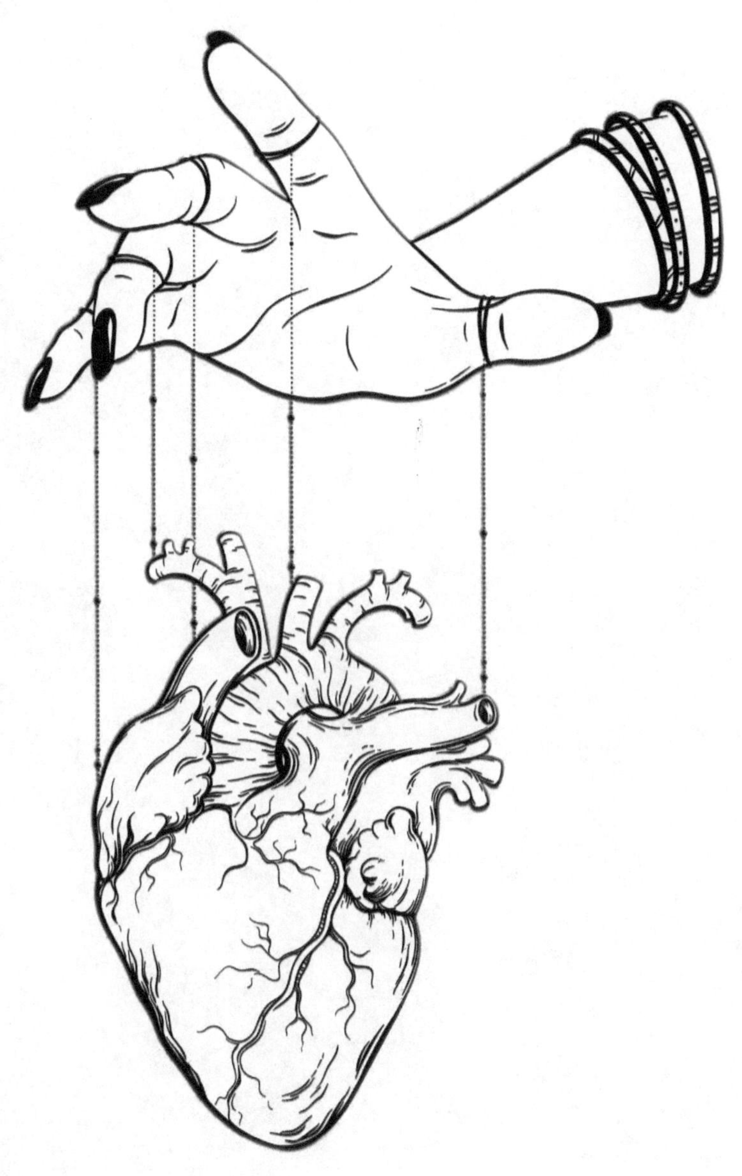

CRIPPLED PLAYTHINGS

THE SHERLOCK HOLMES CASE FILES

Friedrich Nietzsche once said, "He who fights with monsters might take care lest he thereby become a monster. And if you gaze for long into an abyss, the abyss gazes also into you." Looking back on the curious and bizarre incidents of my life with Sherlock Holmes, I often wondered if the great philosopher did not say these things with specific intent toward my dearest friend himself.

It was not until the twilight years of our lives that I came to discover just how fortunate – no, how lucky – the both of us had been. Holmes would no doubt have told me he didn't believe in such madness as luck, were I to have expressed this sentiment to him. Though I watched so many times as Holmes and that proverbial abyss stared eye-to-eye, the darkness threatening to swallow his humanity whole.

The tale I share tonight is one of confusion and desperation, and because of the complex nature I have asked Holmes himself to contribute to its telling. For the truest accounting of events may only come from the consciousness of the man who witnessed these atrocities first-hand.

Sherlock Holmes. New York City, October 18, 1907

I stood at the helm of the airship, watching the people bustle to and fro amid the clouds of coal smoke and city fog. The telegram sent to me by my colleague and friend, Dr. John Watson, rested in my left breast pocket, its contents curious enough to bring me to New Orleans from London by way of New York and Baton Rouge.

My Dearest Holmes,
It has been brought to my attention by local law enforcement that people have begun to vanish. This would pique neither my interest nor yours, except that those vanishing share a similar trait: each missing person is permanently confined to a wheelchair or a bed.
Please come, as the authorities in New Orleans are baffled by the disappearances.
Yours Truly,
John H. Watson, MD

Watson was, of course, spot on when he said it would be of no interest to me. I still found very little interest in the disappearances, but out of sheer boredom I made the attempt to humor my friend by purchasing a ticket for America. As I stood aboard the deck of the great blimp, I found myself wondering how many of those aboard would meet an untimely demise in the world's most sinful city. These pathetic beasts would no doubt follow their baser desires to ultimate doom, smiling and singing as the poison of youth infiltrated their minds and removed what inhibitions might keep them from stepping into the streets in front of a carriage.

Said thought process was interrupted with the addition of a young, wheelchair-laden man. He moved with grace despite the self-propelled contraption bound to his lower half, which immediately told me he and it had been one for quite some time — the majority of his life, as a matter of fact. Withered legs beneath a tattered, tartan blanket emphasized the stout and stocky upper body. He turned the machine toward me by way of the ticking contraption pressed against his right palm, and glided across the uneven deck. The wheels of his chair took the brunt of the impact as they rattled and clattered across the boards, yet he remained upright and supremely unaware of the danger beneath him. I was most fortunate that this young man came to a stop beside me.

"Good evening," he said with a smile and a slight nod of his head. The silk-trimmed straw boater dipped with his head, but remained otherwise immobile. I touched my fingers to the brim of my own top hat and, without appearing obvious, continued with my review of his situation. Worn places on his gloves showed repeated use of his hands — expected for one in such a predicament as him. A tinkerer by trade – and a dying trade at that – his clothes were shabby; the wheelchair even more so, held together by what mismatched bits of metal he could find coupled with this own ingenuity. The weakness of stature was cleverly disguised, however, by additions such as gear sets and pulleys — systems which appeared to make travel easier for him. This man had little money and, if my intuition were correct, had spent his last penny on the ticket for the dirigible on which we stood. This man carried some sort of foolish dream. If he happened to be going my way, it also meant he could be a potential victim.

"Nice evening," I said, the pleasantry extended to glean his intentions.

"It is. I look forward to the fresh air once we lift off." His accent was hard, unrefined, and completely American.

"Are you in Baton Rouge long?"

He shook his head. "Only passing through on my way to New Orleans."

"Business or pleasure?" I prodded. He did not appear flustered by my small talk.

"A bit of both, I suppose. I have an appointment with a doctor who believes he might be able to do something about my...situation." While I considered his comment, he extended a hand to me. "Henry Gaston," he said. "Pleased to meet you, Mr..."

"Holmes," I replied, taking his hand and shaking hard once. "Sherlock Holmes."

His eyes lit up. "The detective from London?" I nodded and a look of glee came over his face. "I love Dr. Watson's stories. I never imagined I might have the chance to meet you in person, though!" I waited for his tirade to end, hoping not to expend the entirety of my patience on his outburst. When his composure returned, he cleared his throat and apologized. "So what brings you to the States, Mr. Holmes?"

"A telegram from Dr. Watson, as a matter of fact," I replied, and quickly changed the subject. "So this doctor of yours... he claims he can cure you?"

Henry shrugged. "He said so. I'm hopeful, but not so naïve that I believe it will work."

I wondered who he was trying to convince: himself or me. "A healthy position," I offered as I watched a young woman come aboard. She stood out to me because of the new, gleaming wheelchair and the air of impatience about her. She was waiting to die.

"To be honest, I am more interested in seeing another part of the world outside of my apartment." He glanced back over his shoulder as the grinding of gears filled the air and the gangplank began to rise. It came to a stop with a shuddering crash, and I had to brace myself against the railing to keep from toppling backwards. Henry never moved. "I have been confined to a chair since childhood. A fever, you see, took my mobility and with it, my freedom." Sadness crossed his face for the briefest moment, replaced quickly by longing. "Because of my condition," he continued as the noise subsided, "I never got to see the world." He sighed. "Those in wheelchairs —however advanced their tinkered accessories may be," he motioned to the gadgets and gears adorning his own chair, "are rarely able to travel with ease. This trip, however, promises to be the beginning of a new life if the doctor can truly work miracles."

Unease came over me. The more this man spoke, the more certain I became of his involvement in this wicked scheme. Almost certainly, this man would be among the missing.

Funny, I thought. *With all the modern conveniences and technological advancements of the twentieth century — we were flying, after all — that the surgeons have yet been unable to repair spines and cure crippling diseases.*

The other occupants of this floating marvel ran to the railings to wave to the rabble below as the floor began to vibrate under the strain of the engines. Slowly, the craft rose from the ground, pitching us into sharp wind currents. Soon, we were far enough above the city of New

York that it appeared as little more than a painting. As we rose the sun sank below the horizon, and the colors of evening faded into the starry blackness of night. Henry politely excused himself and moved to sit beside the lonely woman. He attempted to engage her in conversation, but she refused to speak.

I watched the dim haze of the hamlets slide past on the patchwork ground, each one acknowledged only by flickering streetlamps as the world slept below the dirigible. The girl still refused to speak to Henry, but from the look of her, I could only assume she was on this journey for the same reason as him: to walk. She rolled away, locating a crew member to lift her from her chair and carry her downstairs. Eventually, even Henry gave up and moved to the back of the deck in search of assistance to go below.

The only civilian left on deck, I marveled at the great airship's propellers, studied the feel of the wind against my face – somewhat of a draft created despite the windscreens affront the ship. Overhead the night sky was littered with stars. The moon, little more than a pale sliver, hung low on the horizon. The atmosphere would begin to change color soon—I could feel morning coming.

Two days out of New York, the woman finally began to speak. Georgia Corchoran, I learned, was the victim of a terrible carriage accident which left her with a severed spinal column and no use of her legs. I learned this from Henry, of course, who had no problem at all keeping me apprised of the goings-on of the ship...whether or not I wanted to know. He also appeared particularly interested in an older gentleman with a handlebar moustache. He carried a handkerchief in his left hand and spent the majority of our journey wiping at his nose. In between bouts of allergic distress, he showed a disturbing level of attention to Henry; asked of his home life, his childhood, and the fever. Henry took the questions in stride and, to my surprise, attempted to introduce the gentleman to Miss Corchoran as well.

She, for the most part, ignored him completely.

However, during this grueling process, I learned from Henry a single interesting piece of information: Miss Corchoran had also been told her paralysis could be reversed. The other gentleman, whose name I did not care to learn, was also interested in her plight.

Liar, my better senses told me of the man. *Dangerous*.

From my pocket I removed a small notepad and began to list items of importance — their shared immobility, their similar invitations, and the fact that people much like the two of them were disappearing at an alarming rate from the streets of New Orleans.

With one day to go before docking in Baton Rouge, I needed to use Henry's obvious adoration of me to the fullest extent—by questioning every person aboard the ship for any and all information related to the case. Unfortunately, the line of questioning produced no other useful information.

Once in Baton Rouge, Henry, and I were ushered to a smaller dirigible which would take us to New Orleans. It was early in the morning on a Friday and the air was already thick and humid despite the chill in it. Two others from the New York flight accompanied us; one being the bespectacled gentleman with the dripping nose and deplorable mustache. The other, to my great delight, was Miss Corchoran. Not one, but *two* disabled bodies on the same journey... I was already closer to solving this mystery than the authorities.

From the air, New Orleans glowed. A city of magic, mystery and intrigue. I found myself amused by Henry's open adoration of the city. He marveled at the sparkling blanket of gas lights and coal lamps beneath us. The dirigible's turbines rotated around until the blades lay parallel to the deck, giving us a clearer view of the urban sprawl.

As the aircraft sank closer and closer to solid ground, the sparkles turned to bright orbs and between them in the early morning house movement began. Specks of scurrying energy turned to ants which in turn morphed into people, carriages, and the occasional horseless contraption. On the platform below, I spotted Watson and his wife, Mary, their faces turned up to the bottom of the ship.

As we began the arduous task of debarking, Henry caught me by the wrist.

"Do you think I'm making a mistake, Mr. Holmes? Trusting my fate to a man I've never met?"

"How is trusting me to answer your question any different?" I replied, surprising him. "Only time will tell."

John Watson. New Orleans, October 22, 1907

"Sherlock Holmes, you are a sight for sore eyes," I said, taking my friend's hand. It had been months since our paths crossed, what with my having accompanied Mary stateside for a visit with a childhood friend. As I predicted, Holmes scarcely acknowledged me in favor of embracing my wife.

"Hello, Sherlock," Mary said with a smile. The corners of her mouth creased around her dimples, and when Holmes smiled back at her, tiny lines formed at the corners of his eyes. We were no longer young, I realized, as the symptoms of old age began to show themselves in even our most practiced of motions.

Holmes nodded at her pleasantry as he released her, then immediately began to walk toward our carriage. Mary and I raced to catch up to him, not at all surprised that he'd already begun to speak to us, regardless of the fact that we were out of earshot.

"...so I must keep track of him," Holmes said.

"Who?"

"I just *told* you," he replied tersely.

"Yes, you did," I answered as patiently as I could, "but you told me when I was quite unable to hear you." Holmes made a face at me, but did not argue, which surprised me. He typically argued.

"The man in the self-propelled chair," Holmes said. "I need to keep track of him, as I believe he may be connected to the subject of your letter."

"Sherlock, the authorities –"

"Will not catch the culprit without first finding the next victim," he snapped. A scowl set in on his face as he climbed into the carriage. From inside, he extended a hand to Mary, and once we were all safely inside, we started toward the outskirts of town. Holmes had fallen into a sullen silence, his eyes drifting closed as he processed what information he'd obtained on the flight. We rode in silence until the moment when the carriage stopped. Holmes immediately came to life, giving the driver a new address and pulling me back into the carriage.

"Come, Watson," he said, manic glee settling into his features, "we have a mystery to solve."

The roads on the outskirts of New Orleans were dangerous, to say the least. After the terrible rains from the earlier season, many were deemed impassable by the coachman, who graciously let us out to walk the remainder of the way. Without a moment's hesitation, Holmes stepped down from the carriage, his singular focus on finding the man he'd called Henry Gaston.

"Do you honestly believe a chance meeting on a dirigible is going to lead you to the answer so quickly?" I asked as a struggled to maintain pace with him. For a moment I suspected he would ignore me, then he opened his mouth.

"You know, Watson, that I do not believe in 'luck', and there are no coincidences. I came on this journey the moment I did to solve a possible crime, and should a clue roll up to me and introduce itself, far be it from me to ignore it."

I could have easily argued divine providence, yet chose to keep my mouth tightly closed. The sun, long-since gone below the tree line, was pulling with it the bright colors of day and leaving in its wake a murky sort of sunset which enveloped us in a dismally unnerving calm. Were I on my own, I would have turned back here, but my companion would not be swayed from his task and I knew it.

"Holmes, answer a question for me," I said after another half-mile of our picking over fallen branches and other such debris.

"If I must," he said without affect.

"Forgive me for thinking so strangely, but please explain to me how a man confined to a wheelchair would be able to make the journey down this road on foot." Holmes paused, one foot hanging in midair, and scowled.

"In this age of steam-powered technology," he replied, "anything is possible."

"However improbable."

"*Improbability* has absolutely no bearing on *possibility*. Now come…we must find this boarding house."

But there was no boarding house to be found. The road on which we walked ended very suddenly around the next bend, trickling off into a mass of overgrowth and organic decay. I would have laughed had terror not seized my voice.

"Curious," Holmes said as he examined the trees around us.

"We should turn back," I urged. I expected him to argue, but he did no such thing, instead he turned on his heel and strode back the way we came, stepping over the debris with strides far too wide for my height. I stumbled to keep up, and when we returned to the place where the carriage had deposited us, we found it was gone. "That's just *fantastic*," I snapped. "What do we do now?"

"We walk."

John Watson. New Orleans, October 27, 1907

It would be nearly a week before another clue appeared. Against his will, I delivered Holmes to the local police who gave him very little useful information – crippled men and women disappearing with increasing frequency over the last five months. So far no bodies had been located, nor any living souls returned. Holmes studied maps and walked the roads, often requiring my assistance if for no other reason than to keep him from walking off into a ravine or out in front of a carriage.

It was on one such occasion that a rustling in the underbrush piqued his interest. Expecting to find a small animal, I watched as he, his age showing by the stoop of his shoulders, bent and delved into the brush. A shriek of delight tore from his throat and I rushed forward just as he pulled the twisted remains of a wheelchair frame from the tall grass.

"It could have come from anywhere," I replied to his sudden mania. "As rusted and worn as the frame is, God only knows how long it has been there."

"True," Holmes stated, "but to find it *here*, it does make one curious."

"It does," I admitted. "But it still does not help you locate the missing people – eleven now by the deputy's last estimation."

"Thirteen," he corrected. "Henry and the woman are also part of this wicked scheme."

"You think."

"I *know*."

I wanted to question how he know... but it *was* Sherlock Holmes, and when he said he knew something, he was usually correct. Rather than continue the argument, I conceded the sentiment and allowed him to lead me back toward town, all the while conversing with himself of the many possibilities the chair provided. This case, I assumed, would never be solved even with the help of Sherlock Holmes, as his leads, his deductions, had all turned up nothing.

Then the woman appeared.

As we walked down Canal Street, a desperate woman's voice broke through the bustle of people. Her hysterical tone caught my attention even as it bypassed Holmes' caring…

Until she called his name.

"Holmes…" she gasped, her voice hitching with each and every breath. "Sh-Sherl-lock H-Holmes…" She stumbled out of an alley, clothes torn and dirty, her balance shaky as if she had only just learned to walk. Her fingers tangled into the coats of passersby, people who shoved her away in disgust at her distressed and frightened state. "I h-have to f-f-find H-Holmes…" she gasped. I rushed forward to catch her as she collapsed.

"I am John Watson," I said as I lowered her to sit on the brick sidewalk. "This is Sherlock Holmes." I motioned to my companion who knelt beside us. Her eyes went wide as she looked at him, as if she recognized him.

"Georgia Corchoran," Holmes said, aghast.

"You know this woman?" I asked.

"She was aboard the dirigible from New York. In a wheelchair."

"Henry…" she said, and began to cough. Her dry lips cracked and began to bleed, and with her left hand she toyed with the hem of her skirt. "Henry told me to find

Sherlock Holmes." She pulled the hem of her skirt above her boots. "He didn't lie," she whispered. "I walked again."

The woman fell limp in my arms. Her pulse remained strong and her breathing came in hard, short bursts. This woman was hysterical.

Holmes moved her hand to the side and lifted her skirt. Surprised and mildly disgusted gasps echoed around us and I reached for his hand to stop him – we were on a sidewalk in broad daylight with a growing audience – but he quickly batted me away and tugged aside her petticoat. What he found turned his complexion white as porcelain. "We must get this woman to a hospital. Now." He lifted her into his arms and, despite the crowd, and carried her limp body into the street where he hailed a taxi.

Once safely inside the carriage, he pulled back the cloth to reveal the most grisly display I'd ever seen – her withered legs encased in leather straps and metal gears, held in place with rods and tubes which wormed their way in and out of her skin. The boots themselves appeared to be part of the apparatus, and when Holmes bent her legs, the mechanical whirring of well-oiled gears filled the space.

Sherlock Holmes. New Orleans, October 25, 1907

I waited three days for the woman to wake. I neither ate nor slept, the need for information greater than those bodily functions, and when given the opportunity, studied the contraptions encasing her withered legs. The muscle tone surrounding the bones spoke of a distinct inability to support her weight, yet she'd walked upright—albeit jerkily—into Watson's arms. The tiny gears beside her knees waited patiently, their smooth and shining surfaces glinting in the gaslight of the hospital room. From time to time a nerve would twitch, and the smooth hum of the mechanism would catch my attention. The tubes which ran beneath the surface of her skin distorted the shapely figure of her lower extremities in a most terrible manner. The doctors had attempted to remove her boots, but found it impossible without removing the encasements themselves. As one particularly curious doctor unlaced her left shoe, he discovered that the leather of the boot itself appeared to have been welded to her very skin.

The boots had become a part of her.

The police came and went, examining the handiwork of the "doctor" and quickly departed, quite *greener* than when they arrived. I was questioned and, having a better grasp of the situation than they, grew bored with their mundane inquiries. These poor imbeciles had little, if any, chance of solving this case.

When Miss Corchran regained consciousness, she did so screaming. The doctor and nurse rushed in to sedate her, and when her hysteria subsided, I stepped up to her bedside.

"Tell me what happened to you," I urged.

"The doctor," she whispered, her breath coming in shallow pants. "He is a liar."

I pulled back the blanket from her legs and the grotesque contraptions encasing them. "Is this his work?" She nodded. "Does he have others?" Again, she nodded. "What is his purpose in taking them?"

"I don't know."

"Tell me where he is."

"I…I don't know."

"What do you know?" I snapped, suddenly weary of her tears.

"He's a madman!" she shrieked, which brought the nurse running again. I pushed the door closed and leaned against it to keep her out. "He offered me the chance to walk again after my accident and I willingly took the chance because I wanted my old life back so badly." She coughed to cover a sob and wiped at her eyes. "The pain… oh, God, the pain…" She wailed, her fists balling into the thin sheet covering her abominable legs.

"Why is he doing it?"

She shrugged. "Power, maybe. Money. He…he has servants in the cane fields. I think they may have been like…"

"Like what?" I prodded.

"Like me," she whispered, and blew her nose. "Earlier versions of his work, perhaps. From what I could see through the window…" she trailed off. "You won't believe me if I tell you."

"At this point, Miss Corchoran, I am willing to believe anything."

"He wanted to *use* us."

"For what purpose?"

"I don't know." She coughed indelicately. "Some were in the kitchen, others in the fields. Some were suspended from cables in the ceiling. Those outside…they only ever moved along the same paths – never veering. But every person I spoke to said they had started out just like me."

"I need to know where this place is," I demanded.

"I don't know where it is, exactly," she said. "*Lacrainte*

Parish, I think he said." It was a start. "I… I think I can take you there," she whispered beneath a sniffle.

John Watson. New Orleans, October 31, 1907

We woke to news of another young, crippled woman being stolen from her bed. The newspaper only seemed to agitate Holmes more, and as we prepared to leave he paced the floor as a caged animal, with all the side effects save foaming of the mouth.

Once we finally took to the streets in the carriage, he seemed to relax, though the girl grew increasingly more anxious and withdrawn. I couldn't blame her, as she'd suffered unmentionable nightmares. Children in costumes moved along the streets in packs, some knocking on doors and running away while others attempted to garner treats from those occupying the spaces behind the doors. *Halloween*, I remembered, and the pit of anxiety swelled.

The driver took us out of New Orleans proper in the direction of Raceland, and with each passing moment my sense of unease grew in an exponential manner. Perhaps it was Georgia's anxiety fueling my own, but Holmes as usual remained blissfully unaware of the potential trap into which we were walking.

"Turn right," Georgia said suddenly.

The carriage jolted sharply as the driver took the turn. She sat up straighter, peering out the window at the scenery drifting by. "This is the right way," she continued after some time. "I remember that tree."

"How far away are we?" Holmes asked, his voice monotone and impatient.

"Not far," Georgia replied, and looked at me. "Do you think we can save that girl, Dr. Watson?"

"I hope so," I replied.

The longer the carriage trundled on, the more I began to doubt the accuracy of Georgia's memory. She glanced out the window at regular intervals, her brow furrowing in a combination of anxiety and frustration.

"I know it was here," she muttered under her breath. "We turned from this road. Did we pass it?"

"We have passed nothing," Holmes replied sharply. "Nothing but trees and fields and—"

"There!" she cried, stabbing her finger at the window. "Stop!" she cried to the driver, who pulled the carriage to hasty halt. Unease turned to bald fear as we stepped down from the carriage into the street, and Georgia let out a tiny, stifled cry.

"What is this place?" Holmes asked as we looked out across the fields, watching people move between the rows.

"This is where he *changed* me," she whispered.

"Holmes?" I asked when he didn't respond.

"Take Miss Corchoran back to town and keep her safe. Alert the authorities. I will find the culprit."

Sherlock Holmes. Lecrainte Parish, October 31, 1907

The carriage pulled away, leaving me alone in this wretched place. The sun shined through the dark clouds, as if encasing the entire property beneath a dark shroud. There was no birdsong, no movement of small animals in the underbrush. The cotton was in bloom, its delicate fragrance filling the air. As I approached, I noticed the men and women moving about the fields silently. None looked in my direction, and upon watching them I discovered Miss Corchoran's description to be accurate. They moved along a single path, turning one way then the other, then hoisting their full baskets up and moving back toward the house before returning. Their movements seemed unnatural, and I wanted to know why.

I stepped off the dusty road into the tall grass beside the cotton fields and started forward, only to catch my foot on something and nearly tumble headlong into the plants. Hiding in the growth was a rusted rail, similar to that used on the many freight lines crisscrossing the continent. Curious, I followed it along the road to the point where it intersected another and ran perpendicular into the rows of cotton plants toward the next row. The metal was cold, and the slightest of vibrations brought me closer, pressing my ear and cheek against the bar to listen.

As I continued my investigation, the familiar sound of clockwork mechanisms moved past me. Parting the bushes, I watched as a servant—a young man of Hispanic descent—strode past. Or rather, *rode* past. His lower extremities were encased in an apparatus similar to the girl's , albeit a more primitive model. A series of ropes and pulley systems connected his legs to a pole riding above the track. Chains ran along either side of the harness system atop the track as well. Those chains, I quickly realized, operated the entire contraption.

"Intruder!" a voice boomed above me, and I looked up into the face of the angry servant. "Intruder!" he shouted again and swung a machete at me. I ducked backward s and scrambled out of the cotton rows, thankful the rail system kept him out of range. My coat and shirt became ensnared as I made my retreat, tearing large pieces loose from the bushes.

A chorus of voices rose among the rows and the individual mechanisms screeched in an unholy symphony as the mechanized field hands returned to the manor. A moment later, the thunder of hooves pounded the ground. Two men appeared above me, each wielding a musket.

"What do you want?" the taller of the two demanded as he leveled the barrel of his firearm with my forehead. They did not dismount—*couldn't*, I realized, as their bodies rested in saddles fitted with contraptions similar to the field hands.

"H-help me," I begged, forcing fear and concession into my voice. "I can't w-walk…" I dragged myself forward through the dirt with my hands, my fingers straining with the effort. My legs stayed limp, imitating lifelessness.

"Should we take him?" the shorter man asked under his breath. "Think Doc will want to see 'im?"

"Can't hurt," the other replied. "If Doc don't want him, we'll dispose of him."

I allowed those men to drag me through the dirt. With no small amount of difficulty I managed to maintain a façade of unaffected calm as my knees and shins bounced against the steps of the manor house. The horsemen handed me off to a pair of well-dressed servants whose mechanical workings were nearly as advanced as Georgia's, though quite bulkier. They took me to an expansive sitting room, a high-ceilinged antebellum cavern decorated with high quality reproductions of ancient relics. As I was dropped unceremoniously to the settee, I understood two fundamental things about this "doctor".

First, he valued old things, those that would otherwise be of little to no value to the layperson. Second, he saw his work as a noble cause, however terrible it might be for his "patients". The longer I listened to the silence of the house and the faint sounds of well-lubricated clockwork running just beneath its surface, the more curious I became. A servant passed down a nearby hallway and closed a door behind her, leaving me entirely alone. There were no others on this floor, but the "doctor" would appear soon.

Rising from the settee, I turned the other way to move swiftly and silently up the stairs. The hallways and rooms continued to the point of ridiculousness. Embedded into the ceilings and floors were tracks of varying shapes and styles. Above I noticed the tracks were more intricate, as if the mechanisms suspended from them would serve multiple purposes. What those purposes were, however, I did not know without seeing first seeing the attached apparatuses.

Half-way down the hallway, the faint whirring sound started. I ducked into a room whose door stood jar and watched from the darkness as a servant passed — a servant whose legs were encased in an even more primitive version of the field hands' harnesses and whose torso was suspended by ropes and wire from the ceiling's tracks – her gaze focused only ahead. She was young, her skin pale and ashen beneath her maid's uniform, her hair twisted into a distressed bun. In her hands she carried a tray which contained a bottle of cleaner, a rag, and a feather duster. I moved back into the hallway, following the dead-eyed girl into a room near the end of the house. The tracks turned her abruptly, her head falling to the side in the mechanism's haste. As I entered the room, the smell of cleaner overwhelmed me, momentarily distracting me from the fact that she was nowhere in sight.

I found that the floor tracks ended in the center of the room, but the ceiling tracks circled the perimeter of the room before disappearing behind a wall tapestry. I pushed it back and examined the wall, finding a set of tiny separations which indicated a secret door behind which the track ran. I pushed and the door tipped inward into darkness. The sun, I realized, was gone behind the storm clouds when the first peal of thunder rattled the aging window frames. I stepped into the darkness.

And fell.

Sliding along the hidden laundry chute, I twisted and turned until I came to rest rather abruptly on a cold and damp stone floor. The sudden impact knocked the wind from my lungs, momentarily compacting my spine in a sharp burst of pain. Watson, I discovered, was right. I was growing older, whether or not I wanted to believe it.

"Welcome to my home, Mr. Holmes."

As I regained my breath I glanced toward the voice. A table bisected this basement and behind it sat a shriveled, little man with a bushy moustache. A pair of goggles exaggerated his beady eyes. A closet stood open behind him, stacked deep with tattered clothing and costumes.

"You must be the doctor."

"Bertram Granville," he replied. "I would say it is a pleasure to meet you, but that would be a lie."

Motion in the closet drew my attention. A series of tracks ran across the ceiling, layered across one another as they entered and exited the closet. The moment drew my eye toward the right-hand side. A maid's costume… *no*. Upon closer inspection I discovered the items hanging in it were not clothes. *The maid.* The items in the closet weren't just clothing. They were *people*.

"Why?" I asked as I struggled to my feet. "Why do you do it?"

Bertram moved the goggles to his forehead, replacing them with a pair of round-lensed spectacles. His moustache twitched. "Why?" he echoed, tilting his head to one side. "Why do I do what?"

"What you're doing to these people. Why torture them?"

"Torture?" he replied, affronted by my question. "I do *not* torture these people. I *liberate* them."

My gaze traveled back to the closet full of modified humans. This was… inhumane. Surely men and women stacked in a closet as if they were coats could not be considered liberation. Then I recognized one.

Henry.

"How is entombing them in a closet, only to be used in your grand designs, *liberating*?"

Bertram inhaled deeply through his nose and released it in the same manner, a slight whistle emanating from his sinuses as he did so. "Come with me, Mr. Holmes." Rather than standing, he turned and came around the table, his body settled into Henry's wheelchair. My stomach turned.

"My grandfather built this grand estate," he said as he led me toward the staircase where a pair of metal bars extended into the wheels of the chair at the push of a button. "After the Emancipation Proclamation, we feared the plantation would fall apart, as so many around us did. My father, a physician despite my grandfather's wishes, began accepting volunteers to work in exchange for his services." As I ascended the stairs, the mechanism to which the bars were attached lifted Bertram, bringing him alongside me. "In addition to working the fields, we learned how to work the human body. It is such a beautifully complicated mechanism."

"These people do not appear to be volunteers."

Bertram made a low musing sound. "I have no doubt Miss Corchoran brought you here," he said.

"You kidnapped them."

"Our methods may not always have been so *ethical*," he paused to glance up at me, "but we always had the best interests of the people at heart. As you can clearly see, Miss Corchoran now has full, autonomous use of her legs. How much do you know about her condition?"

"Nothing," I admitted.

"She was involved in a terrible carriage accident which severed her spinal column between the lower lumbar vertebrae and the sacrum. The damage was absolute. She was not meant to walk again."

"So you were going to turn her into another of your puppets?" I asked, bile rising in my throat at the thought of the tortured souls in the basement.

"Absolutely not," he snapped. We reached the main floor and the bars retracted into the wall. We moved down the hallways toward the front of the house. The sound of the storm outside completely drowned out the mechanics of the house and nearly took his voice with it. "Those *unfortunates* in the basement were only steps in the research process. Those who would deny me their gratitude by trying to leave against my will. You see, my technology is expanding. I can *fix them.* I gave that woman her legs back."

"How?" I asked, my curiosity nearly overwhelming.

"The wires beneath her skin," he began, "I fused them to her nervous system at the point of severance. While she has no feeling in her lower extremities, she has the ability to control the mechanisms which control them."

"So using your own technology, she managed to escape you."

"She had assistance," he replied, his voice growing dark.

Henry.

I kept my face a mask of calm as my temper flared. This man had punished Henry for an act of kindness.

"What exactly is your endgame?" I asked, my voice still and steady. He looked up at me in surprise.

"Surely, Mr. Holmes, you have deduced that much."

I swallowed against the bile rising in my throat. "To walk."

"Of course. I lost the use of my legs as a result of an accident with a piece of machinery. My father vowed he would restore full use of my lower extremities." A pause. "Then the fever took him and left me to continue his work" Thunder rattled the foundation of the house and rain pelted the windows. I could scarcely hear myself think, let alone comprehend the madness of this man. So driven, yet so clearly mad. "I do apologize for this," he said, his beady eyes twinkling in the dim light of the house, "but I simply cannot allow you to leave."

A hand came around my throat and the sharp, piercing pain of a needle sank deep into the side of my neck. Before I could fight, my vision blurred, and the last face I saw was that of the man with the drippy nose.

John Watson. Lecrainte Parish, October 31, 1907

Agitation. Frustration. Fear.

An aptly named Parish, I thought wildly as the carriage made its slow trek toward that god-forsaken plantation. Children in brightly-colored masks danced beneath the umbrellas of their parents as we left the town, blissfully unaware of either the rain *or* the madman living not far from their homes. The Halloween festivities only served to rattle my nerves more.

Anyone could be hiding behind those masks, I thought as the crowds dwindled to nothing. Trees replaced the neatly-rowed houses, the occasional driveway or plantation yard sprawling out into the desolation.

The police seemed equally as nervous, though apprehensive. In the many months they'd been chasing this man, they could scarcely accept that Holmes had come in and solved the case in a matter of *days*.

"Can we go any faster?" I asked out the window.

"Afraid not, sir," the young man guiding the carriage called back. "Storm is strong. Almost there, but the roads're almost impassable."

I flung myself back against the uncomfortable seat with a frustrated groan. Holmes' life was at stake here. I didn't want to wait. I wanted to be there. *Now*.

The carriage lurched forward with an ominous screech and crack. Ahead, the frightened horses screamed. The carriage fell to the right, throwing me against the wall with a bone-jarring impact.

"Axle broke, sir!" the young man called out as he pulled open the door. "Can't go on!"

"We have to!" I shouted back and motioned to the two officers disentangling themselves before me. "We are almost there. We'll go on foot!"

Sherlock Holmes. Lecrainte Parish, October 31, 1907

"Monster," I muttered as I woke.

My tongue felt swollen and feathery, my eyes too large for their sockets. My body was immobile, strapped to a surgical table with bloody restraints. The goggles were once again covering Bertram's eyes.

"Welcome to the family, Mr. Holmes," he said, wicked glee dancing on the edges of his words. "You will be my greatest creation… other than myself, of course."

"You didn't create those people," I slurred, my mind foggy from the sedative. "You destroyed them."

"I saved them!" he shouted, rising from the chair by his arms. The anger quickly passed, replaced by his prior serenity as he settled himself back into the chair. *Henry's chair.* "Just as I will save you…from yourself."

I was immobile, unable to extract myself from the stiff restraints and their metal buckles. The man with the moustache stood in the corner, wiping at his nose with the same dirty handkerchief from the dirigible. Cruelty danced in his eyes and the key swung from his other hand. Behind him, curious glances peered over his shoulder, those captives who remained conscious watched in horrified fascination. I found Henry's face in the huddled mass, his right eye bruised and swollen shut. I could see no more of him than his battered face, but he turned ever so slightly. He was still alive.

Near my feet, Bertram sharpened a series of blades. I had to distract him, keep him talking. Keep him from beginning whatever deplorable surgical procedure he had in mind for me. I had to give Watson time to arrive or give myself time to clear the drug-induced haze and get myself loose.

I twisted my wrists slowly against the rough edge of the restraint. Pain clawed at the nerve endings of my left hand. I twisted again. Again. Again.

Warmth pierced the pain and my hand slipped slightly. I twisted again. As Bertram prattled on, his incessant diatribe growing more tedious with each breath, I worked my hand loose, my fingers contorting painfully as they slipped through the restraint. My left arm flew free and the mustached man dove forward. In a smooth, upward stroke, my fist connected with his jaw and sent him tumbling backward, the keys dancing just out of my reach. Bertram, I realized, had turned away, huddled over something on his worktable, giving me the opportunity to unfasten the buckle binding my right hand and that at my waist.

I sat up, the world canting slightly leftward, and reached for the straps immobilizing my legs and feet. His helper stood shakily and advanced on me, his fists balled tightly. I swung again and he danced out of my reach, then took a swing of his own. His right fist connected with my ribcage. Pain flared as I swung again, this time connecting my right fist with his left temple. With a sharp yelp of pain, he went down and did not get up again.

"My, my…you are a resourceful one," Bertram said, and clicked his tongue. He advanced, a syringe and a scalpel clutched in his left hand. "I do respect your work, Mr. Holmes, and I was hoping to be merciful." His expression turned dark. His eyebrows knitted in the center of his forehead and his lips shriveled into a thin line. "But it appears we shall have to do this the hard way."

Bertram jabbed the syringe into my thigh. The drug, Vecuronium if I were to guess from the immediate onset of paralysis throughout my entire nervous system, unleashed a torrent of fire followed by a curious numbness. I remained upright, my muscles frozen in place, but found myself quite unable to move even so much as a fingertip. While the dose was enough to confine me to unwanted stillness, it also guaranteed I was left to watch in horror as the scalpel first removed the leg of my trousers, then sliced into my flesh. Pain unlike any I have ever known flared to life under that dastardly blade, and the man wielding it showed no remorse. As he worked, I fantasized thirty-five ways to remove this monster from his mortal coil, and it was not until the basement door flew open and the cacophony of voices filled the dank space that my mind overloaded and closed down. Somewhere in the din and just as my consciousness began to fade, I heard the one and only voice that could make me believe this scenario would turn out for the best.

John Watson.

John Watson.. Lecrainte Parish, October 31, 1907

At first glance, I did not believe Sherlock Holmes to be alive.

My heart seized in my chest as I looked upon him, lying motionless with his eyes fixed on the ceiling. The officers behind me made quick work of the doctor and his equipment, and as the first two dragged the madman back up the stairs, another shrieked in horror. I turned with my fingers still pressed to Holmes's pulse and found the source of the man's disgust.

Bodies—more than three dozen men and women at final count—hung suspended from tracks in the ceiling of the closet. Most were still alive, though it appeared some had fallen victim to taxidermy and automation. None of them appeared to have even a shred of humanity left…except one.

"John Watson?" the young man near the front asked as I assisted an officer in removing him from the harness around his torso.

"Yes?" I asked, curious to learn how he would know my name.

"Is Mr. Holmes alive?" he asked, his voice weak.

"He is," I confirmed, glancing back over my shoulder as others carried him up the stairs to prepare him for the journey back to the hospital in New Orleans. I looked back into the young man's face, and realized he was the key to this puzzle. "You must be Henry."

"I am."

"What happened to you?"

"The doctor said I would walk again." The harness fell loose and he clutched my arms weakly as I took on his full weight. "Put me down, please."

"Are you certain?"

"No," he said with a sad smile, "but I assume that since you are here, Miss Corchoran's miracle came to her. I can only hope mine will, too."

I carefully lowered him to his feet. The whirring of hidden mechanisms echoed through the space and the men around me stopped to watch, some in amazement and others in horror, as the young man took his full weight onto his legs for the first time in his life. He wobbled slightly, clutching my shoulders for balance, and with the assistance of the machinery took his first step. His legs buckled and he collapsed to the floor, dragging me partially down with him.

"I am exhausted," he said, "but when I regain my strength, I do believe I will walk." A single tear slipped down his cheek. "Could you please help me to my chair, Dr. Watson?" He nodded to the contraption the mad doctor had once occupied. I nodded and lifted Henry, holding the majority of his weight as he took steps, joyous laughter erupting from him as he did so.

When he finally took his seat, he left out a contented sigh. "I never thought I would see the world as other men do," he said. "Now I will. But first, please take me to the hospital. And if you can find Miss Corchoran, I would like to see her as well."

The incident left neither Sherlock Holmes nor myself without psychological scars. The horror of human marionettes — those poor, crippled playthings of a scientist so mad he could not see the error of his ways — will haunt me for the rest of my life.

Sherlock remained in the hospital nine days while the doctors attempted to repair the damage to his leg. After another week and a half in a rehabilitation home, we were given clearance to return to London. Holmes walks with a cane now, as the muscular damage was too great for a complete repair.

Bertram Granville, the mad doctor, was committed to an insane asylum, and has not once spoken of the atrocities he committed, or his intentions toward Sherlock himself. While both Sherlock and I have lost countless hours wondering what the outcome would have been had I not arrived with the cavalry, I have convinced myself that Divine Intervention is what has kept those secrets thus.

Six months after our return to London, we received a letter from Henry in which he stated that he had regained use of his legs, and he and Georgia were hoping that we would return to New York to attend their wedding. While he would never admit it to being touched by the invitation, I do — from time to time — see Sherlock Holmes smile to himself as he sits in his favorite chair with a cup of tea and his violin. His damaged leg remains mostly straight, and he struggles to climb out of his chair now.

Holmes and I are no longer young. Our lives have been far from perfect. But from this most terrible experience sprang something beautiful.

The Memory Remains

THE CAR TRUNDLED DOWN THE TWO-LANE BLACKTOP, a combination of loose belts and a bad alignment causing it to rattle on its chassis. Storm clouds obscured the moon. Thunder rumbled overhead, booming loudly enough to shake the windows in the car. A fine mist fell, just dense enough to leave the road slick and the windshield smeared. It was well after midnight and the highway was mostly deserted, save the occasional logging truck or late-night traveler. The road had long-since grown dark and narrow, weaving in and around old oak trees and creek tributaries. Spanish moss hung low from the boughs, obscuring her long-distance vision…what little her weak headlights illuminated, that was. Sarah turned the radio up another notch and adjusted the dial in an attempt to crowd out the overzealous low-band bible chatter.

The end is near! Save yourselves! Praise Jesus' holy and most precious name or burn in hell for all eterni—

The station she found a little up the dial was spotty, but elicited a staticky, mostly recognizable version of one of the newest songs on the radio. She didn't know the song, but she did recognize the voice as belonging to Rosemary Clooney. Her late mother's favorite singer. Thinking of her recently deceased mother brought tears to her eyes. Sarah swerved to miss a possum in the road, the car fishtailing wildly. She gasped as she white-knuckled the steering wheel, silently praying the car would right itself. It did, finally, and she sighed in shaky relief.

Sarah turned the knob on the radio, taking the half-garbled transmission as loud as it would go. At least she had something decent to listen to as she blew through rural South Carolina. This lonely stretch of Highway 17 taunted her with its false sense of peace. She hadn't passed a house in twenty minutes, and the last traffic signal she saw was over an hour away from this empty stretch of no-man's land. Empty. Dark. Deathly.

Tears leaked from the corners of Sarah's eyes, and she stomped on the gas pedal. Her aging Plymouth groaned at the sudden force, shuddered, and threatened to stall before the speedometer jumped up another five miles an hour. She couldn't wait to get out of this state, and out of the life she so desperately ached to leave behind. She'd already closed her bank account. She could change her name and go off the grid. Live off the land. Maybe join one of those isolated communes in another country, away from political injustice and the threat of war. At least there she wouldn't be judged, or lied to, or hurt. She wouldn't lose another family member to senseless illness. She wouldn't have to worry about someone else taking advantage of her good nature. The last four years had been too much too fast, and she hadn't prepared herself for what she now saw as the inevitable. She resolutely ignored her reflection in the rear view mirror and the sickly green-black lump glaring back at her from her left cheekbone. Sarah never asked for this.

Lost in thoughts of escape, she took the curve too fast and the car hydroplaned. It spun in a wide circle, the headlights illuminating a blurry arc of wet trees and empty, black road. Sarah screamed, and her knuckles popped as she clutched the wheel, but any control she had was lost when the back left tire slid from the ragged asphalt and sank into the soft, muddy earth. The old car skidded off the road, back tires popping, and slid down into a swampy gulley. Its heavy front fenders bouncing against saplings and thick underbrush as it descended. The sudden, crumpling impact as the car made contact with a felled pine tree threw Sarah forward. With a loud, resounding crunch, her forehead connected with the windshield. White light exploded around her in a shower of sparkling pain, and the world went dark.

Sarah came to with a splitting headache. Fiery needles of agony greeted her as she opened her eyes to blurry vision. The lights on the dashboard flickered, and drops of water seeped in through cobweb cracks in the windshield. Rain poured through the forest canopy, and steam rose from the hood of the car. Even in the downpour, she could hear the distinct hiss of the busted radiator. A frightened sob escaped her as she looked through the shattered window at the steam cloud mingling with the rain. Aside from being stuck in a ravine on some desolate highway on the east side of Walterboro, Sarah didn't even know where she was. No one knew she'd even left, so none of the people in her life would think to ask questions, nor would they know where to begin their search once they found her missing.

She leaned back against the headrest, gritting her teeth to keep the hysterics at bay. Thunder rumbled, and lightning flashed through the trees. The storm had landed right on top of her while she'd been out, increasing in intensity tenfold since sending her careening off the highway. She wanted to cry, to scream, to go back in time and take her foot from the gas pedal before making the stupidest decision of her life. Yet despite the fear and the splitting pain in her forehead, Sarah felt the pull of sleep.

Just for a moment…just to clear the fog. Until the rain stopped and she could focus.

Lightning struck the tops of the trees, sending a cascade of exploded and burning branches hurtling toward her. The firebombs bounced on the hood of her car and rolled away, sizzling and smoking as the rain smothered the flames and she nearly crawled backwards over the headrest to escape them. The windshield bowed inward under the weight of one of the larger projectiles. Another would surely send it crumpling toward her and crush her under the flaming logs.

She couldn't wait any longer.

Sarah's heart began to race, pounding against her ribs as the orange haze of panic settled over her vision. Lungs constricting in claustrophobic fear, she clawed at the door handle, suddenly desperate for the outside. It wouldn't budge. Throwing her full weight against the door did nothing but hurt her shoulder. She wiped at the fog on the windows and craned her head around to find the driver's side door pinned shut by a large, smoldering branch. The passenger's side, she found, was not blocked, but the door handle was no longer attached and the place where it used to be was dented in far enough to allow water to seep in around the door's seal. The window was a cobweb of tiny cracks. It matched the windshield, but still held firm. The way the door caved, she would never get it open on her own. As it stood, she was trapped.

Unless…

Sarah turned and, bracing her hands against her seatback and the steering wheel, kicked. Pain flared up her leg and into her knee as her foot connected with the glass. The window crunched and bowed outward, but didn't immediately break.

She cursed and kicked again. The ruined glass slipped from its seal at the top of the window, but still didn't let go completely. Rain poured in, soaking her shoe and her sock. Sarah let out a frustrated wail and thrust her foot outward one final time, forcing every ounce of anger and frustration she had into the movement.

She screamed as pain flared along the bone from her ankle to her knee. The majority of the glass laid over, a few small shards flying outward from the point of impact, yet one sliver held firm, slicing a fine, fiery line up the back of her calf as her leg moved through the now-open window. Fine, white sparks danced before her eyes as she dug her fingers into the seat's upholstery and fought the urge to scream in agony.

All too slowly, the pain subsided. Sarah reeled in her aching, bloody leg and climbed over the gear shift and center console into the passenger's seat. She plucked the bloodstained sliver of glass from its seat in the window frame and threw it out as she glanced out into the darkness. Rain poured in sheets from the forest canopy, coming in sideways through the window and soaking everything around her. Small streams cut through the muddy undergrowth, running downhill away from the road. Getting out of the car, she noticed, would put her in about two inches of rapidly-moving water.

Her umbrella was in the trunk and for the most part useless. By the time she could move her suitcase to get to it, she'd be soaked anyway. Better to get to the road as fast as possible and get to safety. After all, she could always come back and collect her things when the tow truck came to get her car. Sarah took hold of the door frame and hauled herself through the opening, careful of the chunks of glass still clinging there.

Her feet hit the ground and the world began to spin. Cold rain pelted her from every angle and her saddle shoes sank into the loamy earth. Gooseflesh rippled up her bare legs beneath her skirt, like freezing fingers on her bare skin yet stinging as it made its way into the fresh, ragged cut. The muddy water seeping into her socks chilled her to the bone. Thunder and lightning continued their violent concert overhead and as she thought she'd black out again, an odd numbness settled over her.

Fear promptly replaced pain.

She stumbled away from the wreckage, leaving her belongings behind, and followed the wet, broken trail back up to the main road. The embankment was steep and required no small amount of effort to find hand and footholds. She fell more than once, skidding back to the bottom of the hill after a root broke loose or the clump of soggy mud she clutched collapsed under her weight. The constant flood from runoff only compounded her trek.

On Sarah's fourth attempt to crest the hill, she found the right combination and hoisted herself up into the tall grass. Beer cans and empty cigarette packs littered the sides of the road, and the whole area stank of burnt rubber and swamp mildew. The rain still poured in sheets, though Sarah no longer noticed it. She'd become too focused on getting to a visible place to care if she mildewed a little.

The first car that passed blew by without even so much as swerving to miss her. The passenger's side mirror of the speeding Chevy came within inches of striking her, and she staggered backwards to miss it and slipped, landing with a hard thump in the mud. Sarah whimpered as she pushed her palms into the sticky ground and forced herself first to her knees, then to her feet. Soaking wet and dripping with mud, she stumbled back toward the road.

Lightning flashed again, and through the break in the forest canopy it illuminated the road enough for her to see the skid marks left from her car. She stepped onto the slick blacktop and started off in the same direction she'd been heading before the accident.

Sarah walked nearly a mile before another car appeared, the lights behind her illuminating little, white reflectors that had been screwed into the old oak trees flanking the road. She turned, squinting into the brightness, and waved her right hand over her head.

The blue and white car passed her, the reflection of its taillights flickering in the sheen of the road, then stopped. She jogged up to the passenger's side window as it came down. A handsome, young man with wavy hair the color of sand occupied the car. A look of deep concern carved hard lines into his kindly face. His pale eyes twinkled in the dashboard lights.

"What happened to you, sweetheart?" he asked. His voice was deep and gravelly, coated in a slow, southern drawl. Sarah nearly cried.

"My car went off the road about a mile back. I need to get to town, wherever that is."

"Hop in and I'll take you," he replied and leaned over to pull the door latch. It popped open. "Monarch's Crossing is about three miles up the road."

Sarah pulled open the door and climbed in. Cool, dry air greeted her as she relaxed into the plush back seat. The gooseflesh returned, crawling up her arms. She shivered, suddenly desperate for a towel and dry clothes. "Thanks for stopping," she added as the young man maneuvered the car back onto the highway.

"The name's Billy," the man said. "What in Heaven's name were you doing out there?"

"I was going too fast around the curve and lost control. I just need to get to a phone." She coughed once.

"How about I drop you at the police station? Chief Robersen is a good man."

"Thanks again." She settled down into the seat, wrapping her arms around her wet body to hold in what little body heat she could, and leaned her head against the window. The rain finally seemed to be letting up, and when lightning flashed, thunder didn't immediately follow. For the first mile she watched the waterlogged scenery pass. Then her eyes grew heavy, and against her better judgment, Sarah let unconsciousness take her.

Sarah came to behind the wheel of her car with a splitting headache. Her vision blurred as she looked at the cracked windshield, and barbs of pain stabbed at the backs of her eyes. She had no way of telling how long she'd been out, and remembered nothing beyond being on the wet, dark highway and taking the curve too fast.

Steam rose from beneath the crumpled hood, and through the downpour she could hear the hiss of a busted radiator. She reached toward her purse in search of her wallet, but her head began to spin, wiping the thought of her ID from her mind. Darkness threatened at the edges of her vision and she had to clutch the gear shift to keep from slipping into the wet floor.

Panic flooded her mind and Sarah, despite knowing she wouldn't be strong enough to break through, attempted to force the door open. It wouldn't budge, and neither would the passenger's side door. In a last, desperate attempt at freedom, she turned and kicked at the cracked passenger's side window. Pain shot up her leg, but the window cobwebbed. She kicked again and it laid over, the safety glass clinging to itself despite the pressure of her foot and the weight of the rainwater. A single shard remained, slicing a harsh, jagged line up the back of her calf. This new agony pulled the air from her lungs and the thoughts from her head. Cold air and torrential rain poured in as she fought to keep from screaming.

With the pain receding, Sarah slithered out the window, and as her feet touched the ground, her head spun. She clutched the top of the car to steady herself. The dizziness passed, taking with it all sense of feeling. Numbness settled over her, and though logically she knew rain still pelted her, she no longer felt it. She knew her leg still bled, but it no longer throbbed.

With this newfound blankness, Sarah turned away from the steaming wreckage of her car and made her way back up to the roadside. She only slipped once on her ascent, skidding six inches or so before she found a handhold. The old oak trees lining the quaint country road hung heavy with water, and the road shimmered with a combination of rain and oil. She spared one glance at the curve before turning and continuing on in the direction she'd originally headed.

Four cars blew past her, spraying her with greasy road film, but Sarah didn't seem to notice. The first mile passed in a blur of lightning flashes and super-bright headlights. Nobody seemed to notice the waterlogged girl on the side of the road waving her arms over her head. By the end of the second mile, a dull ache had started at the base of her skull. The rain intensified, and more than once hard gusts of wind threatened to knock her off her feet.

Then a horn honked and a car swerved over to the side of the road. She stepped up to the passenger's side window of the big car and leaned down.

"Need a ride, honey?" The old man in the passenger's seat asked across his wife. "It's rainin' like the dickens out here and town is still two miles away."

"If you don't mind, I would love a ride," Sarah replied, relief sweeping through her. The pain in her neck radiated down her spine and thunder rattled overhead. The trees lit up as a lightning bolt hit somewhere in the nearby woods. The passenger door opened as the ear-splitting peal of thunder rattled the car on its chassis. The old woman leaned forward, pulling the seat with her, and Sarah climbed in, careful not to drip too much water on her as she did so.

"What's your name, girl?" the man asked.

"Sarah. Thank you for stopping."

"I'm Jesse," he replied, "and this is my wife, Mae. What on Earth are you doing out here?"

"My car went off the road at the curve and hit a tree."

"Are you okay, sweetie?" Mae asked. Sarah couldn't help but smile at the gentleness in her voice. They seemed like a lovely couple, even if Jesse did drive nearly as slow as she walked.

"Yes, Ma'am. A little banged up, but I'll survive."

"Oh, good," she replied, and the car fell silent. The storm continued outside, the rain pouring down in sideways sheets. Even the oak canopy overhead couldn't break up the downpour. Jesse slowed down a bit more and leaned forward, craning his wizened head up over the steering wheel. He reminded Sarah a little of a turtle. She rode along in silence, listening to the rain as it battered the roof of the car.

When Jesse's car crested a small hill and the flickering lights of a town appeared on the horizon. Excitement pulsed through her. Sarah had begun to think she'd be lost forever.

Welcome to Monarch's Crossing, the Jewel of the South, the hand-painted wooden sign read. She'd never heard of it. In all her life, living just two hours from this very spot, she never saw it on a map, never knew such a place existed.

The town was, as a whole, still asleep.

"Where should we take you, honey?" Jesse asked. Sarah shrugged.

"The police station, I suppose," she replied.

"Oh, well Chief Robersen won't be in until at least seven and they lock the place up tight at night. We can take you to the diner and you can get a cup of coffee until he comes in."

"I don't have any money," Sarah said with a defeated sigh. "I left my purse in my car."

"No worries," Mae replied and hauled her carpetbag purse into her lap. "I can spare a dime."

Sarah accepted the dime in quiet gratitude. The car crawled down Main Street, giving her a good look at the darkened windows. Many of the storefronts appeared to be only that. Brightly-colored signs and awnings remained atop boarded-up windows and doors, a picture perfect façade hiding the face of a specter.

Jesse pulled up to the curb and let her out with instructions to go straight to the diner and wait for Chief Roberson, then pulled away, leaving her standing under the awning for a quaint little ice cream parlor. The rain still poured, and Sarah began to walk, ducking in and out of the relative safety of awnings and umbrellas.

Light peeked between the buildings, drawing her attention. The sky to the east had begun to showcase the spectacle of dawn. She paused in the open space and turned her gaze to the soft pastels gracing the visible slivers of morning horizon. Sarah allowed herself a moment to daydream, to remember the feeling of happiness. The proper meaning of the word still eluded her.

"You lost, child?" The voice seemed to come from nowhere, startling her. Sarah found its owner sitting in an old rocker on the sidewalk, drinking a cup of tea. A long, wide awning graced the top of the building, yet the rain seemed to run away from the spot where the woman sat.

"Yes," Sarah replied. "I'm supposed to go to the diner and wait for Chief Robertson."

"Robersen," the woman corrected. As Sarah neared, she discovered a small, black lady of undeterminable age with small, dark eyes that twinkled even in the darkness. She was old, but not. Young, but too old to be so.

Ageless.

"I'm Sarah," she said to break the sudden, awkward silence.

The old woman nodded, as if coming to some fundamental realization. As if she already knew. "Folk 'round these parts call me Madame Eshe." She emptied the cup in her hand and went about the laborious task of rising from her rocker. "Come with me, child. Let's get you some tea to warm them wet bones." She turned into the store, careful to raise her feet as she stepped over the threshold. Sarah looked down at the line of chalk dust along the lip of the jamb, then she too stepped over it and followed the old woman into the little tea shop, graciously accepting the delicate china cup from Madame Eshe's hand. The tea carried the gentle aroma of lavender, but it did little to warm her. Even as the steaming liquid slid down Sarah's throat, she noted curiously that her skin still felt clammy and her insides trembled.

"I don't know what to do now," Sarah said, breaking the long silence. "My car is destroyed, and I don't even have my pocketbook. Maybe I should go to the police station."

"Could," Madame Eshe replied without affect, "but if you really wants the police, you best go down the street to the diner. Chief Robersen can always be found havin' breakfast down there 'fore he opens up the station." She rose from the stool on which she sat, her bones creaking with each deliberate movement in a telltale sign of age. She passed by Sarah, then turned and waved her hand. "Come on, then. I'll see you down there. Jus' let Chief get two cups ah coffee in 'im before you try an' bother him."

"Thank you," Sarah said for what felt like the hundredth time and rose to follow. They left the shop and walked two doors down toward the slope of the hill. The oversized clock on the back wall of the restaurant read 6:45, and it was obvious the place had just opened. A long table down the center of the room held a group of about fifteen older men.

Most of them wore button-down shirts and nice slacks with well-polished shoes. Two wore what looked to be the trappings of firefighters' uniforms, and three at the far end wore the regulation blue of police. An older, white-haired man in a pristine uniform sat at the head of the table. His left breast held a shining, gold star, and under his right arm rode a sidearm revolver. He had a kind face and a handsome smile, and though he didn't appear entirely awake, he was deep in conversation with his tablemates.

Madame Eshe led Sarah to a small table near where Chief Robersen sat. The waitress, an older woman with her big hair pinned up on her head, placed a sweaty glass of ice water on the table, then turned and walked away without even glancing in Sarah's direction. She started to question the rudeness when the conversation at the big table grabbed her attention.

"What's the story about the car in the woods, Al?" Sarah inwardly sighed in relief. She couldn't believe they'd already found her car. It had only been a few hours, after all. "Did you find anything out there?"

Chief Robersen emptied his coffee cup and placed it back on the table. "We did."

"So Billy weren't crazy after all," someone else said. "He really did see a ghost!" Laughter trickled down the table.

Who's Billy? she wondered. Maybe he was the one who found her car.

"Appears so." The kindly old man heaved a sigh. Sarah gathered he'd had this conversation a time or two already. "Tow truck pulled it out yesterday."

"Yesterday?" Sarah squeaked, and turned her attention to Madame Eshe. "That's not possible… I just got out of it a few hours ago!"

The other woman shushed her. "Listen, child," she whispered. Sarah blinked, because she didn't see Madame Eshe's mouth move.

"What did they find?" someone from the end of the Chief's table called out.

"Wrecked '46 Plymouth," he replied. "The one Charleston Police are looking for as a matter of fact."

"How long was it down there?" another voice asked.

"Can't be sure, but the Coroner said she'd been dead about six days, give or take a day." Another relief. She'd only been out a few hours, and she hadn't talked to anyone named Billy. Jesse and Mae had picked her up.

"The girl was dead?" a third voice called out. The Chief of Police hesitated, then closed his eyes and nodded. A round of gasps rose in the now quiet diner.

"Behind the wheel," he continued. "Bobby checked her out and said it looked like she died on impact. Hit the windshield. Broke her neck and fractured her skull."

Sarah listened, stunned.

They couldn't possibly be talking about *her* car, then. It had to be another Plymouth, and another impact and another girl. After all, she was sitting here listening to this conversation! Yet something about this conversation felt somehow…*wrong.*

"Who was she?" another of the old men asked. The growing lump of dread tightened in the pit of Sarah's stomach. She needed to know, was compelled to hear it, even though she *knew* what he was going to say. His lips parted on a slight inhale, and suddenly she prayed for him to stop.

No…no, no, no… please don't say it. Please… she silently pleaded. It was unnatural, but the truth nonetheless, resonating unspoken through the near-silent diner.

"Her name was—"

Oh please, God, no… don't let him say—

"Sarah Bennett."

…my name.

"Twenty-six years old." Bile rose in her throat and she fell forward, her forehead connecting with the table. It made no noise. "Her husband called the police an' said she'd run away." Chief Robersen sighed. "When Chief Mitchell called her daddy, he found out her mama died a few weeks back an' her old man had taken to beatin' on her. Said she had a nasty shiner last time he saw her."

Murmurs of shock and surprise passed through the aging occupants of the table, but Sarah no longer processed their conversation. She stopped listening after hearing her name fall from the Police Chief's lips. She couldn't believe it. Refused. There couldn't be two of her. She wasn't there and here at the same time, and she didn't believe in ghosts.

"Looks like the rain's finally stopping," someone at another table said in a hushed tone. The words echoed through her head, seemingly as important as the fact that she'd just been identified as the dead girl in the Plymouth down in the woods.

The world lurched, canting sharply to the right as she lifted her head and looked up at the old woman across from her. This...this couldn't be real. They were talking about her as if she weren't there...as if they couldn't see her. As if she were...

"Dead," she said weakly at the end of a gasp. The sound of her voice in the quiet also came with an unnatural chill. "I'm not dead!"

Madame Eshe shrugged and said nothing.

"But Jesse and Mae... and you!" Sarah slammed her fist against the table. Again, it made no sound and the glass of water never showed signs of movement. It was as if she weren't really there. "You can see me, can't you?"

Madame Eshe shook her head, and a look of pity ghosted across her face. "I see you, girl. But I see a lotsa things ain't really there. Talkin' to the spirits'll do that."

"Is...is that what I am?"

The old woman nodded. "Honey, you been dead since the minute you hit that tree. Ain't another soul in this building can see or hear you, and they ain't hearin' me talk to you neither." That was the point when Sarah realized she hadn't been seeing things earlier. Madame Eshe's mouth didn't move when she spoke.

"I don't believe you!" Sarah screamed.

"Girl, you ain't got no choice. Just 'cause you don't 'member the things they said don't mean they ain't happened. You's dead, honey, and ain't no amount of wailin' gonna change that."

Sarah nearly fell as she climbed out of the booth, and tripped twice stumbling out of the diner. The bell on the door didn't ring, and nobody noticed as she fell through the smooth pane of glass without disturbing it at all.

When she landed on her knees in the street, the car rumbling towards her never even touched the brakes as it passed through her form.

She looked down at her body, horrified, expecting to find herself mangled. Sarah found nothing but her white blouse and pink skirt, though they were once again soaking wet and covered in matted smears of blood.

Her blood.

As Sarah came to, she felt as if her head would explode. Pain pulsed at the base of her skull, down into the upper portion of her spine. Her vision doubled, wavered, then started to clear. The windshield cobwebbed out from the point of impact, a wobbly circle which lined up perfectly with her forehead. When she touched her raw skin, her fingers came away coated in blood. Her rising panic intensified as she discovered the front end of her old Plymouth pinned between two trees and crumpled around a third. The storm rumbled overhead, showering the hood of her car in leaves ripped loose by the wind and a torrential downpour. The telltale hiss of the busted radiator told her that unless she broke out a window, she wasn't going anywhere for a very long time.

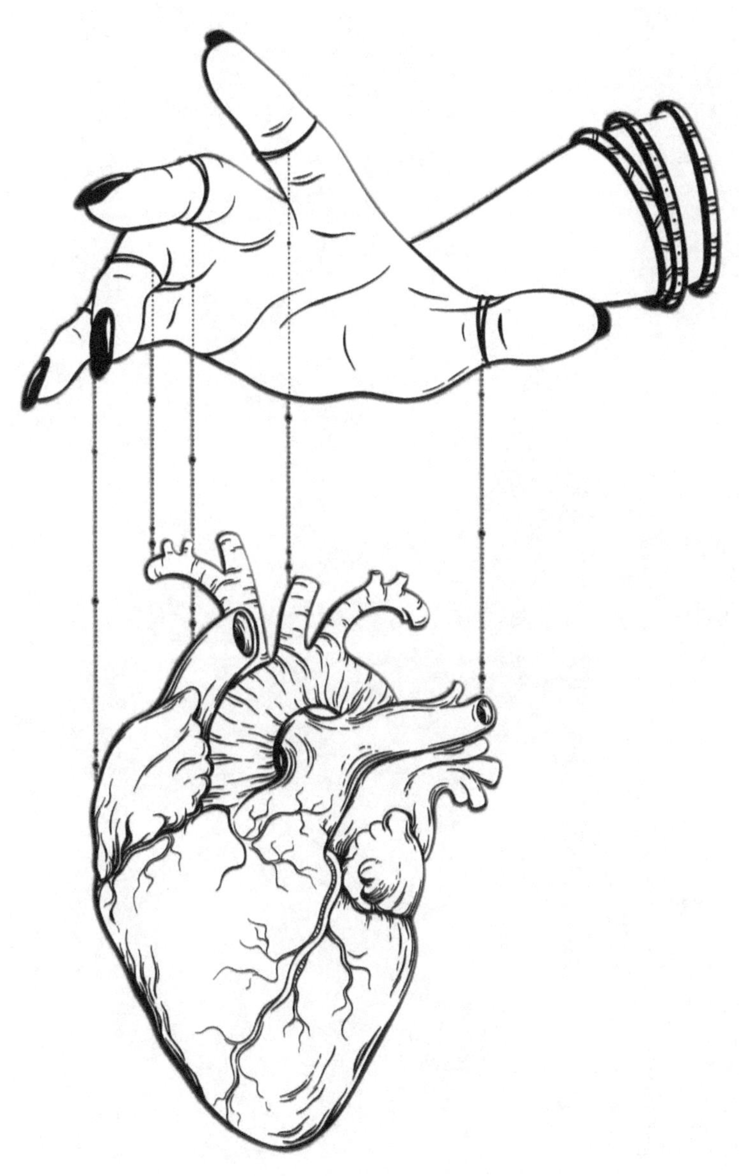

FROZEN GROUND

FOUR SHOTS RANG OUT ON A COLD NOVEMBER afternoon, hard and loud, from the muzzle of a nine-millimeter handgun. The booming sound, reminiscent of cannon-fire, startled the residents of the sleepy neighborhood. Then a single, lonely shot followed, rendering the world silent. The woman lay on the ground, her bullet-riddled body unmoving. A man lay just behind her, his body convulsing as he struggled through the stages of death. The raw wound along the right side of his face–a gnarled, meaty mass of brain tissue and bone fragments–oozed blood. His chest heaved, and a thin dribble of blood trailed down his cheek from the left side of his mouth.

A frightened scream broke the stillness as the first witness spotted the three bloody wounds in her back and followed the trail to the fatal wound in the back of her head. Soon the sound of sirens drowned out even the rumble of the freight train along the tracks across the street.

TWO YEARS LATER

Tuesday

Vaughn stuffed a baseball cap down over his head and turned for the door. He resolutely ignored the mirror hanging in the foyer as he stepped out into the bright November sunlight. Throwing his hand up to shield his eyes, he stepped down onto the uneven cobblestone walkway and started for his motorcycle. He'd just recently learned to ride again after suffering such severe head trauma; he'd lost a good portion of his motor skills in the…

The accident.

He couldn't call it what it was. His father's attorney had been generous and found leniency in a jury. He'd pled no contest, and by reason of insanity found himself sentenced to fourteen months of extensive physical therapy issued in a maximum-security psychiatric facility. His survival had been labeled a miracle and the jury took pity. After all, he'd taken out a good portion of the right side of his skull when he put the gun in his mouth and pulled the trigger. He'd lost a portion of his brain as well as the jaw joint and much of the musculature in the right side of his neck. Vaughn had almost completely lost the ability to speak and was no longer considered able to function on his own, but he could still ride.

He'd been institutionalized, certified, rehabilitated, and released, all in two years. His brother had not only become his primary caregiver and responsible guardian, but had also seen fit to keep up the maintenance on the old, silver Harley. After two unsuccessful rounds of riding, both of which resulted in pretty severe cases of road rash,

Vaughn was ready to try again. It would be a short ride – just around the block a time or two to get his balance back – but it would feel so good. The day was unseasonably warm, even for November in South Carolina, and he couldn't wait to feel the wind on his skin again.

Vaughn held tightly to the handlebars as he swung his leg over the body of the steel horse. He wobbled as if he would fall, his equilibrium still not where it should be, then pitched himself forward to land on the hard, leather seat. His knee cracked against the underside of the handlebar, sending a flare of pain up his leg. Tears sprang to his eyes – pain affected him much more these days – and for a brief moment he considered giving up and going back inside. But he couldn't give up…if he couldn't ride, he couldn't hang. And his street brothers wouldn't suffer his inability much longer.

The beast roared to life between his legs. The heavy rumble of the Harley engine rattled through him, awakening a long-dormant part of his mind. Vaughn breathed a sigh of relief and threw back the kickstand in preparation for his first solo ride in two years. Sliding his fingers into place, he shifted his weight to his right foot and placed his left foot on the foot peg. He took a deep breath and disengaged the clutch. Shifting into first gear, he twisted the throttle and the bike shot forward. The front wheel wobbled as he wrestled for control. Then he leaned into the wind. He shifted into second gear, and gunned the engine. The exhilarating rush of warm air enveloped him, and Vaughn smiled his ruined half-smile. He couldn't help it. He was back, and nobody could stop him now.

He turned onto Lawson Street, moving deeper into his neighborhood where Kelli Brighton jogged on the opposite side of the road. She was sixteen now, and had become quite the looker in his two years away. Vaughn craned his head around to stare at her ass as she ran by, and turning his head threatened his already precarious balance. The bike fishtailed and nearly pitched him into the street.

Vaughn righted himself at the last possible second, breathing a sigh of relief as she turned a corner out of sight. She hadn't seen his near miss. And he wanted to look at her again. He'd checked out her ass, but had been so caught up in realizing who she was that he'd totally forgotten to look at her tits. She lived two blocks over and he was moving faster than she, so he had the opportunity to double back and check out the front.

Which he did. Vaughn took another left, sped down Blackwell Avenue, and swung around the corner headed back to his street. She'd pass in front of his house, but he had the built-in excuse of practicing his riding ready if she questioned. He turned back onto Whitecrest Drive and blew past his house. She came toward him, her ponytail swinging with each stride, but he had his eyes locked squarely on her chest...

High and tight, just as he thought. And bigger than he'd anticipated. Bouncing with each stride. He'd love to get his hands on those funbags and take them for a ride. She didn't look like she'd mind either...if she was as easy as her Mama, he'd have no trouble getting her into his house. As she passed, he glanced up and caught sight of...

Elise.

The bike wobbled again, and this time Vaughn laid it down. He tilted to the left, and as the machine spun out from beneath him, he hit the pavement on his left elbow.

Pain bloomed out from the point of impact, turning to raw fire as the old asphalt chewed up the skin along his forearm and bicep. The screeching sound of metal on blacktop echoed in the quiet afternoon, and Vaughn's skid turned into a roll, his face scraping against the road with each hard tumble. His back bowed around the seat of the bike, knocking the wind from his lungs and throwing his spine into a sharp bend. Yet despite the pain, the he couldn't help but see his dead wife's face on that girl's body. He gasped for breath and, unable to find a connection to reality, slipped into darkness.

Vaughn woke sometime later in a hospital bed. His father and brother stood outside the door, embroiled in a hushed disagreement. He strained to hear, but the heavy glass separating him from his family made it impossible. The world danced around him, double-vision blurring anything but the vague outlines of items and people. The steady beep of a heart monitor echoed around the room, and even under the heavy curtain of painkillers, Vaughn knew he'd done a number on himself. He wondered briefly what had become of his bike, but he couldn't get the sight of Elise's face out of his head.

But it wasn't Elise. She was dead and buried. Two years in the ground, he doubted there was anything left of her but maggots and bones.

Bitch did it to herself, he thought with a bitter pang and closed his eyes against the medication. But in that darkness, he only found her angry scowl, her eyes dark and filled with hatred. The beep of the heart monitor increased. His heart began to pound and his palms, well-wrapped as they were, began to sweat. He needed to get out, to breathe in fresh air and to escape the confines of this hospital bed. God knew he'd spent enough of the last two years strapped to one of these death-machines. So he'd laid his bike down…so what? He didn't want to be here.

Vaughn started to pull the IV from his arm when the nurse came rushing in. She pumped something into the port on the IV tube before he could pull the tape loose. His arm began to burn, and suddenly he forgot why he should be angry. Blessed sleep overtook him, and he let it, hoping Elise's face would be gone when he woke.

But it wasn't. Six hours later he woke with a doctor standing over him, giving his brother, Derrick, directions on how to care for the road rash on his arm and the laceration to his forehead. The IV had long-since been removed, but the oxycodone haze still lingered. The doctor's words came out in a quiet rush, and he heard not English, but the gibberish language associated with the adults from the old Peanuts cartoons. His brother nodded in understanding and accepted the paperwork. Vaughn considered playing at sleep, but every time he closed his eyes he saw his arm extended and the gun in his hand. He also saw Elise's lifeless body lying on the ground at the other end of the gun. His heart thumped hard.

An accident…just an accident.

"Get up and come on," Derrick snapped. The calm façade cracked as soon as the doctor walked away, leaving Vaughn at the mercy of his brother's fury. "Dumbass," he hissed, "what the hell made you think you'd be able to control that motorcycle?" Vaughn's tongue felt thick. He couldn't find the power to make his mouth move, which left him completely defenseless. "I should leave your stupid ass here, but I can't. Doctor won't let me." Derrick grunted as the nurse entered the room with a wheelchair. "Come on. I've got to be to work in an hour and my Sergeant will have my head if I'm late again."

Vaughn stumbled down the hallway, right hand braced on the wall for support as he navigated himself toward his bedroom. Despite his resistance to the truth, Derrick had been right. It had been stupid to take the bike out on his own. He'd paid for it too, between the dogmeat on his arm, the deep gouges to the paint job, and the dent in the gas tank. He lamented the damage to the bike more than himself. He'd heal. The bike? Not so much. Being on disability now meant he had the money to make his bills, but the small stipend left little in the way of play money, and Vaughn wasn't about to get another job. The stupid fucker he'd last worked for couldn't see his worth, and he refused to condescend to be a workhorse for another asshole. Between that goddamn job and Elise, he'd suffered enough.

Vaughn noticed a flicker of movement in the bathroom as he passed. He paused, his heart skipping a beat, and took a step back to turn on the light. The room was empty save his mangled reflection in the vanity mirror. He sighed, annoyed with himself for being so easily startled at his own reflection. Of course he'd seen movement... *his own*. He slapped angrily at the light switch and started back down the hallway toward the bedroom, feeling more than a little sheepish.

His bed was comfortable. Vaughn sank into the old mattress and pulled the covers up under his chin before flipping on the television. He set the timer for two hours, knowing it wouldn't even take that long to pass out, and found one of the nostalgia channels playing old reruns of *Beavis & Butthead*. He'd loved that show, and sometimes wished he could be as cool as those two losers. At least their lives were interesting.

The pain in his arm had yet to return thanks to the high-power narcotics supplied by the hospital, but he was tired and didn't want to wake up in the middle of the night in pain. Vaughn popped the top on the pill bottle on his nightstand and washed down another oxy with a swig of cheap whiskey, then rolled over on his right side to keep his wounds from bleeding through the bandages onto his sheets. They were the only ones he had left and he wasn't about to get up and wash them. Or the set he pissed through last week.

The two losers on television grunted and giggled at juvenile dick and fart jokes as the drugs took hold, and Vaughn began to float into oblivion. In one final moment of clarity before he passed out, he could have sworn he felt the covers rise and the bed dip as someone climbed in beside him.

A slithering sense of dread came over him, but he was helpless against the pull of the medication. Vaughn remained lucid enough to hear the background noise of the television, but told himself the gentle touch of a woman's hand on his shoulder was only his imagination. He was alone in the house. Alone. No one else there.

Certainly not Elise. She was dead.

Vaughn vaulted upward in complete darkness, his heart pounding. Sweat beaded and rolled from his forehead. The television had long-since turned itself off, and he had no clock in the room. In the depths of the house he heard the heavy *tock-tock-tock* of the old grandfather clock she'd been so proud of, but the rest of the house stood still and silent, save his labored breathing.

He didn't realize he'd been asleep until he woke. He'd dreamed, but he couldn't remember what. It had been a strong image, and one that still had his guts rolling and his heart stuttering against his ribcage. As he laid back and his hand came to rest on the empty space beside him and the drugs began to pull him under again, he could have sworn the bed was still warm.

Vaughn crawled out of the bed and staggered back toward the living room. The drugs were really doing a number on him, and he couldn't stand to lay there anymore thinking he might somehow be hallucinating her back into his life. He missed her, yes… at least he told himself he did because that's what husbands were supposed do when their wives were dead. It didn't matter that he'd put the bullets in the back of her head…it just mattered that she was gone and he was alone.

Besides, she'd driven him to it. It was all her fault, the ungrateful bitch. He'd given her everything and she'd thrown it all up in his face. She walked away for no reason, and even after giving up everything he owned, she still couldn't get past her own selfish desires and see her way back to her rightful place. He knew in his heart she'd been fucking around, even if he hadn't caught her. But the oxy called to him again and Vaughn could no longer fight it.

Thursday

The road rash hurt like a son of a bitch, and Vaughn couldn't find his pills. He'd left them on the nightstand and some ignorant fuck had come in and moved them. He needed the pills. Who cared if he didn't have a clue what day it was or when he last bathed? Wasn't anyone's businesses but his. And right now he hurt, goddamn it.

With the whiskey gone, he'd been reduced to chugging cough syrup to get even a little bit of a buzz. Derrick wouldn't return his phone calls and their father was out of the country for another week. He considered calling 911 and getting them to come pick him up just so he could get a shot of something. But he still wanted to know who the fuck took his dope.

Vaughn let out a ragged growl as he swiped three dirty glasses and the empty whiskey bottle from the nightstand with his uninjured arm. The bottle thumped across the carpeted floor. One glass rolled under the bed. The other two crashed together and exploded mid-air, spraying the floor with shiny slivers of glass. The pills still weren't there, and now he was going to have to cut his feet all to hell to get out of the room. His boots and sneakers were still in the hallway and he didn't own another pair of shoes.

And he had no idea how to turn the goddamned vacuum cleaner on.

"Fuck it," he growled, but the words squelched in his throat as if he were talking around a mouth full of mashed potatoes. He'd risk the glass in his feet and go find the ibuprofen. Eight or so might help curb the pain in his arm and let him get back to sleep. Sleep was about all he could stand to do these days. He couldn't ride his bike because it was back in the shop. He didn't have the money to go party because his disability barely covered his bills. He couldn't drive since the State had taken his license because of his brain trauma. And no woman wanted to have sex with him without being paid because he looked like some kind of bell-ringing monster with the raw, red scars zigzagging up and down the side of his mashed-in head.

Vaughn swung his feet around to the back side of the bed and planted them on the floor. Even with the carpet, a cold draft crept across the ground. It seemed to linger around his ankles, to cling to his skin. It was probably the drugs talking, but it almost seemed the cold wanted inside him. It caressed his skin with phantom fingers, raising the thick hairs on his legs and sending gooseflesh rippling up the backs of his knees. Vaughn told himself he didn't feel it and paused long enough to stuff his feet inside an extra pair of socks before beginning the trek around the perimeter of the bedroom.

The extra socks did the job. Only one sliver of glass made it through the extra padding, but didn't burrow itself deep enough to be of any consequence. Besides, the pain in his arm trumped any sting the glass could muster.

He'd get Derrick to vacuum the carpet when he came through with groceries. Until then he'd just sleep on the couch. It meant he'd be closer to the bathroom anyway. Though as Vaughn passed the darkened bathroom, he made a point of not looking toward the room. Last time he'd come down the hall, he'd nearly scared the piss out of himself thinking someone was in there. That shit wasn't happening again. He'd take all the drugs in the house and die before he let himself be such a pussy again.

Vaughn stumbled his way across the living room to the couch, where he sat down and yanked off both pairs of socks. The shard of glass sticking in the arch of his foot came away with the fabric and buried itself somewhere in the carpet. He'd find it later — probably with his skin — but he had bigger problems.

Drugs.

He staggered into the kitchen and jerked open the cabinet where he usually kept his pills. Inside he found a bottle of expired allergy tablets, a male enhancement supplement he'd started taking to help him keep his hard-on going, and a dusty bottle of women's vitamins left behind by Elise.

Elise. Elise. Elise.

Her name repeated in his head until he thought he'd go mad. He hadn't thought of her in almost two years and now...

Now he couldn't get her out of his head.

He snatched the pill bottle out of the cabinet and flung it across the room where it hit the wall and popped open, spraying the floor with pink-and-white caplets. He shifted the other pill bottles around in search of something, anything, to take the edge off the throbbing in his elbow, but came up short. Not only had the fucker — whoever it was — come in and stolen his oxy, but the asshole had also cleaned him out of every over the counter pill he had.

"Fuck!" Vaughn screamed and slammed the cabinet door. The plates and glasses inside rattled under the force. He had to get something. Didn't matter what it was... he just needed a hit.

Elise used to stash money around the house. *Rainy Day Funds*, she'd called her little nest eggs, and she'd gotten so pissed when he found them. Vaughn hated the idea of good money wasting away at the bottom of a cookie jar or in a baggie behind the toilet. He never could understand why she thought taping a twenty to the slats under the bed would save them from complete ruin, but she did.

A week after he came home from the hospital, he'd found forty bucks stuck in a plastic bag at the bottom of the old rooster cookie jar on the counter. It had been enough to score a dime bag from his neighbor's son and a bottle of cheap whiskey from the red-dot store on the corner. Two weeks after that he found the twenty in the toilet and got another bottle of booze with it. The ten in the utility drawer had scored dinner at McDonald's because he was so fucking sick of eating dollar microwave dinners.

Right now, Vaughn needed one of those little money pockets to make itself available. Elise had been beyond useless in life after she decided to stop putting out, but her obsessive-compulsive hoarding of money was about the best thing she could have left him. Vaughn started at one end of the kitchen, pulling open cabinets and looking under stacks of dishes. He checked the back of the refrigerator, felt along the back side of the under-counter CD player, checked under and behind the small TV she kept on the shelf in the corner. He managed to dig three dollars in change out of the utility drawer, but otherwise found no cash stashed in the kitchen. Vaughn moved to the living room, overturning furniture and checking under pillows and cushions. He snatched pictures off the walls and threw Elise's collection of tchotchkes off the shelves in search of one of those financial hidey-holes.

He found one on the back of their hand-painted wedding portrait. The biggest haul yet, Vaughn pulled the baggie off the back of the painting, uncaring that the adhesive from the duct-tape holding it in place ripped the canvas. He didn't need that fucking picture anymore. If anything, it served as a reminder of the worst time in his life.

The bag held three hundred dollars in tens and twenties. That would be enough to score drugs and booze enough to keep him stocked for at least week. And maybe something to eat, too. Thrilled with his new find, Vaughn stuffed his feet into his shoes and, ignoring the pain flaring in his arm, started for the door.

The touch of a feminine hand ghosted across his scarred cheek.

Vaughn spun around, a shock of ice-cold fear rippling down his spine. His blood turned sluggish in his veins and his heart kicked into overdrive, but when he turned he found his living room trashed yet devoid of human life. He was still alone, still a self-made widower, and still jonesing for a hit. But that touch... it was so fucking *real*. The slender fingertips were warm and gentle, and his skin still tingled where they touched. It was a touch he'd experienced so many times in his life; the very thing which had once compelled him to marry. He'd loved that touch, wanted it to be his and his alone for the rest of his life. But it, just like her life, had ended two years ago in a fit of jealous rage. He'd never confirmed it, but he was absolutely certain she'd been sharing those caresses with another man.

The sensation lingered long after it should have, to the point where Vaughn reached up and touched his face. Elise's phantom touch—similar to the cold caress of his ankles—dissipated, that fragile illusion dissolving under the weight of his clunky hand against his ruined cheek. Vaughn shook his head, annoyed with himself for believing something so absurd, even if only for a moment. He reached for the doorknob again, forcing his hand not to hesitate in anticipation of a second touch that never came.

Outside the sun cast a sharp glare over the world. There was not a cloud in the sky and this day was still oddly warm for November. He stumbled once on his trek across the yard, but managed to not fall on his face and cause further damage to his person. The brief thought of that sexy little neighbor of his crossed his mind, but he dismissed it in favor of reining in the pain in his arm.

Vaughn made his way down the sidewalk to the end of the neighborhood and ventured across the highway to the half-empty strip mall rotting on the corner. At one end sat a liquor store—the only reason the facility still stood at all – and half-way down was a "country market", which in reality was little more than a convenience store. Except this place sold bacon and chicken wings cooked on a hotplate in the storage room.

His first stop was the market, where he picked up a bottle of aspirin and some peroxide. The bag of chicken wings and two bags of week-old potato chips were frivolous buys, but there wasn't shit to eat in the house and he'd need something to stave off the munchies when they hit. He moved on to the liquor store, where he walked the floor, careful not to look up at the clerk as he picked up four bottles of cheap whiskey and a selection of flavors from the dollar mini-bottle bucket.

When Vaughn reached the counter, the woman there looked up at him, recoiling in disgust. Her name was Gloria, and two years ago she'd have climbed him like a tree if he'd just given the word. Today, she looked like she wanted to vomit.

The expression passed from her face quickly as she set about ringing up his purchase. She didn't look up at him again and was careful to not touch his hand as he handed her a hundred dollars and change. So he had some scars... he wasn't a fucking leper. Scars didn't give people the right to be assholes toward him.

But being a murderer does.

Elise's voice floated through his mind. Vaughn snatched the paper bag off the counter, nearly dropping it in his rage, and spun for the door. He wanted to give Gloria what-for, to tell her just how much of a bitch she'd become, but he knew the words wouldn't come out right. This permanent case of mush-mouth made his anger hard to express.

Hanging out beside the building was exactly the kid he wanted. The young punk leaned against the corner, a cigarette dangling from his lips as his thumbs flew over the screen of his smartphone. Vaughn cleared his throat. The kid glanced up and immediately dismissed his presence in favor of the gadget in his hand.

"What's your poison, Pop?" the boy asked. Vaughn immediately wanted to slap the bitch off the kid, but he wanted the kid's drugs more.

"What you got?" he asked, focusing all of his attention on making his voice as normal as possible.

"Which family?"

"Painkillers."

"Oxy, percocet, dilaudid. Fentanyl, if you're interested in life-or-death roulette."

Fentanyl? Fuck, this kid's serious... Vaughn thought. He liked the idea of being completely pain-free again. After all, he'd learned just how tasty fentanyl could be after he put a nine-millimeter slug through the side of his face.

"Also got heroin and a decent spread of hallucinogens if you want to party."

"How much is the fentanyl?" Vaughn asked.

"Three hundred for a sucker."

"Fuck."

The kid grinned, and the wicked image burned itself into Vaughn's memory. "Most of my fentanyl users ain't repeat customers, bro."

"What you got for eighty?"

"Two perocet and Angel Dust. Good deal, dude."

"Yeah." Vaughn handed over the cash and accepted a handful of small bags the kid produced from inside his hoodie.

"Thanks, Pop," the kid replied and disappeared around the back of the building.

Finally, Vaughn thought as he turned and started across the street toward his house. He wanted it all right now, but that would be too obvious. He needed to get home so he didn't have to move for awhile.

Vaughn righted the couch cushions and turned the coffee table on its feet before falling into the warped, old piece of furniture with his haul. He peeled the tops off of all three bottles of whiskey and lined up the minis across the edge of the table. Then he popped open both bags of chips and the box of chicken wings. Then, finally, he pulled the baggies out of his pocket and poured their contents onto the table in front of the whiskey bottles.

Three capsules half-full of a crystalline, white powder rolled around, bumping against the two white, coated tablets. He wanted the angel dust, but would be able to enjoy it more if he got rid of the pain first. Plus, the percocet would give him a nice base high.

Vaughn popped the two tablets into his mouth and upended the first bottle of whiskey. The combination of drug and alcohol left a bitter taste in his mouth, which he chased down with a minibottle of cinnamon whiskey. He followed that with another minibottle, some swirling, purple liquid that tasted like potpourri smelled. It was disgusting, and it took two long swigs of his whiskey to kill the flavor.

The walls began to spin. Vaughn fell backwards, bottle in hand, and laid his head against the back of the couch. The pain was already starting to wane, and a delicious, numbing warmth spread through his limbs. This was exactly what the doctor ordered.

"You're an idiot, Vaughn."

He bolted up, sloshing booze down his chest as he looked around. Her voice had been so close, so real, so accusatory. Right in his ear. She could have been sitting in his lap as she used to do when they were young and in love.

"Bitch!" he cried out. "You made me spill my whiskey!"

Vaughn tried to stand, but the combination of substances in his bloodstream made it impossible. He wasn't planning on going anywhere, so he tugged off his wet shirt and tossed it across the room, where it landed across the arm of Elise's antique rocking chair.

Bare-chested and beer-bellied, he leaned back against the couch and picked up the TV remote from the arm. It took almost ten minutes of drunken channel surfing to find something interesting. He didn't have a clue what it was, but the white guy on the screen seemed to hate everything and everyone around him, a familiar sentiment.

Vaughn woke several hours later with a dried line of spittle trailing down his chin and throat. The house had gone cold while he slept, but the television carried on in the background. It was dark outside, but the batteries in the wall clock died a year ago and he hadn't given enough of a shit to replace them. An empty whiskey bottle lay on the floor at his feet, gooseflesh rippled across his chest and down his arms, and three caps of angel dust sat on the table in front of him.

Vaughn slipped one of the three pills into his mouth and chased it with a long swig from the second bottle. It went down smoothly, the burn of the alcohol obscuring any aftertaste the dusty gelatin might have had. Distantly he thought about the contents of that capsule and what it might do to him, but five minutes later he couldn't even feel his face.

Friday

He couldn't remember what it was he was supposed to care about. Hell, he could barely remember his name. All he knew is his arm hurt like a son of a bitch – couldn't remember why either – and the handful of aspirin he took with the booze on the table hadn't done fuck-all to stop it. There was a tiny, niggling thought worming its way through his subconscious, but it took too much effort to figure out what was going on.

The world warped and spun, dancing on its axis while he remained a disassociative onlooker. The silence carried its own song, lilting and turning in time with Vaughn's heartbeat. It spoke to him with a familiar and haunting voice, telling his most intimate secrets to the draft creeping visibly along the floor.

When had that mist come into the house? It was pretty as it slipped over the individual fibers of the carpet, the tiny fingers of the intangible cloud reaching and twisting as they moved toward him. The fingers solidified, took a familiar shape as they continued their path toward his feet. His heart stuttered and his breath caught in his throat as the swirling white cloud took on a soft, pinkish hue and the delicate, curved tips of Elise's fingernails reached toward him from the miasma. He wanted to scream, but the muscles in his throat refused to work. He wanted to crawl up on the couch, to take his feet away from those questing, phantasmal fingers, but his nervous system had already begun to shut down. He couldn't move, could do nothing but sit and watch in frozen terror as her arm followed her hand and those ghostly digits laid themselves against the leg of his jeans. The vision came with the sensation of gentle pressure where cloth collapsed against his skin.

The hand tightened until even in his drug-induced fog he could feel the pressure of each individual finger. His heart beat hard against the inside of his ribcage. His jaw quivered, and tiny, frightened sounds escaped his throat with each whistling breath. The pressure turned to pain.

The hand jerked.

Vaughn consciously experienced the sensation of falling into the cloud of mist, falling forever, then pain blossomed from the back of his head in a cascade of rainbow colors, and the world went dark.

Saturday

Vaughn woke on the kitchen floor with the vague memory of falling. He didn't know if it had been a hallucination, a dream, or something else, but he did know his head hurt like a sonofabitch. He struggled to sit up and his vision blurred in a sickening swirl of light and color. It nearly toppled him back to the floor as he grabbed for his head to steady himself. He drew his hand away, surprised to find a sticky wetness coating the back of his skull. He looked down at his hand and found it covered in a viscous, red substance, flecked with skin and bits of brown…dried blood, he realized. *Drying* blood. His blood.

Whatever happened, he'd banged his head pretty fucking good. Probably even had a concussion. Though through the haze of drugs and alcohol, he really couldn't give a shit. At least his arm didn't hurt.

Small favors, he thought as he struggled to drag himself backward on his elbows and prop himself against the wall. Fuck, his head hurt.

He took several deep breaths. The house was still and silent. He could feel his heart beating in his feet. The back of his head grew warm and he vaguely registered that he'd begun to bleed again. Vaughn closed his eyes, and just as he lost contact with his sight, something moved across the kitchen.

He struggled against the pull of unconsciousness to open his eyes and look around. Once he forced his eyes open, he found the kitchen wrecked but otherwise empty. Despite what he saw, the gnawing sense that he wasn't alone crept over him. He couldn't shake it, even after stretching his good arm over his head and turning on the light.

The kitchen flooded with the blinding glare of the overhead fluorescent, yet it did nothing to dispel his angst. The light intensified the sense of despair, stretching the shadows and illuminating the cracks in the paint.

The drugs...it's the drugs making you paranoid, you fucktard.

The drugs… most of them still lay undisturbed on the table. Vaughn turned and fell into the doorway, collapsing onto his belly before managing to shove his knees under his body and, using the door jamb for support, struggled to his feet. He stumbled into the room, his head doing somersaults on his shoulders. In between the waves in his vision he saw the two small capsules nested safely between the pair of empty liquor bottles.

Three steps into the room he lost his balance and pitched forward, turning just in time to fall into the couch rather than crash down onto the coffee table and destroy his stash. His head pounded like it would explode and a new flow of warmth cascaded down his neck. He should probably call someone and get it looked at, but he needed alcohol first. Something, anything, to dull the pain. Vaughn rolled over and grabbed the last bottle from the table. He started to turn it up and met with resistance. He closed both hands around the neck of the bottle and pulled, but an unseen hand held the bottle tight, suspended in midair a foot and a half from his face. He tugged again, but nothing happened.

Vaughn growled and jerked at the bottle. This time it sprang free from that phantom grasp, nearly slamming into his mouth while sloshing cheap whiskey all over him. He cursed, though the words came out slurred and unintelligible.

The pill stuck in his throat and the whiskey burned. Vaughn coughed, trying to bring it back up, but the gelatin casing had already begun to dissolve, growing tacky and refusing to budge. He crawled from the couch, dizzy from a combination of head injury and lack of air, and stumbled back into the kitchen for a glass of water. The briefest flash of a figure in the door to the hallway caught his attention, but his immediate fear of choking to death on angel dust took precedence. By now the bitter powder had begun to seep through the casing. It made him gag. It burned his throat. He wanted to vomit, to throw himself over a chair, anything to dislodge the bullet of death in his throat.

The edges of Vaughn's vision began to blur and he fell to his knees two steps short of the sink. He tilted forward, ready to go down and resigned to his disgusting fate when the sensation of hands on his shoulders startled him. He was alone in the house, goddamn it. This was just another hallucination.

His imagination's death rattle…

But the pressure remained even. The hands trailed down his back and under his arms. Vaughn watched in paralyzed horror as the hair on his bare chest flattened where arms should have been. The phantom hands closed around him and pulled sharply.

Three hard, rib-cracking thrusts later, the remnants of the pill dislodged, bouncing against the back of his tongue. The arms released, and Vaughn collapsed to the floor, gasping for air.

"Last save, motherfucker," the soft, feminine voice whispered in his ear. Every hair on Vaughn's body stood on end as the sound of Elise's words filled his head, echoing again and again as he took breath after painful breath.

He scrambled to his feet, took a drink of water to wash down the pill and kill the burn of narcotics on his tongue, then stumbled back to the sofa, where he collapsed to wait for the drugs to knock him out.

"Fuck me…" he gurgled, staring up at the stained ceiling. The sensation of being watched retuned, but he didn't dare remove his focus from the dusty space behind the ceiling fan's still blades. He couldn't handle it if the hateful gaze he felt burning from the doorway were actually coming from a real pair of eyes. The thought that she could really be there…

"No… nonononono…" he muttered, shaking his increasingly heavy head back and forth yet keeping his vision sharply focused.

The drugs weren't working fast enough. He wanted that other pill, but his arms wouldn't work to reach it. He could move his fingers and hands up to the wrist, but it felt as though something were holding him in place, strapped to the sofa. The phantom fingers slipped over his cheek again and a tiny, strangled cry of fear escaped his throat. Vaughn was alone, but not. He couldn't see her, but he could *feel* her.

"Elise, please…" he begged, tears springing to his eyes, his base instinct telling him she'd returned. He closed his eyes, forcing the tears away, to no avail. "Please!"

The pressure on his wrists increased to the point of pain, then fell away. He gasped in relief, and when Vaughn opened his eyes again, a spectral version of Elise's form passed through the doorway and down the hall.

The air around him turned deathly cold. Even the ever-present draft under the front door stopped. His breath came in tiny, frantic puffs of opaque cloud. They seemed to crystallize in the air before him and drop to the ground like tiny, icy jewels.

"Oh God, oh God, oh God…" Vaughn chanted, his ruined jaw clicking with each uttered word. He began to shiver, his fingertips losing their color and fading to blue. His legs ached from the cold tremors. He wanted to run, to escape whatever delusion this was. Elise was dead, goddamn it. She was dead and she couldn't be here tormenting him now. But he'd seen her in the bathroom. He'd heard her voice. He'd felt her hands. She *was* here. And she wanted to hurt him. "GET OUT, YOU BITCH!" he screamed into the cold silence.

Disembodied laughter filled the room. It sounded as if there were twenty of her in the house with him, all laughing at once. The sound swelled, rising in volume and intensity until Vaughn thought he'd go deaf. He pressed his cold hands against his ears, but the action did nothing to dull the cacophony.

Then it stopped.

Silence.

Stillness.

Cold.

Vaughn registered each of these things singly; his inebriated mind would only allow one sensation at a time. In the newfound quiet, he had a hard time processing that Elise had been there. It wasn't real. It was a product of the drugs.

"How *fucking* dare you!"

Her image rushed forward, crowding into his face with an angry screech. Her face was a mask of murderous hatred. Her hands reached for him, her fingernails distended and curving. Grasping. Wanting.

A scream tore from Vaughn's throat and he scrambled toward the door. He couldn't find his footing. He could barely get his hands beneath him. He scrabbled across the tile floor, dragging his inebriated body behind him. Tiny, screeching pants echoed against the walls and the floor, mixing with the returned sound of Elise's hideous laughter.

He found the doorknob and turned. The door lurched in his hand, then swung inward, bouncing against his forehead in a flash of pain. Barefoot, Vaughn dragged himself up on the edge of the counter and threw himself into the cold night, Elise's frantic giggles following him into the darkness. He gasped and panted as he stumbled down the sidewalk and out toward the main highway. His toes caught on the cracks in the concrete. The gravel bit into the pads of his feet. More than once his unbalanced equilibrium threatened to shove him to the ground, but he kept on. His heart hammered in his chest, his pulse beating so hard in his throat it threatened to choke him.

Nononononononono... He begged the residual sounds to stop, ignored the horns blowing as he ran into the street, his feet hitting the asphalt with a hard shock. Still he carried on, dragging himself one frantic step at a time farther and farther away from the house, as if putting distance between himself and his abode would erase the presence of his dead wife's ghost.

Vaughn picked up momentum, finding his footing on raw skin and beginning to run. He ran blindly forward, following the twists and turns of the sidewalk as it led him farther and farther away. Then the adrenaline expended itself and his pace began to slow. Out of shape, he began to pant. His heartrate spiked. His hands shook. Vaughn slowed to a walk and focused to remain on his feet in the dew-covered grass.

He'd stumbled far enough away from his home that the streetlights were fewer and farther between. The cold was beginning to set in; an unseasonal cold. And an abnormal quiet. That creeping stillness which threatened to suffocate him. Vaughn stumped his foot against something hard, stumbled, and righted himself, cursing. If the damned drugs had done their job, he wouldn't have felt it. But the cold November air had sobered him. He looked down at the thing over which he'd tripped, and his mouth went dry.

A grave marker.

In his panic, Vaughn had come to the one place he'd never have ventured on his own, day or night. *She* was here. Or what was left of her, anyway. He looked up, straining in the darkness to find the gates. Clouds had moved in, obscuring the moonlight. There were no lights here save the occasional solar bauble placed by a loved one, but even those had gone dim, strained until their energy had been spent. He twisted and turned until his head began to spin. Vaughn stumbled among the rows, his feet aching from the cold and the uneven ground.

A fine, white powder floated down from above, each individual flake a tiny, icy kiss against his battered skin. His heart rate accelerated. Tiny beads of sweat dotted his forehead, ran down his arms. Deeper into the cemetery he stumbled, or closer to the exit...

He couldn't tell anymore.

Vaughn picked his way across the grounds carefully, feeling out each new step with his toes before placing his weight onto his full foot. The thought of walking barefoot across graves disturbed him more than the thought that he may have seen his dead wife's ghost. The crunch of his own feet across the frozen ground echoed back up at him, tripling the anxiety and adrenaline coursing through his body. The snow grew heavier, chilled the air further. He could no longer feel his fingers, but the sound of Elise's laughter had also faded. Out in the crispness of the night, Vaughn was easily able to rationalize what he heard.

I just miss her is all. It's that time of year, and I'm feeling a little guilty. Maybe I want her back more than I thought…

His name echoed through the trees, a feminine whisper on the wind. Intangible fingers fluttered down the side of his head, tickling along the scar. Vaughn spun on his heel, losing his balance and falling face-down into the soft dirt. No one was behind him.

"Alone. I'm alone," he told himself, but the words came out in a jumbled mess.

Laughter filled the air. *Her* laughter.

He screamed.

The sound echoed through the still November night, then fell silent, truncated by the falling snow. The ground, he realized, had been recently disturbed.

Maybe he *wasn't* alone.

The drugs… it's the drugs. Dry leaves crunched as he struggled to his hands and knees. His own labored breathing scraped against the stillness.

"Vaughn…"

He began to laugh. Tears and snot streamed down his face, catching in the stubble on his chin. "Go away!" he screamed. Laughter turned to hysterical sobs.

"Tell me you love me, Vaughn," the spectral voice said. "Tell me you love me."

"No!"

"Tell me…" The voice was gaining strength, becoming more like…

"Elise…" her name fell from his lips, a pleading sob. "Please…"

"Tell me you love me." She was angry. He knew that tone.

He couldn't feel his toes. She was dead. He was cold. A twig snapped behind the gravestone. He was alone. This was a product of the drugs. He was going to die.

He knew the last with absolute certainty.

The gentle touch returned, caressing his bald head. She always loved to touch his head. She was so sweet, so loving. She always loved him, even when he didn't deserve it.

Even now, after he killed her.

"Elise," he pleaded, "I'm so sorry. I love you." His breath hitched as he placed his hands on the stone in front of him to steady himself. "P-please, Elise…" he continued into the still silence, "forgive me."

The snow came down heavier, muting the world around him. He shivered hard against the creeping cold, against the hypothermia settling into his body. But she didn't answer. The air around him remained still and silent.

"Please…" he sobbed, the sound nearly lost under the quiet shuffle of snow. "Please…"

Then the fingers touched his head again. He shrieked and tried to pull away, but the touch followed, sliding delicately over his skin. He tried to push away from the gravestone, but he couldn't move. His legs refused to work. His fingers did not register the feel of frozen marble beneath him.

"Vaughn..." his name rang in his head in her voice, soft and sweet. Beautiful.

The gentle caresses turned hard, fingers biting into his skin, digging at his arms and shoulders, pushing him forward. He collapsed under the weight, his voice gone to the cold, yet his mouth opened around a silent scream when he realized the grave was hers.

Freshly disturbed.

Empty, he'd bet.

A second name rested on that wide stone.

His.

Fingers twined through with his in the soft earth, and with one swift pull he was trapped to his shoulders, his arms locked into the frozen dirt. She held firm while he struggled. He couldn't move. Couldn't breathe.

"Elise, please... please, no..."

Another soft caress of her fingers across his head brought his attention back above-ground. He turned and she lay on the ground beside him, her face to the sky, smiling her sweet, playful smile.

"Vaughn," she said, her voice a distant echo as the snow began to cover his cooling body. Tears slipped over his cheeks and sank into the cold earth.

She turned to face him, dead eyes locking onto his, and leaned forward to kiss his lips softly.

"Tell me you love me, Vaughn," she said again, and her spectral hands sank through the material of his shirt, their cold touch closing around his heart.

About the Author

Susan H. Roddey writes dark speculative fiction and works as a book formatter, cover designer, and developmental editor, both for hire and for several independent presses. She is also a voracious reader, wanna-be chef, amateur gamer, and owner of The Snark Shop, a handcrafted internet market. She lives in the Piedmont area of South Carolina with a house full of humans, cats, books, and yarn, and spends entirely too much time yelling at her sewing machine. She's also very food-motivated and can be bought with chocolate chip cookies and cheesecake.

For more information on Susan, her imagination, and the things she writes, visit www.linktr.ee/shroddey.

ALSO BY
SUSAN H. RODDEY

THESE PRECIOUS THINGS (COMING AUGUST 2025)

THE WONDERLAND WARS SERIES
from Watertower Hill Publishing
In Spades
Diamonds & Rust (Coming February 2026)

THE SOUL COLLECTORS SERIES
Devil's Daughter
Armageddon Rising

THE SHADOW COUNCIL CASE FILES
from Falstaff Books
Gods & Monsters
Blood & Bone
Between the Dim & The Dark